World Classic Reading Book

20 GREAT SHORT STORIES Vol. 02

[English Version]

by Various Writers

20 Great Short Stories Vol. 02
[English Version]

발 행 | 2021년 03월 10일
저 자 | Various Writers
펴낸이 | 한건희
펴낸곳 | 주식회사 부크크
출판사등록 | 2014.07.15.(제2014—16호)
주 소 | 서울 금천구 가산디지털1로 119 SK트윈테크타워 A동 305-7호
전 화 | 1670—8316
이메일 | info@bookk.co.kr

ISBN | 979-11-372-3900-5

www.bookk.co.kr

이 책은 'English Version' 영어 원서와 국가별(예, 러시아 / 프랑스 등) 작품을 영어 번역한 도서로 이름, 지명 등 일부 단어는 그 나라의 언어로 표기로 되어 있습니다.

World Classic Reading Book

20 Great Short Stories Vol. 02

[English Version]

by Various Writers

CONTENTS

20 Great Short Stories Vol. 02

20 GREAT SHORT STORIES Vol. 02

by Various Writers

The Last Leaf

O. Henry

In a little district west of Washington Square the streets have run crazy and broken themselves into small strips called "places." These "places" make strange angles and curves. One street crosses itself a time or two. An artist once discovered a valuable possibility in this street. Suppose a collector with a bill for paints, paper and canvas should, in traversing this route, suddenly meet himself coming back, without a cent having been paid on account!

So, to quaint old Greenwich Village the art people soon came prowling, hunting for north windows and eighteenth-century gables and Dutch attics and low rents. Then they imported some pewter mugs and a chafing dish or two from Sixth avenue, and became a "colony."

At the top of a squatty, three-story brick Sue and Johnsy had their studio. "Johnsy" was familiar for Joanna. One was from Maine; the other from California. They had met at the table d'hote of an Eighth street "Delmonico's," and found their tastes in art, chicory salad and bishop sleeves so congenial that the joint studio resulted.

That was in May. In November a cold, unseen stranger, whom the doctors called Pneumonia, stalked about the colony, touching one here and there with his icy fingers.

Over on the east side this ravager strode boldly, smiting his victims by scores, but his feet trod slowly through the maze of the narrow and moss-grown "places."

Mr. Pneumonia was not what you would call a chivalric old gentleman. A mite of a little woman with blood thinned by California zephyrs was hardly fair game for the red-fisted, short-breathed old duffer. But Johnsy he smote; and she lay, scarcely moving, on her painted iron bedstead, looking through the small Dutch window-panes at the blank side of the next brick house.

One morning the busy doctor invited Sue into the hallway with a shaggy, gray eyebrow.

"She has one chance in—let us say, ten," he said, as he shook down the mercury in his clinical thermometer. "And that chance is for her to want to live. This way people have of lining-up on the side of the undertaker makes the entire pharmacopeia look silly. Your little lady has made up her mind that she's not going to get well. Has she anything on her mind?"

"She—she wanted to paint the Bay of Naples some day," said Sue.

"Paint?—bosh! Has she anything on her mind worth thinking about twice—a man, for instance?"

"A man?" said Sue, with a jew's-harp twang in her voice. "Is a man worth—but, no, doctor; there is nothing of the kind."

"Well, it is the weakness, then," said the doctor. "I will do all that science, so far as it may filter through my efforts, can accomplish. But whenever my patient begins to count the carriages in her funeral procession I subtract 50 per cent. from the curative power of medicines. If you will get her to ask one question about the new winter styles in cloak sleeves I will promise you a one-in-five chance for her, instead of one in ten."

After the doctor had gone Sue went into the workroom and cried a Japanese napkin to a pulp. Then she swaggered into Johnsy's room with her drawing board, whistling ragtime.

Johnsy lay, scarcely making a ripple under the bedclothes, with her face toward the window. Sue stopped whistling, thinking she was asleep.

She arranged her board and began a pen-and-ink drawing to illustrate a magazine story. Young artists must pave their way to Art by drawing pictures for magazine stories that young authors write to pave their way to Literature.

As Sue was sketching a pair of elegant horseshow riding trousers and a monocle on the figure of the hero, an Idaho cowboy, she heard a low sound, several times repeated. She went quickly to the bedside.

Johnsy's eyes were open wide. She was looking out the window and counting—counting backward.

"Twelve," she said, and a little later "eleven;" and then "ten," and "nine;" and then "eight" and "seven," almost together.

Sue looked solicitously out the window. What was there

to count? There was only a bare, dreary yard to be seen, and the blank side of the brick house twenty feet away. An old, old ivy vine, gnarled and decayed at the roots, climbed half way up the brick wall. The cold breath of autumn had stricken its leaves from the vine until its skeleton branches clung, almost bare, to the crumbling bricks.

"What is it, dear?" asked Sue.

"Six," said Johnsy, in almost a whisper. "They're falling faster now. Three days ago there were almost a hundred. It made my head ache to count them. But now it's easy. There goes another one. There are only five left now."

"Five what, dear. Tell your Sudie."

"Leaves. On the ivy vine. When the last one falls I must go, too. I've known that for three days. Didn't the doctor tell you?"

"Oh, I never heard of such nonsense," complained Sue, with magnificent scorn. "What have old ivy leaves to do with your getting well? And you used to love that vine so, you naughty girl. Don't be a goosey. Why, the doctor told me this morning that your chances for getting well real soon were—let's see exactly what he said—he said the chances were ten to one! Why, that's almost as good a chance as we have in New York when we ride on the street cars or walk past a new building. Try to take some broth now, and let Sudie go back to her drawing, so she can sell the editor man with it, and buy port wine for her sick child, and pork chops for her greedy self."

"You needn't get any more wine," said Johnsy, keeping her eyes fixed out the window. "There goes another. No, I don't want any broth. That leaves just four. I want to see the last one fall before it gets dark. Then I'll go, too."

"Johnsy, dear," said Sue, bending over her, "will you promise me to keep your eyes closed, and not look out the window until I am done working? I must hand those drawings in by to-morrow. I need the light, or I would draw the shade down."

"Couldn't you draw in the other room?" asked Johnsy, coldly.

"I'd rather be here by you," said Sue. "Besides I don't want you to keep looking at those silly ivy leaves."

"Tell me as soon as you have finished," said Johnsy, closing her eyes, and lying white and still as a fallen statue, "because I want to see the last one fall. I'm tired of waiting. I'm tired of thinking. I want to turn loose my hold on everything, and go sailing down, down, just like one of those poor, tired leaves."

"Try to sleep," said Sue. "I must call Behrman up to be my model for the old hermit miner. I'll not be gone a minute. Don't try to move 'till I come back."

Old Behrman was a painter who lived on the ground floor beneath them. He was past sixty and had a Michael Angelo's Moses beard curling down from the head of a satyr along the body of an imp. Behrman was a failure in art. Forty years he had wielded the brush without getting near enough to touch the hem of his Mistress's robe. He had been always about to paint a masterpiece, but had never yet begun it. For several years he had painted nothing except now and then a daub in the line of commerce or advertising. He earned a little by serving as a model to those young artists in the colony who could not pay the price of a professional. He drank gin to excess, and still talked of his coming masterpiece. For the rest he was a fierce little old man, who scoffed terribly at softness in any one, and who regarded himself as especial mastiff-in-waiting to protect the two young artists in the studio above.

Sue found Behrman smelling strongly of juniper berries in his dimly lighted den below. In one corner was a blank canvas on an easel that had been waiting there for twenty-five years to receive the first line of the masterpiece. She told him of Johnsy's fancy, and how she feared she would, indeed, light and fragile as a leaf herself, float away when her slight hold upon the world grew weaker.

Old Behrman, with his red eyes, plainly streaming, shouted his contempt and derision for such idiotic imaginings.

"Vass!" he cried. "Is dere people in de world mit der foolishness to die because leafs dey drop off from a confounded vine? I haf not heard of such a thing. No, I will not bose as a model for your fool hermit-dunderhead. Vy do you allow dot silly pusiness to come in der prain of her? Ach, dot poor lettle Miss Johnsy."

"She is very ill and weak," said Sue, "and the fever has left her mind morbid and full of strange fancies. Very well, Mr. Behrman, if you do not care to pose for me, you needn't. But I think you are a horrid old—old flibbertigibbet."

"You are just like a woman!" yelled Behrman. "Who said I will not bose? Go on. I come mit you. For half an hour I haf peen trying to say dot I am ready to bose. Gott! dis is not any blace in which one so goot as Miss Yohnsy shall lie sick. Some day I vill baint a masterpiece, and ve shall all go away. Gott! yes."

Johnsy was sleeping when they went upstairs. Sue pulled the shade down to the window-sill, and motioned Behrman into the other room. In there they peered out the window fearfully at the ivy vine. Then they looked at each other for a moment without speaking. A persistent, cold rain was falling, mingled with snow. Behrman, in his old blue shirt, took his seat as the hermit-miner on an upturned kettle for a rock.

When Sue awoke from an hour's sleep the next morning she found Johnsy with dull, wide-open eyes staring at the drawn green shade.

"Pull it up; I want to see," she ordered, in a whisper.

Wearily Sue obeyed.

But, lo! after the beating rain and fierce gusts of wind that had endured through the livelong night, there yet stood out against the brick wall one ivy leaf. It was the last on the vine. Still dark green near its stem, but with its serrated edges tinted with the yellow of dissolution and decay, it hung bravely from a branch some twenty feet above the ground.

"It is the last one," said Johnsy. "I thought it would surely fall during the night. I heard the wind. It will fall to-day, and I shall die at the same time."

"Dear, dear!" said Sue, leaning her worn face down to the pillow, "think of me, if you won't think of yourself. What would I do?"

But Johnsy did not answer. The lonesomest thing in all the world is a soul when it is making ready to go on its mysterious, far journey. The fancy seemed to possess her more strongly as one by one the ties that bound her to friendship and to earth were loosed.

The day wore away, and even through the twilight they could see the lone ivy leaf clinging to its stem against the wall. And then, with the coming of the night the north wind was again loosed, while the rain still beat against the windows and pattered down from the low Dutch eaves.

When it was light enough Johnsy, the merciless, commanded that the shade be raised.

The ivy leaf was still there.

Johnsy lay for a long time looking at it. And then she called to Sue, who was stirring her chicken broth over the gas stove.

"I've been a bad girl, Sudie," said Johnsy. "Something has made that last leaf stay there to show me how wicked I was. It is a sin to want to die. You may bring me a little broth now, and some milk with a little port in it, and—no; bring me a hand-mirror first, and then pack some pillows about me, and I will sit up and watch you cook."

An hour later she said.

"Sudie, some day I hope to paint the Bay of Naples."

The doctor came in the afternoon, and Sue had an excuse to go into the hallway as he left.

"Even chances," said the doctor, taking Sue's thin, shaking hand in his. "With good nursing you'll win. And now I must see another case I have downstairs. Behrman, his name is—some kind of an artist, I believe. Pneumonia, too. He is an old, weak man, and the attack is acute. There is no hope for him; but he goes to the hospital to-day to be made more comfortable."

The next day the doctor said to Sue: "She's out of danger. You've won. Nutrition and care now—that's all."

And that afternoon Sue came to the bed where Johnsy lay, contentedly knitting a very blue and very useless woolen shoulder scarf, and put one arm around her, pillows and all.

"I have something to tell you, white mouse," she said. "Mr. Behrman died of pneumonia to-day in the hospital. He was ill only two days. The janitor found him on the morning of the first day in his room downstairs helpless with pain. His shoes and clothing were wet through and icy cold. They couldn't imagine where he had been on such a dreadful night. And then they found a lantern, still lighted, and a ladder that had been dragged from its place, and some scattered brushes, and a palette with green and yellow colors mixed on it, and—look out the window, dear, at the last ivy leaf on the wall. Didn't you wonder why it never fluttered or moved when the wind blew? Ah, darling, it's Behrman's masterpiece—he painted it there the night that the last leaf fell."

The Diamond Necklace

Guy de Maupassant

The girl was one of those pretty and charming young creatures who sometimes are born, as if by a slip of fate, into a family of clerks. She had no dowry, no expectations, no way of being known, understood, loved, married by any rich and distinguished man; so she let herself be married to a little clerk of the Ministry of Public Instruction.

She dressed plainly because she could not dress well, but she was unhappy as if she had really fallen from a higher station; since with women there is neither caste nor rank, for beauty, grace and charm take the place of family and birth. Natural ingenuity, instinct for what is elegant, a supple mind are their sole hierarchy, and often make of women of the people the equals of the very greatest ladies.

Mathilde suffered ceaselessly, feeling herself born to enjoy all delicacies and all luxuries. She was distressed at the poverty of her dwelling, at the bareness of the walls, at the shabby chairs, the ugliness of the curtains. All those things, of which another woman of her rank would never even have been conscious, tortured her and made her angry. The sight of the little Breton peasant who did her humble housework aroused in her despairing regrets and bewildering dreams. She thought of silent antechambers hung with Oriental tapestry, illumined by tall bronze candelabra, and of two great footmen in knee breeches who sleep in the big armchairs, made drowsy by the oppressive heat of the stove. She thought of long reception halls hung with ancient silk, of the dainty cabinets containing priceless curiosities and of the little coquettish perfumed reception rooms made for chatting at five o'clock with intimate friends, with men famous and sought after, whom all women envy and whose attention they all desire.

When she sat down to dinner, before the round table covered with a tablecloth in use three days, opposite her husband, who uncovered the soup tureen and declared with a delighted air, "Ah, the good soup! I don't know anything better than that," she thought of dainty dinners, of shining silverware, of tapestry that peopled the walls with ancient personages and with strange birds flying in the midst of a fairy forest; and she thought of delicious dishes served on marvellous plates and of the whispered gallantries to which you listen with a sphinxlike smile while you are eating the pink meat of a trout or the wings of a quail.

She had no gowns, no jewels, nothing. And she loved nothing but that. She felt made for that. She would have liked so much to please, to be envied, to be charming, to be sought after.

She had a friend, a former schoolmate at the convent, who was rich, and whom she did not like to go to see any more because she felt so sad when she came home.

But one evening her husband reached home with a triumphant air and holding a large envelope in his hand.

"There," said he, "there is something for you."

She tore the paper quickly and drew out a printed card which bore these words:

The Minister of Public Instruction and Madame Georges Ramponneau

request the honor of M. and Madame Loisel's company at the palace of

the Ministry on Monday evening, January 18th.

Instead of being delighted, as her husband had hoped, she threw the invitation on the table crossly, muttering:

"What do you wish me to do with that?"

"Why, my dear, I thought you would be glad. You never go out, and this is such a fine opportunity. I had great trouble to get it. Every one wants to go; it is very select, and they are not giving many invitations to clerks. The whole official world will be there." She looked at him with an irritated glance and said impatiently:

"And what do you wish me to put on my back?"

He had not thought of that. He stammered:

"Why, the gown you go to the theatre in. It looks very well to me."

He stopped, distracted, seeing that his wife was weeping. Two great tears ran slowly from the corners of her eyes toward the corners of her mouth.

"What's the matter? What's the matter?" he answered.

By a violent effort she conquered her grief and replied in a calm voice, while she wiped her wet cheeks:

"Nothing. Only I have no gown, and, therefore, I can't go to this ball. Give your card to some colleague whose wife is better equipped than I am." He was in despair. He resumed:

"Come, let us see, Mathilde. How much would it cost, a suitable gown, which you could use on other occasions—something very simple?" She reflected several seconds, making her calculations and wondering also what sum she could ask without drawing on herself an immediate refusal and a frightened exclamation from the economical clerk.

Finally she replied hesitating:

"I don't know exactly, but I think I could manage it with four hundred francs."

He grew a little pale, because he was laying aside just that amount to buy a gun and treat himself to a little shooting next summer on the plain of Nanterre, with several friends who went to shoot larks there of a Sunday.

But he said:

"Very well. I will give you four hundred francs. And try to have a pretty gown."

The day of the ball drew near and Madame Loisel seemed sad, uneasy, anxious. Her frock was ready, however. Her husband said to her one evening: "What is the matter? Come, you have seemed very queer these last three days."

And she answered:

"It annoys me not to have a single piece of jewelry, not a single ornament, nothing to put on. I shall look poverty-stricken. I would almost rather not go at all."

"You might wear natural flowers," said her husband. "They're very stylish at this time of year. For ten francs you can get two or three magnificent roses." She was not convinced.

"No; there's nothing more humiliating than to look poor among other women who are rich."

"How stupid you are!" her husband cried. "Go look up your friend, Madame Forestier, and ask her to lend you some jewels. You're intimate enough with her to do that." She uttered a cry of joy:

"True! I never thought of it."

The next day she went to her friend and told her of her distress.

Madame Forestier went to a wardrobe with a mirror, took out a large jewel box, brought it back, opened it and said to Madame Loisel: "Choose, my dear."

She saw first some bracelets, then a pearl necklace, then a Venetian gold cross set with precious stones, of admirable workmanship. She tried on the ornaments before the mirror, hesitated and could not make up her mind to part with them, to give them back. She kept asking: "Haven't you any more?"

"Why, yes. Look further; I don't know what you like."

Suddenly she discovered, in a black satin box, a superb diamond necklace, and her heart throbbed with an immoderate desire. Her hands trembled as she took it. She fastened it round her throat, outside her high-necked waist, and was lost in ecstasy at her reflection in the mirror.

Then she asked, hesitating, filled with anxious doubt:

"Will you lend me this, only this?"

"Why, yes, certainly."

She threw her arms round her friend's neck, kissed her passionately, then fled with her treasure.

The night of the ball arrived. Madame Loisel was a great success. She was prettier than any other woman present, elegant, graceful, smiling and wild with joy. All the men looked at her, asked her name, sought to be introduced. All the attaches of the Cabinet wished to waltz with her. She was remarked by the minister himself.

She danced with rapture, with passion, intoxicated by pleasure, forgetting all in the triumph of her beauty, in the glory of her success, in a sort of cloud of happiness comprised of all this homage, admiration, these awakened desires and of that sense of triumph which is so sweet to woman's heart.

She left the ball about four o'clock in the morning. Her husband had been sleeping since midnight in a little deserted anteroom with three other gentlemen whose wives were enjoying the ball.

He threw over her shoulders the wraps he had brought, the modest wraps of common life, the poverty of which contrasted with the elegance of the ball dress. She felt this and wished to escape so as not to be remarked by the other women, who were enveloping themselves in costly furs.

Loisel held her back, saying: "Wait a bit. You will catch cold outside. I will call a cab."

But she did not listen to him and rapidly descended the stairs. When they reached the street they could not find a carriage and began to look for one, shouting after the cabmen passing at a distance.

They went toward the Seine in despair, shivering with cold. At last they found on the quay one of those ancient night cabs which, as though they were ashamed to show their shabbiness during the day, are never seen round Paris until after dark.

It took them to their dwelling in the Rue des Martyrs, and sadly they mounted the stairs to their flat. All was ended for her. As to him, he reflected that he must be at the ministry at ten o'clock that morning.

She removed her wraps before the glass so as to see herself once more in all her glory. But suddenly she uttered a cry. She no longer had the necklace around her neck!

"What is the matter with you?" demanded her husband, already half undressed.

She turned distractedly toward him.

"I have—I have—I've lost Madame Forestier's necklace," she cried.

He stood up, bewildered.

"What!—how? Impossible!"

They looked among the folds of her skirt, of her cloak, in her pockets, everywhere, but did not find it.

"You're sure you had it on when you left the ball?" he asked.

"Yes, I felt it in the vestibule of the minister's house."

"But if you had lost it in the street we should have heard it fall. It must be in the cab."

"Yes, probably. Did you take his number?"

"No. And you—didn't you notice it?"

"No."

They looked, thunderstruck, at each other. At last Loisel put on his clothes.

"I shall go back on foot," said he, "over the whole route, to see whether I can find it."

He went out. She sat waiting on a chair in her ball dress, without strength to go to bed, overwhelmed, without any fire, without a thought.

Her husband returned about seven o'clock. He had found nothing.

He went to police headquarters, to the newspaper offices to offer a reward; he went to the cab companies—everywhere, in fact, whither he was urged by the least spark of hope.

She waited all day, in the same condition of mad fear

before this terrible calamity.

Loisel returned at night with a hollow, pale face. He had discovered nothing.

"You must write to your friend," said he, "that you have broken the clasp of her necklace and that you are having it mended. That will give us time to turn round." She wrote at his dictation.

At the end of a week they had lost all hope. Loisel, who had aged five years, declared:

"We must consider how to replace that ornament."

The next day they took the box that had contained it and went to the jeweler whose name was found within. He consulted his books.

"It was not I, madame, who sold that necklace; I must simply have furnished the case."

Then they went from jeweler to jeweler, searching for a necklace like the other, trying to recall it, both sick with chagrin and grief.

They found, in a shop at the Palais Royal, a string of diamonds that seemed to them exactly like the one they had lost. It was worth forty thousand francs. They could have it for thirty-six.

So they begged the jeweler not to sell it for three days yet. And they made a bargain that he should buy it back for thirty-four thousand francs, in case they should find the lost necklace before the end of February.

Loisel possessed eighteen thousand francs which his father had left him. He would borrow the rest.

He did borrow, asking a thousand francs of one, five hundred of another, five louis here, three louis there. He gave notes, took up ruinous obligations, dealt with usurers and all the race of lenders. He compromised all the rest of his life, risked signing a note without even knowing whether he could meet it; and, frightened by the trouble yet to come, by the black misery that was about to fall upon him, by the prospect of all the physical privations and moral tortures that he was to suffer, he went to get the new necklace, laying upon the jeweler's counter thirty-six thousand francs.

When Madame Loisel took back the necklace Madame Forestier said to her with a chilly manner:

"You should have returned it sooner; I might have needed it."

She did not open the case, as her friend had so much feared. If she had detected the substitution, what would she have thought, what would she have said? Would she not have taken Madame Loisel for a thief?

Thereafter Madame Loisel knew the horrible existence of the needy. She bore her part, however, with sudden heroism. That dreadful debt must be paid. She would pay it. They dismissed their servant; they changed their lodgings; they rented a garret under the roof.

She came to know what heavy housework meant and the odious cares of the kitchen. She washed the dishes, using her dainty fingers and rosy nails on greasy pots and pans. She washed the soiled linen, the shirts and the dishcloths, which she dried upon a line; she carried the slops down to the street every morning and carried up the water, stopping for breath at every landing. And dressed like a woman of the people, she went to the fruiterer, the grocer, the butcher, a basket on her arm, bargaining, meeting with impertinence, defending her miserable money, sou by sou.

Every month they had to meet some notes, renew others, obtain more time.

Her husband worked evenings, making up a tradesman's accounts, and late at night he often copied manuscript for five sous a page.

This life lasted ten years.

At the end of ten years they had paid everything, everything, with the rates of usury and the accumulations of the compound interest.

Madame Loisel looked old now. She had become the woman of impoverished households—strong and hard and rough. With frowsy hair, skirts askew and red hands, she talked loud while washing the floor with great swishes of water. But sometimes, when her husband was at the office, she sat down near the window and she thought of that gay evening of long ago, of that ball where she had been so beautiful and so admired.

What would have happened if she had not lost that necklace? Who knows? who knows? How strange and changeful is life! How small a thing is needed to make or ruin us!

But one Sunday, having gone to take a walk in the Champs Elysees to refresh herself after the labors of the week, she suddenly perceived a woman who was leading a child. It was Madame Forestier, still young, still beautiful, still charming.

Madame Loisel felt moved. Should she speak to her? Yes, certainly. And now that she had paid, she would tell her all about it. Why not?

She went up.

"Good-day, Jeanne."

The other, astonished to be familiarly addressed by this plain good-wife, did not recognize her at all and stammered: "But—madame!—I do not know—You must have mistaken."

"No. I am Mathilde Loisel."

Her friend uttered a cry.

"Oh, my poor Mathilde! How you are changed!"

"Yes, I have had a pretty hard life, since I last saw you, and great poverty—and that because of you!"

"Of me! How so?"

"Do you remember that diamond necklace you lent me to wear at the ministerial ball?"

"Yes. Well?"

"Well, I lost it."

"What do you mean? You brought it back."

"I brought you back another exactly like it. And it has taken us ten years to pay for it. You can understand that it was not easy for us, for us who had nothing. At last it is ended, and I am very glad." Madame Forestier had stopped.

"You say that you bought a necklace of diamonds to replace mine?"

"Yes. You never noticed it, then! They were very similar."

And she smiled with a joy that was at once proud and ingenuous.

Madame Forestier, deeply moved, took her hands.

"Oh, my poor Mathilde! Why, my necklace was paste! It was worth at most only five hundred francs!"

The Betrothed

Anton Pavlovich Chekhov

I

IT was ten o'clock in the evening and the full moon was shining over the garden. In the Shumins' house an evening service celebrated at the request of the grandmother, Marfa Mihalovna, was just over, and now Nadya—she had gone into the garden for a minute—could see the table being laid for supper in the dining-room, and her grandmother bustling about in her gorgeous silk dress; Father Andrey, a chief priest of the cathedral, was talking to Nadya's mother, Nina Ivanovna, and now in the evening light through the window her mother for some reason looked very young; Andrey Andreitch, Father Andrey's son, was standing by listening attentively.

It was still and cool in the garden, and dark peaceful shadows lay on the ground. There was a sound of frogs croaking, far, far away beyond the town. There was a feeling of May, sweet May! One drew deep breaths and longed to fancy that not here but far away under the sky, above the trees, far away in the open country, in the fields and the woods, the life of spring was unfolding now, mysterious, lovely, rich and holy beyond the understanding of weak, sinful man. And for some reason one wanted to cry.

She, Nadya, was already twenty-three. Ever since she

was sixteen she had been passionately dreaming of marriage and at last she was engaged to Andrey Andreitch, the young man who was standing on the other side of the window; she liked him, the wedding was already fixed for July 7, and yet there was no joy in her heart, she was sleeping badly, her spirits drooped. . . . She could hear from the open windows of the basement where the kitchen was the hurrying servants, the clatter of knives, the banging of the swing door; there was a smell of roast turkey and pickled cherries, and for some reason it seemed to her that it would be like that all her life, with no change, no end to it.

Some one came out of the house and stood on the steps; it was Alexandr Timofeitch, or, as he was always called, Sasha, who had come from Moscow ten days before and was staying with them. Years ago a distant relation of the grandmother, a gentleman's widow called Marya Petrovna, a thin, sickly little woman who had sunk into poverty, used to come to the house to ask for assistance. She had a son Sasha. It used for some reason to be said that he had talent as an artist, and when his mother died Nadya's grandmother had, for the salvation of her soul, sent him to the Komissarovsky school in Moscow; two years later he went into the school of painting, spent nearly fifteen years there, and only just managed to scrape through the leaving examination in the section of architecture. He did not set up as an architect, however, but took a job at a lithographer's. He used to come almost every year, usually very ill, to stay with Nadya's grandmother to rest and recover.

He was wearing now a frock-coat buttoned up, and shabby canvas trousers, crumpled into creases at the bottom. And his shirt had not been ironed and he had somehow all over a look of not being fresh. He was very thin, with big eyes, long thin fingers and a swarthy bearded face, and all the same he was handsome. With the Shumins he was like one of the family, and in their house felt he was at home. And the room in which he lived when he was there had for years been called Sasha's room. Standing on the steps he saw Nadya, and went up to her.

"It's nice here," he said.

"Of course it's nice, you ought to stay here till the autumn."

"Yes, I expect it will come to that. I dare say I shall stay with you till September."

He laughed for no reason, and sat down beside her.

"I'm sitting gazing at mother," said Nadya. "She looks so young from here! My mother has her weaknesses, of course," she added, after a pause, "but still she is an exceptional woman."

"Yes, she is very nice . . ." Sasha agreed. "Your mother, in her own way of course, is a very good and sweet woman, but . . . how shall I say? I went early this morning into your kitchen and there I found four servants sleeping on the floor, no bedsteads, and rags for bedding, stench, bugs, beetles . . . it is just as it was twenty years ago, no change at all. Well, Granny, God bless her, what else can you expect of Granny? But your mother speaks French, you know, and acts in private theatricals. One would think she might understand." As Sasha talked, he used to stretch out two long wasted fingers before the listener's face.

"It all seems somehow strange to me here, now I am out of the habit of it," he went on. "There is no making it out. Nobody ever does anything. Your mother spends the whole day walking about like a duchess, Granny does nothing either, nor you either. And your Andrey Andreitch never does anything either." Nadya had heard this the year before and, she fancied, the year before that too, and she knew that Sasha could not make any other criticism, and in old days this had amused her, but now for some reason she felt annoyed.

"That's all stale, and I have been sick of it for ages," she said and got up. "You should think of something a little newer."

He laughed and got up too, and they went together toward the house. She, tall, handsome, and well-made, beside him looked very healthy and smartly dressed; she was conscious of this and felt sorry for him and for some reason awkward.

"And you say a great deal you should not," she said. "You've just been talking about my Andrey, but you see you don't know him."

"My Andrey. . . . Bother him, your Andrey. I am sorry for your youth."

They were already sitting down to supper as the young people went into the dining-room. The grandmother, or Granny as she was called in the household, a very stout, plain old lady with bushy eyebrows and a little moustache, was talking loudly, and from her voice and manner of speaking it could be seen that she was the person of most importance in the house. She owned rows of shops in the market, and the old-fashioned house with columns and the garden, yet she prayed every morning that God might save her from ruin and shed tears as she did so. Her daughter-in-law, Nadya's mother, Nina Ivanovna, a fair-haired woman tightly laced in, with a pince-nez, and diamonds on every finger, Father Andrey, a lean, toothless old man whose face always looked as though he were just going to say something amusing, and his son, Andrey Andreitch, a stout and handsome young man with curly hair looking like an artist or an actor, were all talking of hypnotism.

"You will get well in a week here," said Granny, addressing Sasha. "Only you must eat more. What do you look like!" she sighed. "You are really dreadful! You are a regular prodigal son, that is what you are."

"After wasting his father's substance in riotous living," said Father Andrey slowly, with laughing eyes. "He fed with senseless beasts."

"I like my dad," said Andrey Andreitch, touching his

father on the shoulder. "He is a splendid old fellow, a dear old fellow."

Everyone was silent for a space. Sasha suddenly burst out laughing and put his dinner napkin to his mouth.

"So you believe in hypnotism?" said Father Andrey to Nina Ivanovna.

"I cannot, of course, assert that I believe," answered Nina Ivanovna, assuming a very serious, even severe, expression; "but I must own that there is much that is mysterious and incomprehensible in nature."

"I quite agree with you, though I must add that religion distinctly curtails for us the domain of the mysterious."

A big and very fat turkey was served. Father Andrey and Nina Ivanovna went on with their conversation. Nina Ivanovna's diamonds glittered on her fingers, then tears began to glitter in her eyes, she grew excited.

"Though I cannot venture to argue with you," she said, "you must admit there are so many insoluble riddles in life!"

"Not one, I assure you."

After supper Andrey Andreitch played the fiddle and Nina Ivanovna accompanied him on the piano. Ten years before he had taken his degree at the university in the Faculty of Arts, but had never held any post, had no definite work, and only from time to time took part in concerts for charitable objects; and in the town he was regarded as a musician.

Andrey Andreitch played; they all listened in silence.

The samovar was boiling quietly on the table and no one but Sasha was drinking tea. Then when it struck twelve a violin string suddenly broke; everyone laughed, bustled about, and began saying good-bye.

After seeing her fiancé out, Nadya went upstairs where she and her mother had their rooms (the lower storey was occupied by the grandmother). They began putting the lights out below in the dining-room, while Sasha still sat on drinking tea. He always spent a long time over tea in the Moscow style, drinking as much as seven glasses at a time. For a long time after Nadya had undressed and gone to bed she could hear the servants clearing away downstairs and Granny talking angrily. At last everything was hushed, and nothing could be heard but Sasha from time to time coughing on a bass note in his room below.

II

When Nadya woke up it must have been two o'clock, it was beginning to get light. A watchman was tapping somewhere far away. She was not sleepy, and her bed felt very soft and uncomfortable. Nadya sat up in her bed and fell to thinking as she had done every night in May. Her thoughts were the same as they had been the night before, useless, persistent thoughts, always alike, of how Andrey Andreitch had begun courting her and had made her an offer, how she had accepted him and then little by little had come to appreciate the kindly, intelligent man. But for some reason now when there was hardly a month left before the wedding, she began to feel dread and uneasiness as though something vague and oppressive were before her.

"Tick-tock, tick-tock . . ." the watchman tapped lazily. ". . . Tick-tock."

Through the big old-fashioned window she could see the garden and at a little distance bushes of lilac in full flower, drowsy and lifeless from the cold; and the thick white mist was floating softly up to the lilac, trying to cover it. Drowsy rooks were cawing in the far-away trees.

"My God, why is my heart so heavy?"

Perhaps every girl felt the same before her wedding. There was no knowing! Or was it Sasha's influence? But for several years past Sasha had been repeating the same thing, like a copybook, and when he talked he seemed naïve and queer. But why was it she could not get Sasha out of her head? Why was it?

The watchman left off tapping for a long while. The birds were twittering under the windows and the mist had disappeared from the garden. Everything was lighted up by the spring sunshine as by a smile. Soon the whole garden, warm and caressed by the sun, returned to life, and dewdrops like diamonds glittered on the leaves and the old neglected garden on that morning looked young and gaily decked.

Granny was already awake. Sasha's husky cough began. Nadya could hear them below, setting the samovar and moving the chairs. The hours passed slowly, Nadya had been up and walking about the garden for a long while and still the morning dragged on.

At last Nina Ivanovna appeared with a tear-stained face, carrying a glass of mineral water. She was interested in spiritualism and homeopathy, read a great deal, was fond of talking of the doubts to which she was subject, and to Nadya it seemed as though there were a deep mysterious significance in all that.

Now Nadya kissed her mother and walked beside her.

"What have you been crying about, mother?" she asked.

"Last night I was reading a story in which there is an old man and his daughter. The old man is in some office and his chief falls in love with his daughter. I have not finished it, but there was a passage which made it hard to keep from tears," said Nina Ivanovna and she sipped at her glass. "I thought of it this morning and shed tears again." "I have been so depressed all these days," said Nadya after a pause. "Why is it I don't sleep at night!"

"I don't know, dear. When I can't sleep I shut my eyes very tightly, like this, and picture to myself Anna Karenin moving about and talking, or something historical from the ancient world. . . ."

Nadya felt that her mother did not understand her and was incapable of understanding. She felt this for the first time in her life, and it positively frightened her and made her want to hide herself; and she went away to her own room.

At two o'clock they sat down to dinner. It was Wednesday, a fast day, and so vegetable soup and bream with boiled grain were set before Granny.

To tease Granny Sasha ate his meat soup as well as the vegetable soup. He was making jokes all through dinner-time, but his jests were laboured and invariably with a moral bearing, and the effect was not at all amusing when before making some witty remark he raised his very long, thin, deathly-looking fingers; and when one remembered that he was very ill and would probably not be much longer in this world, one felt sorry for him and ready to weep.

After dinner Granny went off to her own room to lie down. Nina Ivanovna played on the piano for a little, and then she too went away.

"Oh, dear Nadya!" Sasha began his usual afternoon conversation, "if only you would listen to me! If only you would!"

She was sitting far back in an old-fashioned armchair, with her eyes shut, while he paced slowly about the room from corner to corner.

"If only you would go to the university," he said. "Only enlightened and holy people are interesting, it's only they who are wanted. The more of such people there are, the sooner the Kingdom of God will come on earth. Of your town then not one stone will be left, everything will be blown up from the foundations, everything will be changed as though by magic. And then there will be immense, magnificent houses here, wonderful gardens, marvellous fountains, remarkable people. . . . But that's not what matters most. What matters most is that the crowd, in our sense of the word, in the sense in which it exists now—that evil will not exist then, because every man will believe and every man will know what he is living for and no one will seek moral support in the crowd. Dear Nadya, darling girl, go away! Show them all that you are sick of this stagnant, grey, sinful life. Prove it to yourself at least!" "I can't, Sasha, I'm going to be married."

"Oh nonsense! What's it for!"

They went out into the garden and walked up and down a little.

"And however that may be, my dear girl, you must think, you must realize how unclean, how immoral this idle life of yours is," Sasha went on. "Do understand that if, for instance, you and your mother and your grandmother do nothing, it means that someone else is working for you, you are eating up someone else's life, and is that clean, isn't it filthy?" Nadya wanted to say "Yes, that is true"; she wanted to say that she understood, but tears came into her eyes, her spirits drooped, and shrinking into herself she went off to her room.

Towards evening Andrey Andreitch arrived and as usual played the fiddle for a long time. He was not given to much talk as a rule, and was fond of the fiddle, perhaps because one could be silent while playing. At eleven o'clock when he was about to go home and had put on his greatcoat, he embraced Nadya and began greedily kissing her face, her shoulders, and her hands.

"My dear, my sweet, my charmer," he muttered. "Oh how happy I am! I am beside myself with rapture!"

And it seemed to her as though she had heard that long, long ago, or had read it somewhere . . . in some old tattered novel thrown away long ago. In the dining-room Sasha was sitting at the table drinking tea with the saucer poised on his five long fingers; Granny was laying out patience; Nina Ivanovna was reading. The flame crackled in the ikon lamp and everything, it seemed, was quiet and going well. Nadya said good-night, went upstairs to her room, got into bed and fell asleep at once. But just as on the night before, almost before it was light, she woke up. She was not sleepy, there was an uneasy, oppressive feeling in her heart. She sat up with her head on her knees and thought of her fiancé and her marriage. . . . She for some reason remembered that her mother had not loved her father and now had nothing and lived in complete dependence on her mother-in-law, Granny. And however much Nadya pondered she could not imagine why she had hitherto seen in her mother something special and exceptional, how it was she had not noticed that she was a simple, ordinary, unhappy woman.

And Sasha downstairs was not asleep, she could hear

him coughing. He is a queer, naïve man, thought Nadya, and in all his dreams, in all those marvellous gardens and wonderful fountains one felt there was something absurd. But for some reason in his naïveté, in this very absurdity there was something so beautiful that as soon as she thought of the possibility of going to the university, it sent a cold thrill through her heart and her bosom and flooded them with joy and rapture.

"But better not think, better not think . . ." she whispered. "I must not think of it."

"Tick-tock," tapped the watchman somewhere far away. "Tick-tock . . . tick-tock. . . ."

III

In the middle of June Sasha suddenly felt bored and made up his mind to return to Moscow.

"I can't exist in this town," he said gloomily. "No water supply, no drains! It disgusts me to eat at dinner; the filth in the kitchen is incredible. . . ."

"Wait a little, prodigal son!" Granny tried to persuade him, speaking for some reason in a whisper, "the wedding is to be on the seventh."

"I don't want to."

"You meant to stay with us until September!"

"But now, you see, I don't want to. I must get to work."

The summer was grey and cold, the trees were wet, everything in the garden looked dejected and uninviting, it certainly did make one long to get to work. The sound of unfamiliar women's voices was heard downstairs and upstairs, there was the rattle of a sewing machine in Granny's room, they were working hard at the trousseau. Of fur coats alone, six were provided for Nadya, and the cheapest of them, in Granny's words, had cost three hundred roubles! The fuss irritated Sasha; he stayed in his own room and was cross, but everyone persuaded him to remain, and he promised not to go before the first of July.

Time passed quickly. On St. Peter's day Andrey Andreitch went with Nadya after dinner to Moscow Street to look once more at the house which had been taken and made ready for the young couple some time before. It was a house of two storeys, but so far only the upper floor had been furnished. There was in the hall a shining floor painted and parqueted, there were Viennese chairs, a piano, a violin stand; there was a smell of paint. On the wall hung a big oil painting in a gold frame—a naked lady and beside her a purple vase with a broken handle.

"An exquisite picture," said Andrey Andreitch, and he gave a respectful sigh. "It's the work of the artist Shismatchevsky."

Then there was the drawing-room with the round table, and a sofa and easy chairs upholstered in bright blue. Above the sofa was a big photograph of Father Andrey wearing a priest's velvet cap and decorations. Then they went into the dining-room in which there was a sideboard; then into the bedroom; here in the half dusk stood two bedsteads side by side, and it looked as though the bedroom had been decorated with the idea that it would always be very agreeable there and could not possibly be anything else. Andrey Andreitch led Nadya about the rooms, all the while keeping his arm round her waist; and she felt weak and conscience-stricken. She hated all the rooms, the beds, the easy chairs; she was nauseated by the naked lady. It was clear to her now that she had ceased to love Andrey Andreitch or perhaps had never loved him at all; but how to say this and to whom to say it and with what object she did not understand, and could not understand, though she was thinking about it all day and all night. . . . He held her round the waist, talked so affectionately, so modestly, was so happy, walking about this house of his; while she saw nothing in it all but vulgarity, stupid, naïve, unbearable vulgarity, and his arm round her waist felt as hard and cold as an iron hoop. And every minute she was on the point of running away, bursting into sobs, throwing herself out of a window. Andrey Andreitch led her into the bathroom and here he touched a tap fixed in the wall and at once water flowed.

"What do you say to that?" he said, and laughed. "I had a tank holding two hundred gallons put in the loft, and so now we shall have water."

They walked across the yard and went out into the street and took a cab. Thick clouds of dust were blowing, and it seemed as though it were just going to rain.

"You are not cold?" said Andrey Andreitch, screwing up his eyes at the dust.

She did not answer.

"Yesterday, you remember, Sasha blamed me for doing nothing," he said, after a brief silence. "Well, he is right, absolutely right! I do nothing and can do nothing. My precious, why is it? Why is it that the very thought that I may some day fix a cockade on my cap and go into the government service is so hateful to me? Why do I feel so uncomfortable when I see a lawyer or a Latin master or a member of the Zemstvo? O Mother Russia! O Mother Russia! What a burden of idle and useless people you still carry! How many like me are upon you, long-suffering Mother!" And from the fact that he did nothing he drew generalizations, seeing in it a sign of the times.

"When we are married let us go together into the country, my precious; there we will work! We will buy ourselves a little piece of land with a garden and a river, we will labour and watch life. Oh, how splendid that will be!" He took off his hat, and his hair floated in the wind, while she listened to him and thought: "Good God, I wish I were home!"

When they were quite near the house they overtook Father Andrey.

"Ah, here's father coming," cried Andrey Andreitch, delighted, and he waved his hat. "I love my dad really," he said as he paid the cabman. "He's a splendid old fellow, a dear old fellow."

Nadya went into the house, feeling cross and unwell, thinking that there would be visitors all the evening, that she would have to entertain them, to smile, to listen to the fiddle, to listen to all sorts of nonsense, and to talk of nothing but the wedding.

Granny, dignified, gorgeous in her silk dress, and haughty as she always seemed before visitors, was sitting before the samovar. Father Andrey came in with his sly smile.

"I have the pleasure and blessed consolation of seeing you in health," he said to Granny, and it was hard to tell whether he was joking or speaking seriously.

IV

The wind was beating on the window and on the roof; there was a whistling sound, and in the stove the house spirit was plaintively and sullenly droning his song. It was past midnight; everyone in the house had gone to bed, but no one was asleep, and it seemed all the while to Nadya as though they were playing the fiddle below. There was a sharp bang; a shutter must have been torn off. A minute later Nina Ivanovna came in in her nightgown, with a candle.

"What was the bang, Nadya?" she asked.

Her mother, with her hair in a single plait and a timid smile on her face, looked older, plainer, smaller on that stormy night. Nadya remembered that quite a little time ago she had thought her mother an exceptional woman and had listened with pride to the things she said; and now she could not remember those things, everything that came into her mind was so feeble and useless.

In the stove was the sound of several bass voices in chorus, and she even heard "O-o-o my G-o-od!" Nadya sat on her bed, and suddenly she clutched at her hair and burst into sobs.

"Mother, mother, my own," she said. "If only you knew what is happening to me! I beg you, I beseech you, let me go away! I beseech you!"

"Where?" asked Nina Ivanovna, not understanding, and she sat down on the bedstead. "Go where?"

For a long while Nadya cried and could not utter a word.

"Let me go away from the town," she said at last. "There must not and will not be a wedding, understand that! I don't love that man . . . I can't even speak about him."

"No, my own, no!" Nina Ivanovna said quickly, terribly alarmed. "Calm yourself—it's just because you are in low spirits. It will pass, it often happens. Most likely you have had a tiff with Andrey; but lovers' quarrels always end in kisses!" "Oh, go away, mother, oh, go away," sobbed Nadya.

"Yes," said Nina Ivanovna after a pause, "it's not long since you were a baby, a little girl, and now you are engaged to be married. In nature there is a continual transmutation of substances. Before you know where you are you will be a mother yourself and an old woman, and will have as rebellious a daughter as I have." "My darling, my sweet, you are clever you know, you are unhappy," said Nadya. "You are very unhappy; why do you say such very dull, commonplace things? For God's sake, why?"

Nina Ivanovna tried to say something, but could not utter a word; she gave a sob and went away to her own room. The bass voices began droning in the stove again, and Nadya felt suddenly frightened. She jumped out of bed and went quickly to her mother. Nina Ivanovna, with tear-stained face, was lying in bed wrapped in a pale blue quilt and holding a book in her hands.

"Mother, listen to me!" said Nadya. "I implore you, do understand! If you would only understand how petty and degrading our life is. My eyes have been opened, and I see it all now. And what is your Andrey Andreitch? Why, he is not intelligent, mother! Merciful heavens, do understand, mother, he is stupid!" Nina Ivanovna abruptly sat up.

"You and your grandmother torment me," she said with a sob. "I want to live! to live," she repeated, and twice she beat her little fist upon her bosom. "Let me be free! I am still young, I want to live, and you have made me an old woman between you!" She broke into bitter tears, lay down and curled up under the quilt, and looked so small, so pitiful, so foolish. Nadya went to her room, dressed, and sitting at the window fell to waiting for the morning. She sat all night thinking, while someone seemed to be tapping on the shutters and whistling in the yard.

In the morning Granny complained that the wind had blown down all the apples in the garden, and broken down an old plum tree. It was grey, murky, cheerless, dark enough for candles; everyone complained of the cold, and the rain lashed on the windows. After tea Nadya went into Sasha's room and without saying a word knelt down before an armchair in the corner and hid her face in her hands.

"What is it?" asked Sasha.

"I can't . . ." she said. "How I could go on living here before, I can't understand, I can't conceive! I despise the man I am engaged to, I despise myself, I despise all this idle, senseless existence."

"Well, well," said Sasha, not yet grasping what was meant. "That's all right . . . that's good."

"I am sick of this life," Nadya went on. "I can't endure another day here. To-morrow I am going away. Take me with you for God's sake!"

For a minute Sasha looked at her in astonishment; at last he understood and was delighted as a child. He waved his arms and began pattering with his slippers as though he were dancing with delight.

"Splendid," he said, rubbing his hands. "My goodness,

how fine that is!"

And she stared at him without blinking, with adoring eyes, as though spellbound, expecting every minute that he would say something important, something infinitely significant; he had told her nothing yet, but already it seemed to her that something new and great was opening before her which she had not known till then, and already she gazed at him full of expectation, ready to face anything, even death.

"I am going to-morrow," he said after a moment's thought. "You come to the station to see me off. . . . I'll take your things in my portmanteau, and I'll get your ticket, and when the third bell rings you get into the carriage, and we'll go off. You'll see me as far as Moscow and then go on to Petersburg alone. Have you a passport?" "Yes."

"I can promise you, you won't regret it," said Sasha, with conviction. "You will go, you will study, and then go where fate takes you. When you turn your life upside down everything will be changed. The great thing is to turn your life upside down, and all the rest is unimportant. And so we will set off to-morrow?" "Oh yes, for God's sake!"

It seemed to Nadya that she was very much excited, that her heart was heavier than ever before, that she would spend all the time till she went away in misery and agonizing thought; but she had hardly gone upstairs and lain down on her bed when she fell asleep at once, with traces of tears and a smile on her face, and slept soundly till evening.

V

A cab had been sent for. Nadya in her hat and overcoat went upstairs to take one more look at her mother, at all her belongings. She stood in her own room beside her still warm bed, looked about her, then went slowly in to her mother. Nina Ivanovna was asleep; it was quite still in her room. Nadya kissed her mother, smoothed her hair, stood still for a couple of minutes . . . then walked slowly downstairs.

It was raining heavily. The cabman with the hood pulled down was standing at the entrance, drenched with rain.

"There is not room for you, Nadya," said Granny, as the servants began putting in the luggage. "What an idea to see him off in such weather! You had better stop at home. Goodness, how it rains!"

Nadya tried to say something, but could not. Then Sasha helped Nadya in and covered her feet with a rug. Then he sat down beside her.

"Good luck to you! God bless you!" Granny cried from the steps. "Mind you write to us from Moscow, Sasha!"

"Right. Good-bye, Granny."

"The Queen of Heaven keep you!"

"Oh, what weather!" said Sasha.

It was only now that Nadya began to cry. Now it was clear to her that she certainly was going, which she had not really believed when she was saying good-bye to Granny, and when she was looking at her mother. Good-bye, town! And she suddenly thought of it all: Andrey, and his father and the new house and the naked lady with the vase; and it all no longer frightened her, nor weighed upon her, but was naïve and trivial and continually retreated further away. And when they got into the railway carriage and the train began to move, all that past which had been so big and serious shrank up into something tiny, and a vast wide future which till then had scarcely been noticed began unfolding before her. The rain pattered on the carriage windows, nothing could be seen but the green fields, telegraph posts with birds sitting on the wires flitted by, and joy made her hold her breath; she thought that she was going to freedom, going to study, and this was just like what used, ages ago, to be called going off to be a free Cossack.

She laughed and cried and prayed all at once.

"It's a-all right," said Sasha, smiling. "It's a-all right."

VI

Autumn had passed and winter, too, had gone. Nadya had begun to be very homesick and thought every day of her mother and her grandmother; she thought of Sasha too. The letters that came from home were kind and gentle, and it seemed as though everything by now were forgiven and forgotten. In May after the examinations she set off for home in good health and high spirits, and stopped on the way at Moscow to see Sasha. He was just the same as the year before, with the same beard and unkempt hair, with the same large beautiful eyes, and he still wore the same coat and canvas trousers; but he looked unwell and worried, he seemed both older and thinner, and kept coughing, and for some reason he struck Nadya as grey and provincial.

"My God, Nadya has come!" he said, and laughed gaily. "My darling girl!"

They sat in the printing room, which was full of tobacco smoke, and smelt strongly, stiflingly of Indian ink and paint; then they went to his room, which also smelt of tobacco and was full of the traces of spitting; near a cold samovar stood a broken plate with dark paper on it, and there were masses of dead flies on the table and on the floor. And everything showed that Sasha ordered his personal life in a slovenly way and lived anyhow, with utter contempt for comfort, and if anyone began talking to him of his personal happiness, of his personal life, of affection for him, he would not have understood and would have only laughed.

"It is all right, everything has gone well," said Nadya hurriedly. "Mother came to see me in Petersburg in the autumn; she said that Granny is not angry, and only keeps going into my room and making the sign of the cross over the walls." Sasha looked cheerful, but he kept coughing, and talked in a cracked voice, and Nadya kept looking at him, unable to decide whether he really were seriously ill or whether it were only her fancy.

"Dear Sasha," she said, "you are ill."

"No, it's nothing, I am ill, but not very . . ."

"Oh, dear!" cried Nadya, in agitation. "Why don't you go to a doctor? Why don't you take care of your health? My dear, darling Sasha," she said, and tears gushed from her eyes and for some reason there rose before her imagination Andrey Andreitch and the naked lady with the vase, and all her past which seemed now as far away as her childhood; and she began crying because Sasha no longer seemed to her so novel, so cultured, and so interesting as the year before. "Dear Sasha, you are very, very ill . . . I would do anything to make you not so pale and thin. I am so indebted to you! You can't imagine how much you have done for me, my good Sasha! In reality you are now the person nearest and dearest to me." They sat on and talked, and now, after Nadya had spent a winter in Petersburg, Sasha, his works, his smile, his whole figure had for her a suggestion of something out of date, old-fashioned, done with long ago and perhaps already dead and buried.

"I am going down the Volga the day after tomorrow," said Sasha, "and then to drink koumiss. I mean to drink koumiss. A friend and his wife are going with me. His wife is a wonderful woman; I am always at her, trying to persuade her to go to the university. I want her to turn her life upside down." After having talked they drove to the station. Sasha got her tea and apples; and when the train began moving and he waved his handkerchief at her, smiling, it could be seen even from his legs that he was very ill and would not live long.

Nadya reached her native town at midday. As she drove home from the station the streets struck her as very wide and the houses very small and squat; there were no people about, she met no one but the German piano-tuner in a rusty greatcoat. And all the houses looked as though they were covered with dust. Granny, who seemed to have grown quite old, but was as fat and plain as ever, flung her arms round Nadya and cried for a long time with her face on Nadya's shoulder, unable to tear herself away. Nina Ivanovna looked much older and plainer and seemed shrivelled up, but was still tightly laced, and still had diamonds flashing on her fingers.

"My darling," she said, trembling all over, "my darling!"

Then they sat down and cried without speaking. It was evident that both mother and grandmother realized that the past was lost and gone, never to return; they had now no position in society, no prestige as before, no right to invite visitors; so it is when in the midst of an easy careless life the police suddenly burst in at night and made a search, and it turns out that the head of the family has embezzled money or committed forgery—and goodbye then to the easy careless life for ever!

Nadya went upstairs and saw the same bed, the same windows with naïve white curtains, and outside the windows the same garden, gay and noisy, bathed in sunshine. She touched the table, sat down and sank into thought. And she had a good dinner and drank tea with delicious rich cream; but something was missing, there was a sense of emptiness in the rooms and the ceilings were so low. In the evening she went to bed, covered herself up and for some reason it seemed to her to be funny lying in this snug, very soft bed.

Nina Ivanovna came in for a minute; she sat down as people who feel guilty sit down, timidly, and looking about her.

"Well, tell me, Nadya," she enquired after a brief pause, "are you contented? Quite contented?"

"Yes, mother."

Nina Ivanovna got up, made the sign of the cross over Nadya and the windows.

"I have become religious, as you see," she said. "You know I am studying philosophy now, and I am always thinking and thinking. . . . And many things have become as clear as daylight to me. It seems to me that what is above all necessary is that life should pass as it were through a prism." "Tell me, mother, how is Granny in health?"

"She seems all right. When you went away that time with Sasha and the telegram came from you, Granny fell on the floor as she read it; for three days she lay without moving. After that she was always praying and crying. But now she is all right again." She got up and walked about the room.

"Tick-tock," tapped the watchman. "Tick-tock, tick-tock. . . ."

"What is above all necessary is that life should pass as it were through a prism," she said; "in other words, that life in consciousness should be analyzed into its simplest elements as into the seven primary colours, and each element must be studied separately." What Nina Ivanovna said further and when she went away, Nadya did not hear, as she quickly fell asleep.

May passed; June came. Nadya had grown used to being at home. Granny busied herself about the samovar, heaving deep sighs. Nina Ivanovna talked in the evenings about her philosophy; she still lived in the house like a poor relation, and had to go to Granny for every farthing. There were lots of flies in the house, and the ceilings seemed to become lower and lower. Granny and Nina Ivanovna did not go out in the streets for fear of meeting Father Andrey and Andrey Andreitch. Nadya walked about the garden and the streets, looked at the grey fences, and it seemed to her that everything in the town had grown old, was out of date and was only waiting either for the end, or for the beginning of something young and fresh. Oh, if only that new, bright life would come more quickly—that life in which one will be able to face one's fate boldly and directly, to know that one is right, to be light-hearted and free! And sooner or later such a life will come. The time will come when of Granny's house, where things are so arranged that the four servants can only live in one room in filth in the basement—the time will come when of that house not a trace will remain, and it will be forgotten, no one will remember it. And Nadya's only entertainment was from the boys next door; when she walked about the garden they knocked on the fence and shouted in mockery: "Betrothed! Betrothed!" A letter from Sasha arrived from Saratov. In his gay dancing handwriting he told them that his journey on the Volga had been a complete success, but that he had been taken rather ill in Saratov, had lost his voice, and had been for the last fortnight in the hospital. She knew what that meant, and she was overwhelmed with a foreboding that was like a conviction. And it vexed her that this foreboding and the thought of Sasha did not distress her so much as before. She had a passionate desire for life, longed to be in Petersburg, and her friendship with Sasha seemed now sweet but something far, far away! She did not sleep all night, and in the morning sat at the window, listening. And she did in fact hear voices below; Granny, greatly agitated, was asking questions rapidly. Then some one began crying. . . . When Nadya went downstairs Granny was standing in the corner, praying before the ikon and her face was tearful. A telegram lay on the table.

For some time Nadya walked up and down the room, listening to Granny's weeping; then she picked up the telegram and read it.

It announced that the previous morning Alexandr

Timofeitch, or more simply, Sasha, had died at Saratov of consumption.

Granny and Nina Ivanovna went to the church to order a memorial service, while Nadya went on walking about the rooms and thinking. She recognized clearly that her life had been turned upside down as Sasha wished; that here she was, alien, isolated, useless and that everything here was useless to her; that all the past had been torn away from her and vanished as though it had been burnt up and the ashes scattered to the winds. She went into Sasha's room and stood there for a while.

"Good-bye, dear Sasha," she thought, and before her mind rose the vista of a new, wide, spacious life, and that life, still obscure and full of mysteries, beckoned her and attracted her.

She went upstairs to her own room to pack, and next morning said good-bye to her family, and full of life and high spirits left the town—as she supposed for ever.

The Last Lesson

Alphonse Daudet

I started for school very late that morning and was in great dread of a scolding, especially because M. Hamel had said that he would question us on participles, and I did not know the first word about them. For a moment I thought of running away and spending the day out of doors. It was so warm, so bright! The birds were chirping at the edge of the woods; and in the open field back of the saw-mill the Prussian soldiers were drilling. It was all much more tempting than the rule for participles, but I had the strength to resist, and hurried off to school.

When I passed the town hall there was a crowd in front of the bulletin-board. For the last two years all our bad news had come from there—the lost battles, the draft, the orders of the commanding officer—and I thought to myself, without stopping:

"What can be the matter now?"

Then, as I hurried by as fast as I could go, the blacksmith, Wachter, who was there, with his apprentice, reading the bulletin, called after me:

"Don't go so fast, bub; you'll get to your school in plenty of time!"

I thought he was making fun of me, and reached M. Hamel's little garden all out of breath.

Usually, when school began, there was a great bustle,

which could be heard out in the street, the opening and closing of desks, lessons repeated in unison, very loud, with our hands over our ears to understand better, and the teacher's great ruler rapping on the table. But now it was all so still! I had counted on the commotion to get to my desk without being seen; but, of course, that day everything had to be as quiet as Sunday morning. Through the window I saw my classmates, already in their places, and M. Hamel walking up and down with his terrible iron ruler under his arm. I had to open the door and go in before everybody. You can imagine how I blushed and how frightened I was.

But nothing happened, M. Hamel saw me and said very kindly:

"Go to your place quickly, little Franz. We were beginning without you."

I jumped over the bench and sat down at my desk. Not till then, when I had got a little over my fright, did I see that our teacher had on his beautiful green coat, his frilled shirt, and the little black silk cap, all embroidered, that he never wore except on inspection and prize days. Besides, the whole school seemed so strange and solemn. But the thing that surprised me most was to see, on the back benches that were always empty, the village people sitting quietly like ourselves; old Hauser, with his three-cornered hat, the former mayor, the former postmaster, and several others besides. Everybody looked sad; and Hauser had brought an old primer, thumbed at the edges, and he held it open on his knees with his great spectacles lying across the pages.

While I was wondering about it all, M. Hamel mounted his chair, and, in the same grave and gentle tone which he had used to me, said:

"My children, this is the last lesson I shall give you. The order has come from Berlin to teach only German in the schools of Alsace and Lorraine. The new master comes to-morrow. This is your last French lesson. I want you to be very attentive."

What a thunder-clap these words were to me!

Oh, the wretches; that was what they had put up at the town-hall!

My last French lesson! Why, I hardly knew how to write! I should never learn any more! I must stop there, then! Oh, how sorry I was for not learning my lessons, for seeking birds' eggs, or going sliding on the Saar! My books, that had seemed such a nuisance a while ago, so heavy to carry, my grammar, and my history of the saints, were old friends now that I couldn't give up. And M. Hamel, too; the idea that he was going away, that I should never see him again, made me forget all about his ruler and how cranky he was.

Poor man! It was in honor of this last lesson that he had put on his fine Sunday-clothes, and now I understood why the old men of the village were sitting there in the back of the room. It was because they were sorry, too, that they had not gone to school more. It was their way of thanking our master for his forty years of faithful service and of showing their respect for the country that was theirs no more.

While I was thinking of all this, I heard my name called. It was my turn to recite. What would I not have given to be able to say that dreadful rule for the participle all through, very loud and clear, and without one mistake? But I got mixed up on the first words and stood there, holding on to my desk, my heart beating, and not daring to look up. I heard M. Hamel say to me: "I won't scold you, little Franz; you must feel bad enough. See how it is! Every day we have said to ourselves: 'Bah! I've plenty of time. I'll learn it to-morrow.' And now you see where we've come out. Ah, that's the great trouble with Alsace; she puts off learning till to-morrow. Now those fellows out there will have the right to say to you: 'How is it; you pretend to be Frenchmen, and yet you can neither speak nor write your own language?' But you are not the worst, poor little Franz. We've all a great deal to reproach ourselves with.

"Your parents were not anxious enough to have you learn. They preferred to put you to work on a farm or at the mills, so as to have a little more money. And I? I've been to blame also. Have I not often sent you to water my flowers instead of learning your lessons? And when I wanted to go fishing, did I not just give you a holiday?" Then, from one thing to another, M. Hamel went on to talk of the French language, saying that it was the most beautiful language in the world—the clearest, the most logical; that we must guard it among us and never forget it, because when a people are enslaved, as long as they hold fast to their language it is as if they had the key to their prison. Then he opened a grammar and read us our lesson. I was amazed to see how well I understood it. All he said seemed so easy, so easy! I think, too, that I had never listened so carefully, and that he had never explained everything with so much patience. It seemed almost as if the poor man wanted to give us all he knew before going away, and to put it all into our heads at one stroke.

After the grammar, we had a lesson in writing. That day M. Hamel had new copies for us, written in a beautiful round hand: France, Alsace, France, Alsace. They looked like little flags floating everywhere in the school-room, hung from the rod at the top of our desks. You ought to have seen how every one set to work, and how quiet it was! The only sound was the scratching of the pens over the paper. Once some beetles flew in; but nobody paid any attention to them, not even the littlest ones, who worked right on tracing their fish-hooks, as if that was French, too. On the roof the pigeons cooed very low, and I thought to myself: "Will they make them sing in German, even the pigeons?"

Whenever I looked up from my writing I saw M. Hamel sitting motionless in his chair and gazing first at one thing, then at another, as if he wanted to fix in his mind just how everything looked in that little school-room. Fancy! For forty years he had been there in the same place, with his garden outside the window and his class in front of him, just like that. Only the desks and benches had been worn smooth; the walnut-trees in the garden were taller, and the hop-vine, that he had planted himself twined about the windows to the roof. How it must have broken his heart to leave it all, poor man; to hear his sister moving about in the room above, packing their trunks! For they must leave the country next day.

But he had the courage to hear every lesson to the very last. After the writing, we had a lesson in history, and then the babies chanted their ba, be, bi, bo, bu. Down there at the back of the room old Hauser had put on his spectacles and, holding his primer in both hands, spelled the letters with them. You could see that he, too, was crying; his voice trembled with emotion, and it was so funny to hear him that we all wanted to laugh and cry. Ah, how well I remember it, that last lesson!

All at once the church-clock struck twelve. Then the Angelus. At the same moment the trumpets of the Prussians, returning from drill, sounded under our windows. M. Hamel stood up, very pale, in his chair. I never saw him look so tall.

"My friends," said he, "I—I—" But something choked him. He could not go on.

Then he turned to the blackboard, took a piece of

chalk, and, bearing on with all his might, he wrote as large as he could:

"Vive La France!"

Then he stopped and leaned his head against the wall, and, without a word, he made a gesture to us with his hand; "School is dismissed—you may go."

The Fall of the House of Usher

Edgar Allan Po

Son cœur est un luth suspendu;
 Sitôt qu'on le touche il résonne..

—De Béranger.

During the whole of a dull, dark, and soundless day in the autumn of the year, when the clouds hung oppressively low in the heavens, I had been passing alone, on horseback, through a singularly dreary tract of country; and at length found myself, as the shades of the evening drew on, within view of the melancholy House of Usher. I know not how it was—but, with the first glimpse of the building, a sense of insufferable gloom pervaded my spirit. I say insufferable; for the feeling was unrelieved by any of that half-pleasurable, because poetic, sentiment, with which the mind usually receives even the sternest natural images of the desolate or terrible. I looked upon the scene before me—upon the mere house, and the simple landscape features of the domain—upon the bleak walls—upon the vacant eye-like windows—upon a few rank sedges—and upon a few white trunks of decayed trees—with an utter depression of soul which I can compare to no earthly sensation more properly than to the after-dream of the reveller upon opium—the bitter lapse into everyday life—the hideous dropping off of the veil. There was an iciness, a sinking, a sickening of the heart—an unredeemed dreariness of thought which no goading of the imagination could torture into aught of the sublime. What was it—I paused to think—what was it that so unnerved me in the contemplation of the House of Usher? It was a mystery all insoluble; nor could I grapple with the shadowy fancies that crowded upon me as I pondered. I was forced to fall back upon the unsatisfactory conclusion, that while, beyond doubt, there are combinations of very simple natural objects which have the power of thus affecting us, still the analysis of this power lies among considerations beyond our depth. It was possible, I reflected, that a mere different arrangement of the particulars of the scene, of the details of the picture, would be sufficient to modify, or perhaps to annihilate its capacity for sorrowful impression; and, acting upon this idea, I reined my horse to the precipitous brink of a black and lurid tarn that lay in unruffled lustre by the dwelling, and gazed down—but with a shudder even more thrilling than before—upon the remodelled and inverted images of the gray sedge, and the ghastly tree-stems, and the vacant and eye-like windows.

Nevertheless, in this mansion of gloom I now proposed to myself a sojourn of some weeks. Its proprietor, Roderick Usher, had been one of my boon companions in boyhood; but many years had elapsed since our last meeting. A letter, however, had lately reached me in a distant part of the country—a letter from him—which, in its wildly importunate nature, had admitted of no other than a personal reply. The MS. gave evidence of nervous agitation. The writer spoke of acute bodily illness—of a mental disorder which oppressed him—and of an earnest desire to see me, as his best, and indeed his only personal friend, with a view of attempting, by the cheerfulness of my society, some alleviation of his malady. It was the manner in which all this, and much more, was said—it was the apparent heart that went with his request—which allowed me no room for hesitation; and I accordingly obeyed forthwith what I still considered a very singular summons.

Although, as boys, we had been even intimate associates, yet I really knew little of my friend. His reserve had been always excessive and habitual. I was aware, however, that his very ancient family had been noted, time out of mind, for a peculiar sensibility of temperament, displaying itself, through long ages, in many works of exalted art, and manifested, of late, in repeated deeds of munificent yet unobtrusive charity, as well as in a passionate devotion to the intricacies, perhaps even more than to the orthodox and easily recognisable beauties, of musical science. I had learned, too, the very remarkable fact, that the stem of the Usher race, all time-honored as it was, had put forth, at no period, any enduring branch; in other words, that the entire family lay in the direct line of descent, and had always, with very trifling and very temporary variation, so lain. It was this deficiency, I considered, while running over in thought the perfect keeping of the character of the premises with the accredited character of the people, and while speculating upon the possible influence which the one, in the long lapse of centuries, might have exercised upon the other—it was this deficiency, perhaps, of collateral issue, and the consequent undeviating transmission, from sire to son, of the patrimony with the name, which had, at length, so identified the two as to merge the original title of the estate in the quaint and equivocal appellation of the "House of Usher"—an appellation which seemed to include, in the minds of the peasantry who used it, both the family and the family mansion.

I have said that the sole effect of my somewhat childish experiment—that of looking down within the tarn—had been to deepen the first singular impression. There can be no doubt that the consciousness of the rapid increase of my superstition—for why should I not so term it?—served mainly to accelerate the increase itself. Such, I have long known, is the paradoxical law of all sentiments having terror as a basis. And it might have been for this reason only, that, when I again uplifted my eyes to the house itself, from its image in the pool, there grew in my mind a strange fancy—a fancy so ridiculous, indeed, that I but mention it to show the vivid force of the sensations which oppressed me. I had so worked upon my imagination as really to believe that about the whole mansion and domain there hung an atmosphere peculiar to themselves and their immediate vicinity—an atmosphere which had no affinity with the air of heaven, but which had reeked up from the decayed trees, and the gray wall, and the silent tarn—a pestilent and mystic vapor, dull, sluggish, faintly discernible, and leaden-hued.

Shaking off from my spirit what must have been a dream, I scanned more narrowly the real aspect of the building. Its principal feature seemed to be that of an excessive antiquity. The discoloration of ages had been great. Minute fungi overspread the whole exterior, hanging in a fine tangled web-work from the eaves. Yet all this was apart from any extraordinary dilapidation. No portion of the masonry had fallen; and there appeared to be a wild inconsistency between its still perfect adaptation of parts, and the crumbling condition of the individual stones. In this there was much that reminded me of the specious totality of old wood-work which has rotted for long years in some neglected vault, with no disturbance from the breath of the external air. Beyond this indication of extensive decay, however, the fabric gave little token of instability. Perhaps the eye of a scrutinizing observer might have discovered a barely perceptible fissure, which, extending from the roof of the building in front, made its way down the wall in a zigzag direction, until it became lost in the sullen waters of the tarn.

Noticing these things, I rode over a short causeway to the house. A servant in waiting took my horse, and I entered the Gothic archway of the hall. A valet, of stealthy step, thence conducted me, in silence, through many dark and intricate passages in my progress to the studio of his master. Much that I encountered on the way contributed, I know not how, to heighten the vague sentiments of which I have already spoken. While the objects around me—while the carvings of the ceilings, the sombre tapestries of the walls, the ebon blackness of the floors, and the phantasmagoric armorial trophies which rattled as I strode, were but matters to which, or to such as which, I had been accustomed from my infancy—while I hesitated not to acknowledge how familiar was all this—I still wondered to find how unfamiliar were the fancies which ordinary images were stirring up. On one of the staircases, I met the physician of the family. His countenance, I thought, wore a mingled expression of low cunning and perplexity. He accosted me with trepidation and passed on. The valet now threw open a door and ushered me into the presence of his master.

The room in which I found myself was very large and lofty. The windows were long, narrow, and pointed, and at so vast a distance from the black oaken floor as to be altogether inaccessible from within. Feeble gleams of encrimsoned light made their way through the trellissed panes, and served to render sufficiently distinct the more prominent objects around; the eye, however, struggled in vain to reach the remoter angles of the chamber, or the recesses of the vaulted and fretted ceiling. Dark draperies hung upon the walls. The general furniture was profuse, comfortless, antique, and tattered. Many books and musical instruments lay scattered about, but failed to give any vitality to the scene. I felt that I breathed an atmosphere of sorrow. An air of stern, deep, and irredeemable gloom hung over and pervaded all.

Upon my entrance, Usher arose from a sofa on which he had been lying at full length, and greeted me with a vivacious warmth which had much in it, I at first thought, of an overdone cordiality—of the constrained effort of the ennuyé man of the world. A glance, however, at his countenance, convinced me of his perfect sincerity. We sat down; and for some moments, while he spoke not, I gazed upon him with a feeling half of pity, half of awe. Surely, man had never before so terribly altered, in so brief a period, as had Roderick Usher! It was with difficulty that I could bring myself to admit the identity of the wan being before me with the companion of my early boyhood. Yet the character of his face had been at all times remarkable. A cadaverousness of complexion; an eye large, liquid, and luminous beyond comparison; lips somewhat thin and very pallid, but of a surpassingly beautiful curve; a nose of a delicate Hebrew model, but with a breadth of nostril unusual in similar formations; a finely moulded chin, speaking, in its want of prominence, of a want of moral energy; hair of a more than web-like softness and tenuity; these features, with an inordinate expansion above the regions of the temple, made up altogether a countenance not easily to be forgotten. And now in the mere exaggeration of the prevailing character of these features, and of the expression they were wont to convey, lay so much of change that I doubted to whom I spoke. The now ghastly pallor of the skin, and the now miraculous lustre of the eye, above all things startled and even awed me. The silken hair, too, had been suffered to grow all unheeded, and as, in its wild gossamer texture, it floated rather than fell about the face, I could not, even with effort, connect its Arabesque expression with any idea of simple humanity.

In the manner of my friend I was at once struck with an incoherence—an inconsistency; and I soon found this to arise from a series of feeble and futile struggles to overcome an habitual trepidancy—an excessive nervous agitation. For something of this nature I had indeed been prepared, no less by his letter, than by reminiscences of certain boyish traits, and by conclusions deduced from his peculiar physical conformation and temperament. His action was alternately vivacious and sullen. His voice varied rapidly from a tremulous indecision (when the animal spirits seemed utterly in abeyance) to that species of energetic concision—that abrupt, weighty, unhurried, and hollow-sounding enunciation—that leaden, self-balanced and perfectly modulated guttural utterance, which may be observed in the lost drunkard, or the irreclaimable eater of opium, during the periods of his most intense excitement.

It was thus that he spoke of the object of my visit, of his earnest desire to see me, and of the solace he expected me to afford him. He entered, at some length, into what he conceived to be the nature of his malady. It was, he said, a constitutional and a family evil, and one for which he despaired to find a remedy—a mere nervous affection, he immediately added, which would undoubtedly soon pass off. It displayed itself in a host of unnatural sensations. Some of these, as he detailed them, interested and bewildered me; although, perhaps, the terms, and the general manner of the narration had their weight. He suffered much from a morbid acuteness of the senses; the most insipid food was alone endurable; he could wear only garments of certain texture; the odors of all flowers were oppressive; his eyes were tortured by even a faint light; and there were but peculiar sounds, and these from stringed instruments, which did not inspire him with horror.

To an anomalous species of terror I found him a bounden slave. "I shall perish," said he, "I must perish in this deplorable folly. Thus, thus, and not otherwise, shall I be lost. I dread the events of the future, not in themselves, but in their results. I shudder at the thought of any, even the most trivial, incident, which may operate upon this intolerable agitation of soul. I have, indeed, no abhorrence of danger, except in its absolute effect—in terror. In this unnerved—in this pitiable condition—I feel that the period will sooner or later arrive when I must abandon life and reason together, in some struggle with the grim phantasm, FEAR." I learned, moreover, at intervals, and through broken and equivocal hints, another singular feature of his mental condition. He was enchained by certain superstitious impressions in regard to the dwelling which he tenanted, and whence, for many years, he had never ventured forth—in regard to an influence whose supposititious force was conveyed in terms too shadowy here to be re-stated—an influence which some peculiarities in the mere form and substance of his family mansion, had, by dint of long sufferance, he said, obtained over his spirit—an effect which the physique of the gray walls and turrets, and of the dim tarn into which they all looked down, had, at length, brought about upon the morale of his existence.

He admitted, however, although with hesitation, that much of the peculiar gloom which thus afflicted him could be traced to a more natural and far more palpable origin—to the severe and long-continued illness—indeed to the evidently approaching dissolution—of a tenderly beloved sister—his sole companion for long years—his last and only relative on earth. "Her decease," he said, with a bitterness which I can never forget, "would leave him (him the hopeless and the frail) the last of the ancient race of the Ushers." While he spoke, the lady Madeline (for so was she called) passed slowly through a remote portion of the apartment, and, without having noticed my presence, disappeared. I regarded her with an utter astonishment not unmingled with dread—and yet I found it impossible to account for such feelings. A sensation of stupor oppressed me, as my eyes followed her retreating steps. When a door, at length, closed upon her, my glance sought instinctively and eagerly the countenance of the brother—but he had buried his face in his hands, and I could only perceive that a far more than ordinary wanness had overspread the emaciated fingers through which trickled many passionate tears.

The disease of the lady Madeline had long baffled the skill of her physicians. A settled apathy, a gradual wasting away of the person, and frequent although transient affections of a partially cataleptical character, were the unusual diagnosis. Hitherto she had steadily borne up against the pressure of her malady, and had not betaken herself finally to bed; but, on the closing in of the evening of my arrival at the house, she succumbed (as her brother told me at night with inexpressible agitation) to the prostrating power of the destroyer; and I learned that the glimpse I had obtained of her person would thus probably be the last I should obtain—that the lady, at least while living, would be seen by me no more.

For several days ensuing, her name was unmentioned by either Usher or myself; and during this period I was busied in earnest endeavors to alleviate the melancholy of my friend. We painted and read together; or I listened, as if in a dream, to the wild improvisations of his speaking guitar. And thus, as a closer and still closer intimacy admitted me more unreservedly into the recesses of his spirit, the more bitterly did I perceive the futility of all attempt at cheering a mind from which darkness, as if an inherent positive quality, poured forth upon all objects of the moral and physical universe, in one unceasing radiation of gloom.

I shall ever bear about me a memory of the many solemn hours I thus spent alone with the master of the House of Usher. Yet I should fail in any attempt to convey an idea of the exact character of the studies, or of the occupations, in which he involved me, or led me the way. An excited and highly distempered ideality threw a sulphureous lustre over all. His long improvised dirges will ring forever in my ears. Among other things, I hold painfully in mind a certain singular perversion and amplification of the wild air of the last waltz of Von Weber. From the paintings over which his elaborate fancy brooded, and which grew, touch by touch, into vaguenesses at which I shuddered the more thrillingly, because I shuddered knowing not why—from these paintings (vivid as their images now are before me) I would in vain endeavor to educe more than a small portion which should lie within the compass of merely written words. By the utter simplicity, by the nakedness of his designs, he arrested and overawed attention. If ever mortal painted an idea, that mortal was Roderick Usher. For me at least—in the circumstances then surrounding me—there arose out of the pure abstractions which the hypochondriac contrived to throw upon his canvass, an intensity of intolerable awe, no shadow of which felt I ever yet in the contemplation of the certainly glowing yet too concrete reveries of Fuseli.

One of the phantasmagoric conceptions of my friend, partaking not so rigidly of the spirit of abstraction, may be shadowed forth, although feebly, in words. A small picture presented the interior of an immensely long and rectangular vault or tunnel, with low walls, smooth, white, and without interruption or device. Certain accessory points of the design served well to convey the idea that this excavation lay at an exceeding depth below the surface of the earth. No outlet was observed in any portion of its vast extent, and no torch, or other artificial source of light was discernible; yet a flood of intense rays rolled throughout, and bathed the whole in a ghastly and inappropriate splendor.

I have just spoken of that morbid condition of the auditory nerve which rendered all music intolerable to the sufferer, with the exception of certain effects of stringed instruments. It was, perhaps, the narrow limits to which he thus confined himself upon the guitar, which gave birth, in great measure, to the fantastic character of his performances. But the fervid facility of his impromptus could not be so accounted for. They must have been, and were, in the notes, as well as in the words of his wild fantasias (for he not unfrequently accompanied himself with rhymed verbal improvisations), the result of that intense mental collectedness and concentration to which I have previously alluded as observable only in particular moments of the highest artificial excitement. The words of one of these rhapsodies I have easily remembered. I was, perhaps, the more forcibly impressed with it, as he gave it, because, in the under or mystic current of its meaning, I fancied that I perceived, and for the first time, a full consciousness on the part of Usher of the tottering of his lofty reason upon her throne. The verses, which were entitled "The Haunted Palace," ran very nearly, if not accurately, thus:

I.

In the greenest of our valleys,
By good angels tenanted,
Once a fair and stately palace—
Radiant palace—reared its head.
In the monarch Thought's dominion—
It stood there!
Never seraph spread a pinion
Over fabric half so fair.

II.

Banners yellow, glorious, golden,
On its roof did float and flow;
(This—all this—was in the olden
Time long ago)
And every gentle air that dallied,
In that sweet day,
Along the ramparts plumed and pallid,
A winged odor went away.

III.

Wanderers in that happy valley
Through two luminous windows saw
Spirits moving musically
To a lute's well-tunéd law,
Round about a throne, where sitting
(Porphyrogene!)
In state his glory well befitting,
The ruler of the realm was seen.

IV.

And all with pearl and ruby glowing
Was the fair palace door,
Through which came flowing, flowing, flowing,
And sparkling evermore,
A troop of Echoes whose sweet duty
Was but to sing,

In voices of surpassing beauty,
The wit and wisdom of their king.

V.

But evil things, in robes of sorrow,
Assailed the monarch's high estate;
(Ah, let us mourn, for never morrow
Shall dawn upon him, desolate!)
And, round about his home, the glory
That blushed and bloomed
Is but a dim-remembered story
Of the old time entombed.

VI.

And travellers now within that valley,
Through the red-litten windows, see
Vast forms that move fantastically
To a discordant melody;
While, like a rapid ghastly river,
Through the pale door,
A hideous throng rush out forever,
And laugh—but smile no more.

I well remember that suggestions arising from this ballad, led us into a train of thought wherein there became manifest an opinion of Usher's which I mention not so much on account of its novelty, (for other men * have thought thus,) as on account of the pertinacity with which he maintained it. This opinion, in its general form, was that of the sentience of all vegetable things. But, in his disordered fancy, the idea had assumed a more daring character, and trespassed, under certain conditions, upon the kingdom of inorganization. I lack words to express the full extent, or the earnest abandon of his persuasion. The belief, however, was connected (as I have previously hinted) with the gray stones of the home of his forefathers. The conditions of the sentience had been here, he imagined, fulfilled in the method of collocation of these stones—in the order of their arrangement, as well as in that of the many fungi which overspread them, and of the decayed trees which stood around—above all, in the long undisturbed endurance of this arrangement, and in its reduplication in the still waters of the tarn. Its evidence—the evidence of the sentience—was to be seen, he said, (and I here started as he spoke,) in the gradual yet certain condensation of an atmosphere of their own about the waters and the walls. The result was discoverable, he added, in that silent, yet importunate and terrible influence which for centuries had moulded the destinies of his family, and which made him what I now saw him—what he was. Such opinions need no comment, and I will make none.

* Watson, Dr. Percival, Spallanzani, and especially the Bishop of Landaff.—See "Chemical Essays," vol v.

Our books—the books which, for years, had formed no small portion of the mental existence of the invalid—were, as might be supposed, in strict keeping with this character of phantasm. We pored together over such works as the Ververt et Chartreuse of Gresset; the Belphegor of Machiavelli; the Heaven and Hell of Swedenborg; the Subterranean Voyage of Nicholas Klimm by Holberg; the Chiromancy of Robert Flud, of Jean D'Indaginé, and of De la Chambre; the Journey into the Blue Distance of Tieck; and the City of the Sun of Campanella. One favorite volume was a small octavo edition of the Directorium Inquisitorium, by the Dominican Eymeric de Gironne; and there were passages in Pomponius Mela, about the old African Satyrs and OEgipans, over which Usher would sit dreaming for hours. His chief delight, however, was found in the perusal of an exceedingly rare and curious book in quarto Gothic—the manual of a forgotten church—the Vigiliae Mortuorum secundum Chorum Ecclesiae Maguntinae.

I could not help thinking of the wild ritual of this work, and of its probable influence upon the hypochondriac, when, one evening, having informed me abruptly that the lady Madeline was no more, he stated his intention of preserving her corpse for a fortnight, (previously to its final interment,) in one of the numerous vaults within the main walls of the building. The worldly reason, however, assigned for this singular proceeding, was one which I did not feel at liberty to dispute. The brother had been led to his resolution (so he told me) by consideration of the unusual character of the malady of the deceased, of certain obtrusive and eager inquiries on the part of her medical men, and of the remote and exposed situation of the burial-ground of the family. I will not deny that when I called to mind the sinister countenance of the person whom I met upon the staircase, on the day of my arrival at the house, I had no desire to oppose what I regarded as at best but a harmless, and by no means an unnatural, precaution.

At the request of Usher, I personally aided him in the arrangements for the temporary entombment. The body having been encoffined, we two alone bore it to its rest. The vault in which we placed it (and which had been so long unopened that our torches, half smothered in its oppressive atmosphere, gave us little opportunity for investigation) was small, damp, and entirely without means of admission for light; lying, at great depth, immediately beneath that portion of the building in which was my own sleeping apartment. It had been used, apparently, in remote feudal times, for the worst purposes of a donjon-keep, and, in later days, as a place of deposit for powder, or some other highly combustible substance, as a portion of its floor, and the whole interior of a long archway through which we reached it, were carefully sheathed with copper. The door, of massive iron, had been, also, similarly protected. Its immense weight caused an unusually sharp grating sound, as it moved upon its hinges.

Having deposited our mournful burden upon tressels within this region of horror, we partially turned aside the yet unscrewed lid of the coffin, and looked upon the face of the tenant. A striking similitude between the brother and sister now first arrested my attention; and Usher, divining, perhaps, my thoughts, murmured out some few words from which I learned that the deceased and himself had been twins, and that sympathies of a scarcely intelligible nature had always existed between them. Our glances, however, rested not long upon the dead—for we could not regard her unawed. The disease which had thus entombed the lady in the maturity of youth, had left, as usual in all maladies of a strictly cataleptical character, the mockery of a faint blush upon the bosom and the face, and that suspiciously lingering smile upon the lip which is so terrible in death. We replaced and screwed down the lid, and, having secured the door of iron, made our way, with toil, into the scarcely less gloomy apartments of the upper portion of the house.

And now, some days of bitter grief having elapsed, an observable change came over the features of the mental disorder of my friend. His ordinary manner had vanished. His ordinary occupations were neglected or forgotten. He roamed from chamber to chamber with hurried, unequal, and objectless step. The pallor of his countenance had assumed, if possible, a more ghastly hue—but the luminousness of his eye had utterly gone out. The once occasional huskiness of his tone was heard no more; and a tremulous quaver, as if of extreme terror, habitually characterized his utterance. There were times, indeed, when I thought his unceasingly agitated mind was laboring with some oppressive secret, to divulge which he struggled for the necessary courage. At times, again, I was obliged to resolve all into the mere inexplicable vagaries of madness, for I beheld him gazing upon vacancy for long hours, in an attitude of the profoundest attention, as if listening to some imaginary sound. It was no wonder that his condition terrified—that it infected me. I felt creeping upon me, by slow yet certain degrees, the wild influences of his own fantastic yet impressive superstitions.

It was, especially, upon retiring to bed late in the night of the seventh or eighth day after the placing of the lady Madeline within the donjon, that I experienced the full power of such feelings. Sleep came not near my couch—while the hours waned and waned away. I struggled to reason off the nervousness which had dominion over me. I endeavored to believe that much, if not all of what I felt, was due to the bewildering influence of the gloomy furniture of the room—of the dark and tattered draperies, which, tortured into motion by the breath of a rising tempest, swayed fitfully to and fro upon the walls, and rustled uneasily about the decorations of the bed. But my efforts were fruitless. An irrepressible tremor gradually pervaded my frame; and, at length, there sat upon my very heart an incubus of utterly causeless alarm. Shaking this off with a gasp and a struggle, I uplifted myself upon the pillows, and, peering earnestly within the intense darkness of the chamber, harkened—I know not why, except that an instinctive spirit prompted me—to certain low and indefinite sounds which came, through the pauses of the storm, at long intervals, I knew not whence. Overpowered by an intense sentiment of horror, unaccountable yet unendurable, I threw on my clothes with haste (for I felt that I should sleep no more during the night), and endeavored to arouse myself from the pitiable condition into which I had fallen, by pacing rapidly to and fro through the apartment.

I had taken but few turns in this manner, when a light step on an adjoining staircase arrested my attention. I presently recognised it as that of Usher. In an instant afterward he rapped, with a gentle touch, at my door, and entered, bearing a lamp. His countenance was, as usual, cadaverously wan—but, moreover, there was a species of mad hilarity in his eyes—an evidently restrained hysteria in his whole demeanor. His air appalled me—but anything was preferable to the solitude which I had so long endured, and I even welcomed his presence as a relief.

"And you have not seen it?" he said abruptly, after having stared about him for some moments in silence—

"you have not then seen it?—but, stay! you shall." Thus speaking, and having carefully shaded his lamp, he hurried to one of the casements, and threw it freely open to the storm.

The impetuous fury of the entering gust nearly lifted us from our feet. It was, indeed, a tempestuous yet sternly beautiful night, and one wildly singular in its terror and its beauty. A whirlwind had apparently collected its force in our vicinity; for there were frequent and violent alterations in the direction of the wind; and the exceeding density of the clouds (which hung so low as to press upon the turrets of the house) did not prevent our perceiving the life-like velocity with which they flew careering from all points against each other, without passing away into the distance. I say that even their exceeding density did not prevent our perceiving this—yet we had no glimpse of the moon or stars—nor was there any flashing forth of the lightning. But the under surfaces of the huge masses of agitated vapor, as well as all terrestrial objects immediately around us, were glowing in the unnatural light of a faintly luminous and distinctly visible gaseous exhalation which hung about and enshrouded the mansion.

"You must not—you shall not behold this!" said I, shudderingly, to Usher, as I led him, with a gentle violence, from the window to a seat. "These appearances, which bewilder you, are merely electrical phenomena not uncommon—or it may be that they have their ghastly origin in the rank miasma of the tarn. Let us close this casement;—the air is chilling and dangerous to your frame. Here is one of your favorite romances. I will read, and you shall listen;—and so we will pass away this terrible night together." The antique volume which I had taken up was the "Mad Trist" of Sir Launcelot Canning; but I had called it a favorite of Usher's more in sad jest than in earnest; for, in truth, there is little in its uncouth and unimaginative prolixity which could have had interest for the lofty and spiritual ideality of my friend. It was, however, the only book immediately at hand; and I indulged a vague hope that the excitement which now agitated the hypochondriac, might find relief (for the history of mental disorder is full of similar anomalies) even in the extremeness of the folly which I should read. Could I have judged, indeed, by the wild overstrained air of vivacity with which he harkened, or apparently harkened, to the words of the tale, I might well have congratulated myself upon the success of my design.

I had arrived at that well-known portion of the story where Ethelred, the hero of the Trist, having sought in vain for peaceable admission into the dwelling of the hermit, proceeds to make good an entrance by force. Here, it will be remembered, the words of the narrative run thus:

"And Ethelred, who was by nature of a doughty heart, and who was now mighty withal, on account of the powerfulness of the wine which he had drunken, waited no longer to hold parley with the hermit, who, in sooth, was of an obstinate and maliceful turn, but, feeling the rain upon his shoulders, and fearing the rising of the tempest, uplifted his mace outright, and, with blows, made quickly room in the plankings of the door for his gauntleted hand; and now pulling therewith sturdily, he so cracked, and ripped, and tore all asunder, that the noise of the dry and hollow-sounding wood alarummed and reverberated throughout the forest." At the termination of this sentence I started, and for a moment, paused; for it appeared to me (although I at once concluded that my excited fancy had deceived me)—it appeared to me that, from some very remote portion of the mansion, there came, indistinctly, to my ears, what might have been, in its exact similarity of character, the echo (but a stifled and dull one certainly) of the very cracking and ripping sound which Sir Launcelot had so particularly described. It was, beyond doubt, the coincidence alone which had arrested my attention; for, amid the rattling of the sashes of the casements, and the ordinary commingled noises of the still increasing storm, the sound, in itself, had nothing, surely, which should have interested or disturbed me. I continued the story: "But the good champion Ethelred, now entering within the door, was sore enraged and amazed to perceive no signal of the maliceful hermit; but, in the stead thereof, a dragon of a scaly and prodigious demeanor, and of a fiery tongue, which sate in guard before a palace of

gold, with a floor of silver; and upon the wall there hung a shield of shining brass with this legend enwritten—
Who entereth herein, a conqueror hath bin;
Who slayeth the dragon, the shield he shall win;

And Ethelred uplifted his mace, and struck upon the head of the dragon, which fell before him, and gave up his pesty breath, with a shriek so horrid and harsh, and withal so piercing, that Ethelred had fain to close his ears with his hands against the dreadful noise of it, the like whereof was never before heard."

Here again I paused abruptly, and now with a feeling of wild amazement—for there could be no doubt whatever that, in this instance, I did actually hear (although from what direction it proceeded I found it impossible to say) a low and apparently distant, but harsh, protracted, and most unusual screaming or grating sound—the exact counterpart of what my fancy had already conjured up for the dragon's unnatural shriek as described by the romancer.

Oppressed, as I certainly was, upon the occurrence of this second and most extraordinary coincidence, by a thousand conflicting sensations, in which wonder and extreme terror were predominant, I still retained sufficient presence of mind to avoid exciting, by any observation, the sensitive nervousness of my companion. I was by no means certain that he had noticed the sounds in question; although, assuredly, a strange alteration had, during the last few minutes, taken place in his demeanor. From a position fronting my own, he had gradually brought round his chair, so as to sit with his face to the door of the chamber; and thus I could but partially perceive his features, although I saw that his lips trembled as if he were murmuring inaudibly. His head had dropped upon his breast—yet I knew that he was not asleep, from the wide and rigid opening of the eye as I caught a glance of it in profile. The motion of his body, too, was at variance with this idea—for he rocked from side to side with a gentle yet constant and uniform sway. Having rapidly taken notice of all this, I resumed the narrative of Sir Launcelot, which thus proceeded: "And now, the champion, having escaped from the terrible fury of the dragon, bethinking himself of the brazen shield, and of the breaking up of the enchantment which was upon it, removed the carcass from out of the way before him, and approached valorously over the silver pavement of the castle to where the shield was upon the wall; which in sooth tarried not for his full coming, but feel down at his feet upon the silver floor, with a mighty great and terrible ringing sound." No sooner had these syllables passed my lips, than—as if a shield of brass had indeed, at the moment, fallen heavily upon a floor of silver—I became aware of a distinct, hollow, metallic, and clangorous, yet apparently muffled reverberation. Completely unnerved, I leaped to my feet; but the measured rocking movement of Usher was undisturbed. I rushed to the chair in which he sat. His eyes were bent fixedly before him, and throughout his whole countenance there reigned a stony rigidity. But, as I placed my hand upon his shoulder, there came a strong shudder over his whole person; a sickly smile quivered about his lips; and I saw that he spoke in a low, hurried, and gibbering murmur, as if unconscious of my presence. Bending closely over him, I at length drank in the hideous import of his words.

"Not hear it?—yes, I hear it, and have heard it. Long—long—long—many minutes, many hours, many days, have I heard it—yet I dared not—oh, pity me, miserable wretch that I am!—I dared not—I dared not speak! We have put her living in the tomb! Said I not that my senses were acute? I now tell you that I heard her first feeble movements in the hollow coffin. I heard them—many, many days ago—yet I dared not—I dared not speak! And now—to-night—Ethelred—ha! ha!—the breaking of the hermit's door, and the death-cry of the dragon, and the clangor of the shield!—say, rather, the rending of her coffin, and the grating of the iron hinges of her prison, and her struggles within the coppered archway of the vault! Oh whither shall I fly? Will she not be here anon? Is she not hurrying to upbraid me for my haste? Have I not heard her footstep on the stair? Do I not distinguish that heavy and horrible beating of her heart? Madman!"—here he sprang furiously to his feet, and shrieked out his syllables, as if in the effort he were giving up his soul—"Madman! I tell you that she now stands without the door!" As if in the superhuman energy of his utterance there had been found the potency of a spell—the huge antique pannels to which the speaker pointed, threw slowly back, upon the instant, their ponderous and ebony jaws. It was the work of the rushing gust—but then without those doors there did stand the lofty and enshrouded figure of the lady Madeline of Usher. There was blood upon her white robes, and the evidence of some bitter struggle upon every portion of her emaciated frame. For a moment she remained trembling and reeling to and fro upon the threshold—then, with a low moaning cry, fell heavily inward upon the person of her brother, and in her violent and now final death-agonies, bore him to the floor a corpse, and a victim to the terrors he had anticipated.

From that chamber, and from that mansion, I fled aghast. The storm was still abroad in all its wrath as I found myself crossing the old causeway. Suddenly there shot along the path a wild light, and I turned to see whence a gleam so unusual could have issued; for the vast house and its shadows were alone behind me. The radiance was that of the full, setting, and blood-red moon, which now shone vividly through that once barely-discernible fissure, of which I have before spoken as extending from the roof of the building, in a zigzag direction, to the base. While I gazed, this fissure rapidly widened—there came a fierce breath of the whirlwind—the entire orb of the satellite burst at once upon my sight—my brain reeled as I saw the mighty walls rushing asunder—there was a long tumultuous shouting sound like the voice of a thousand waters—and the deep and dank tarn at my feet closed sullenly and silently over the fragments of the "House of Usher."

Three Questions

Leo Tolstoy

It once occurred to a certain king, that if he always knew the right time to begin everything; if he knew who were the right people to listen to, and whom to avoid; and, above all, if he always knew what was the most important thing to do, he would never fail in anything he might undertake.

And this thought having occurred to him, he had it proclaimed throughout his kingdom that he would give a great reward to any one who would teach him what was the right time for every action, and who were the most necessary people, and how he might know what was the most important thing to do.

And learned men came to the King, but they all answered his questions differently.

In reply to the first question, some said that to know the right time for every action, one must draw up in advance, a table of days, months and years, and must live strictly according to it. Only thus, said they, could everything be done at its proper time. Others declared that it was impossible to decide beforehand the right time for every action; but that, not letting oneself be absorbed in idle pastimes, one should always attend to all that was going on, and then do what was most needful. Others, again, said that however attentive the

King might be to what was going on, it was impossible for one man to decide correctly the right time for every action, but that he should have a Council of wise men, who would help him to fix the proper time for everything.

But then again others said there were some things which could not wait to be laid before a Council, but about which one had at once to decide whether to undertake them or not. But in order to decide that, one must know beforehand what was going to happen. It is only magicians who know that; and, therefore, in order to know the right time for every action, one must consult magicians.

Equally various were the answers to the second question. Some said, the people the King most needed were his councillors; others, the priests; others, the doctors; while some said the warriors were the most necessary.

To the third question, as to what was the most important occupation: some replied that the most important thing in the world was science. Others said it was skill in warfare; and others, again, that it was religious worship.

All the answers being different, the King agreed with none of them, and gave the reward to none. But still wishing to find the right answers to his questions, he decided to consult a hermit, widely renowned for his wisdom.

The hermit lived in a wood which he never quitted, and

he received none but common folk. So the King put on simple clothes, and before reaching the hermit's cell dismounted from his horse, and, leaving his body-guard behind, went on alone.

When the King approached, the hermit was digging the ground in front of his hut. Seeing the King, he greeted him and went on digging. The hermit was frail and weak, and each time he stuck his spade into the ground and turned a little earth, he breathed heavily.

The King went up to him and said: "I have come to you, wise hermit, to ask you to answer three questions: How can I learn to do the right thing at the right time? Who are the people I most need, and to whom should I, therefore, pay more attention than to the rest? And, what affairs are the most important, and need my first attention?" The hermit listened to the King, but answered nothing. He just spat on his hand and recommenced digging.

"You are tired," said the King, "let me take the spade and work awhile for you."

"Thanks!" said the hermit, and, giving the spade to the King, he sat down on the ground.

When he had dug two beds, the King stopped and repeated his questions. The hermit again gave no answer, but rose, stretched out his hand for the spade, and said:

"Now rest awhile-and let me work a bit."

But the King did not give him the spade, and continued to dig. One hour passed, and another. The sun began to sink behind the trees, and the King at last stuck the spade into the ground, and said:

"I came to you, wise man, for an answer to my questions. If you can give me none, tell me so, and I will return home."

"Here comes some one running," said the hermit, "let us see who it is."

The King turned round, and saw a bearded man come running out of the wood. The man held his hands pressed against his stomach, and blood was flowing from under them. When he reached the King, he fell fainting on the ground moaning feebly. The King and the hermit unfastened the man's clothing. There was a large wound in his stomach. The King washed it as best he could, and bandaged it with his handkerchief and with a towel the hermit had. But the blood would not stop flowing, and the King again and again removed the bandage soaked with warm blood, and washed and rebandaged the wound. When at last the blood ceased flowing, the man revived and asked for something to drink. The King brought fresh water and gave it to him. Meanwhile the sun had set, and it had become cool. So the King, with the hermit's help, carried the wounded man into the hut and laid him on the bed. Lying on the bed the man closed his eyes and was quiet; but the King was so tired with his walk and with the work he had done, that he crouched down on the threshold, and also fell asleep—so soundly that he slept all through the short summer night.

When he awoke in the morning, it was long before he could remember where he was, or who was the strange bearded man lying on the bed and gazing intently at him with shining eyes.

"Forgive me!" said the bearded man in a weak voice, when he saw that the King was awake and was looking at him.

"I do not know you, and have nothing to forgive you for," said the King.

"You do not know me, but I know you. I am that enemy of yours who swore to revenge himself on you, because you executed his brother and seized his property. I knew you had gone alone to see the hermit, and I resolved to kill you on your way back. But the day passed and you did not return. So I came out from my ambush to find you, and I came upon your bodyguard, and they recognized me, and wounded me. I escaped from them, but should have bled to death had you not dressed my wound. I wished to kill you, and you have saved my life. Now, if I live, and if you wish it, I will serve you as your most faithful slave, and will bid my sons do the same. Forgive me!" The King was very glad to have made peace with his enemy so easily, and to have gained him for a friend, and he not only forgave him, but said he would send his servants and his own physician to attend him, and promised to restore his property.

Having taken leave of the wounded man, the King went

out into the porch and looked around for the hermit. Before going away he wished once more to beg an answer to the questions he had put. The hermit was outside, on his knees, sowing seeds in the beds that had been dug the day before.

The King approached him, and said:

"For the last time, I pray you to answer my questions, wise man."

"You have already been answered!" said the hermit, still crouching on his thin legs, and looking up at the King, who stood before him.

"How answered? What do you mean?" asked the King.

"Do you not see," replied the hermit. "If you had not pitied my weakness yesterday, and had not dug those beds for me, but had gone your way, that man would have attacked you, and you would have repented of not having stayed with me. So the most important time was when you were digging the beds; and I was the most important man; and to do me good was your most important business. Afterwards when that man ran to us, the most important time was when you were attending to him, for if you had not bound up his wounds he would have died without having made peace with you. So he was the most important man, and what you did for him was your most important business. Remember then: there is only one time that is important—Now! It is the most important time because it is the only time when we have any power. The most necessary man is he with whom you are, for no man knows whether he will ever have dealings with any one else: and the most important affair is, to do him good, because for that purpose alone was man sent into this life!"

The Ice Palace

Francis Scott Key Fitzgerald

I

The sunlight dripped over the house like golden paint over an art jar, and the freckling shadows here and there only intensified the rigor of the bath of light. The Butterworth and Larkin houses flanking were entrenched behind great stodgy trees; only the Happer house took the full sun, and all day long faced the dusty road-street with a tolerant kindly patience. This was the city of Tarleton in southernmost Georgia, September afternoon.

Up in her bedroom window Sally Carrol Happer rested her nineteen-year-old chin on a fifty-two-year-old sill and watched Clark Darrow's ancient Ford turn the corner. The car was hot—being partly metallic it retained all the heat it absorbed or evolved—and Clark Darrow sitting bolt upright at the wheel wore a pained, strained expression as though he considered himself a spare part, and rather likely to break. He laboriously crossed two dust ruts, the wheels squeaking indignantly at the encounter, and then with a terrifying expression he gave the steering-gear a final wrench and deposited self and car approximately in front of the Happer steps. There was a heaving sound, a death-rattle, followed by a short silence; and then the air was rent by a startling whistle.

Sally Carrol gazed down sleepily. She started to yawn,

but finding this quite impossible unless she raised her chin from the window-sill, changed her mind and continued silently to regard the car, whose owner sat brilliantly if perfunctorily at attention as he waited for an answer to his signal. After a moment the whistle once more split the dusty air.

"Good mawnin'."

With difficulty Clark twisted his tall body round and bent a distorted glance on the window.

"Tain't mawnin', Sally Carrol."

"Isn't it, sure enough?"

"What you doin'?"

"Eatin' 'n apple."

"Come on go swimmin'—want to?"

"Reckon so."

"How 'bout hurryin' up?"

"Sure enough."

Sally Carrol sighed voluminously and raised herself with profound inertia from the floor where she had been occupied in alternately destroyed parts of a green apple and painting paper dolls for her younger sister. She approached a mirror, regarded her expression with a pleased and pleasant languor, dabbed two spots of rouge on her lips and a grain of powder on her nose, and covered her bobbed corn-colored hair with a rose-littered sunbonnet. Then she kicked over the painting water, said, "Oh, damn!"—but let it lay—and left the room.

"How you, Clark?" she inquired a minute later as she

slipped nimbly over the side of the car.

"Mighty fine, Sally Carrol."

"Where we go swimmin'?"

"Out to Walley's Pool. Told Marylyn we'd call by an' get her an' Joe Ewing."

Clark was dark and lean, and when on foot was rather inclined to stoop. His eyes were ominous and his expression somewhat petulant except when startlingly illuminated by one of his frequent smiles. Clark had "a income"—just enough to keep himself in ease and his car in gasolene—and he had spent the two years since he graduated from Georgia Tech in dozing round the lazy streets of his home town, discussing how he could best invest his capital for an immediate fortune.

Hanging round he found not at all difficult; a crowd of little girls had grown up beautifully, the amazing Sally Carrol foremost among them; and they enjoyed being swum with and danced with and made love to in the flower-filled summery evenings—and they all liked Clark immensely. When feminine company palled there were half a dozen other youths who were always just about to do something, and meanwhile were quite willing to join him in a few holes of golf, or a game of billiards, or the consumption of a quart of "hard yella licker." Every once in a while one of these contemporaries made a farewell round of calls before going up to New York or Philadelphia or Pittsburgh to go into business, but mostly they just stayed round in this languid paradise of dreamy skies and firefly evenings and noisy nigger street fairs—and especially of gracious, soft-voiced girls, who were brought up on memories instead of money.

The Ford having been excited into a sort of restless resentful life Clark and Sally Carrol rolled and rattled down Valley Avenue into Jefferson Street, where the dust road became a pavement; along opiate Millicent Place, where there were half a dozen prosperous, substantial mansions; and on into the down-town section. Driving was perilous here, for it was shopping time; the population idled casually across the streets and a drove of low-moaning oxen were being urged along in front of a placid street-car; even the shops seemed only yawning their doors and blinking their windows in the sunshine before retiring into a state of utter and finite coma.

"Sally Carrol," said Clark suddenly, "it a fact that you're engaged?"

She looked at him quickly.

"Where'd you hear that?"

"Sure enough, you engaged?"

"'At's a nice question!"

"Girl told me you were engaged to a Yankee you met up in Asheville last summer."

Sally Carrol sighed.

"Never saw such an old town for rumors."

"Don't marry a Yankee, Sally Carrol. We need you round here."

Sally Carrol was silent a moment.

"Clark," she demanded suddenly, "who on earth shall I marry?"

"I offer my services."

"Honey, you couldn't support a wife," she answered cheerfully. "Anyway, I know you too well to fall in love with you."

"'At doesn't mean you ought to marry a Yankee," he persisted.

"S'pose I love him?"

He shook his head.

"You couldn't. He'd be a lot different from us, every way."

He broke off as he halted the car in front of a rambling, dilapidated house. Marylyn Wade and Joe Ewing appeared in the doorway.

"'Lo Sally Carrol."

"Hi!"

"How you-all?"

"Sally Carrol," demanded Marylyn as they started of again, "you engaged?"

"Lawdy, where'd all this start? Can't I look at a man 'thout everybody in town engagin' me to him?"

Clark stared straight in front of him at a bolt on the clattering wind-shield.

"Sally Carrol," he said with a curious intensity, "don't you 'like us?"

"What?"

"Us down here?"

"Why, Clark, you know I do. I adore all you boys."
"Then why you gettin' engaged to a Yankee?"
"Clark, I don't know. I'm not sure what I'll do, but—well, I want to go places and see people. I want my mind to grow. I want to live where things happen on a big scale."
"What you mean?"
"Oh, Clark, I love you, and I love Joe here and Ben Arrot, and you-all, but you'll—you'll——"
"We'll all be failures?"
"Yes. I don't mean only money failures, but just sort of—of ineffectual and sad, and—oh, how can I tell you?"
"You mean because we stay here in Tarleton?"
"Yes, Clark; and because you like it and never want to change things or think or go ahead."
He nodded and she reached over and pressed his hand.
"Clark," she said softly, "I wouldn't change you for the world. You're sweet the way you are. The things that'll make you fail I'll love always—the living in the past, the lazy days and nights you have, and all your carelessness and generosity."
"But you're goin' away?"
"Yes—because I couldn't ever marry you. You've a place in my heart no one else ever could have, but tied down here I'd get restless. I'd feel I was—wastin' myself. There's two sides to me, you see. There's the sleepy old side you love an' there's a sort of energy—the feeling that makes me do wild things. That's the part of me that

may be useful somewhere, that'll last when I'm not beautiful any more."

She broke of with characteristic suddenness and sighed, "Oh, sweet cooky!" as her mood changed.

Half closing her eyes and tipping back her head till it rested on the seat-back she let the savory breeze fan her eyes and ripple the fluffy curls of her bobbed hair. They were in the country now, hurrying between tangled growths of bright-green coppice and grass and tall trees that sent sprays of foliage to hang a cool welcome over the road. Here and there they passed a battered negro cabin, its oldest white-haired inhabitant smoking a corncob pipe beside the door, and half a dozen scantily clothed pickaninnies parading tattered dolls on the wild-grown grass in front. Farther out were lazy cotton-fields where even the workers seemed intangible shadows lent by the sun to the earth, not for toil, but to while away some age-old tradition in the golden September fields. And round the drowsy picturesqueness, over the trees and shacks and muddy rivers, flowed the heat, never hostile, only comforting, like a great warm nourishing bosom for the infant earth.

"Sally Carrol, we're here!"

"Poor chile's soun' asleep."

"Honey, you dead at last outa sheer laziness?"

"Water, Sally Carrol! Cool water waitin' for you!"

Her eyes opened sleepily.

"Hi!" she murmured, smiling.

II

In November Harry Bellamy, tall, broad, and brisk, came down from his Northern city to spend four days. His intention was to settle a matter that had been hanging fire since he and Sally Carrol had met in Asheville, North Carolina, in midsummer. The settlement took only a quiet afternoon and an evening in front of a glowing open fire, for Harry Bellamy had everything she wanted; and, beside, she loved him—loved him with that side of her she kept especially for loving. Sally Carrol had several rather clearly defined sides.

On his last afternoon they walked, and she found their steps tending half-unconsciously toward one of her favorite haunts, the cemetery. When it came in sight, gray-white and golden-green under the cheerful late sun, she paused, irresolute, by the iron gate.

"Are you mournful by nature, Harry?" she asked with a faint smile.

"Mournful? Not I."

"Then let's go in here. It depresses some folks, but I like it."

They passed through the gateway and followed a path that led through a wavy valley of graves—dusty-gray and mouldy for the fifties; quaintly carved with flowers and jars for the seventies; ornate and hideous for the nineties, with fat marble cherubs lying in sodden sleep on stone pillows, and great impossible growths of nameless granite flowers.

Occasionally they saw a kneeling figure with tributary flowers, but over most of the graves lay silence and withered leaves with only the fragrance that their own shadowy memories could waken in living minds.

They reached the top of a hill where they were fronted by a tall, round head-stone, freckled with dark spots of damp and half grown over with vines.

"Margery Lee," she read; "1844-1873. Wasn't she nice? She died when she was twenty-nine. Dear Margery Lee," she added softly. "Can't you see her, Harry?"

"Yes, Sally Carrol."

He felt a little hand insert itself into his.

"She was dark, I think; and she always wore her hair with a ribbon in it, and gorgeous hoop-skirts of Alice blue and old rose."

"Yes."

"Oh, she was sweet, Harry! And she was the sort of girl born to stand on a wide, pillared porch and welcome folks in. I think perhaps a lot of men went away to war meanin' to come back to her; but maybe none of 'em ever did."

He stooped down close to the stone, hunting for any record of marriage.

"There's nothing here to show."

"Of course not. How could there be anything there better than just 'Margery Lee,' and that eloquent date?"

She drew close to him and an unexpected lump came into his throat as her yellow hair brushed his cheek.

"You see how she was, don't you Harry?"

"I see," he agreed gently. "I see through your precious eyes. You're beautiful now, so I know she must have been."

Silent and close they stood, and he could feel her shoulders trembling a little. An ambling breeze swept up the hill and stirred the brim of her floppidy hat.

"Let's go down there!"

She was pointing to a flat stretch on the other side of the hill where along the green turf were a thousand grayish-white crosses stretching in endless, ordered rows like the stacked arms of a battalion.

"Those are the Confederate dead," said Sally Carrol simply.

They walked along and read the inscriptions, always only a name and a date, sometimes quite indecipherable.

"The last row is the saddest—see, 'way over there. Every cross has just a date on it and the word 'Unknown.'"

She looked at him and her eyes brimmed with tears.

"I can't tell you how real it is to me, darling—if you don't know."

"How you feel about it is beautiful to me."

"No, no, it's not me, it's them—that old time that I've tried to have live in me. These were just men, unimportant evidently or they wouldn't have been 'unknown'; but they died for the most beautiful thing in the world—the dead South. You see," she continued, her voice still husky, her eyes glistening with tears, "people have these dreams they fasten onto things, and I've always grown up with that dream. It was so easy because it was all dead and there weren't any disillusions comin' to me. I've tried in a way to live up to those past standards of noblesse oblige—there's just the last remnants of it, you know, like the roses of an old garden dying all round us—streaks of strange courtliness and chivalry in some of these boys an' stories I used to hear from a Confederate soldier who lived next door, and a few old darkies. Oh, Harry, there was something, there was something! I couldn't ever make you understand but it was there."

"I understand," he assured her again quietly.

Sally Carol smiled and dried her eyes on the tip of a handkerchief protruding from his breast pocket.

"You don't feel depressed, do you, lover? Even when I cry I'm happy here, and I get a sort of strength from it."

Hand in hand they turned and walked slowly away. Finding soft grass she drew him down to a seat beside her with their backs against the remnants of a low broken wall.

"Wish those three old women would clear out," he complained. "I want to kiss you, Sally Carrol."

"Me, too."

They waited impatiently for the three bent figures to move off, and then she kissed him until the sky seemed to fade out and all her smiles and tears to vanish in an ecstasy of eternal seconds.

Afterward they walked slowly back together, while on the corners twilight played at somnolent black-and-white checkers with the end of day.

"You'll be up about mid-January," he said, "and you've got to stay a month at least. It'll be slick. There's a winter carnival on, and if you've never really seen snow it'll be like fairy-land to you. There'll be skating and skiing and tobogganing and sleigh-riding, and all sorts of torchlight parades on snow-shoes. They haven't had one for years, so they're gong to make it a knock-out."

"Will I be cold, Harry?" she asked suddenly.

"You certainly won't. You may freeze your nose, but you won't be shivery cold. It's hard and dry, you know."

"I guess I'm a summer child. I don't like any cold I've ever seen."

She broke off and they were both silent for a minute.

"Sally Carol," he said very slowly, "what do you say to—March?"

"I say I love you."

"March?"

"March, Harry."

III

All night in the Pullman it was very cold. She rang for the porter to ask for another blanket, and when he couldn't give her one she tried vainly, by squeezing down into the bottom of her berth and doubling back the bedclothes, to snatch a few hours' sleep. She wanted to look her best in the morning.

She rose at six and sliding uncomfortably into her clothes stumbled up to the diner for a cup of coffee. The snow had filtered into the vestibules and covered the door with a slippery coating. It was intriguing this cold, it crept in everywhere. Her breath was quite visible and she blew into the air with a naïve enjoyment. Seated in the diner she stared out the window at white hills and valleys and scattered pines whose every branch was a green platter for a cold feast of snow. Sometimes a solitary farmhouse would fly by, ugly and bleak and lone on the white waste; and with each one she had an instant of chill compassion for the souls shut in there waiting for spring.

As she left the diner and swayed back into the Pullman she experienced a surging rush of energy and wondered if she was feeling the bracing air of which Harry had spoken. This was the North, the North—her land now!

"Then blow, ye winds, heighho!
A-roving I will go,"

she chanted exultantly to herself.

"What's 'at?" inquired the porter politely.

"I said: 'Brush me off.'"

The long wires of the telegraph poles doubled, two tracks ran up beside the train—three—four; came a succession of white-roofed houses, a glimpse of a trolley-car with frosted windows, streets—more streets—the city.

She stood for a dazed moment in the frosty station before she saw three fur-bundled figures descending upon her.

"There she is!"

"Oh, Sally Carrol!"

Sally Carrol dropped her bag.

"Hi!"

A faintly familiar icy-cold face kissed her, and then she was in a group of faces all apparently emitting great clouds of heavy smoke; she was shaking hands. There were Gordon, a short, eager man of thirty who looked like an amateur knocked-about model for Harry, and his wife, Myra, a listless lady with flaxen hair under a fur automobile cap. Almost immediately Sally Carrol thought of her as vaguely Scandinavian. A cheerful chauffeur adopted her bag, and amid ricochets of half-phrases, exclamations and perfunctory listless "my dears" from Myra, they swept each other from the station.

Then they were in a sedan bound through a crooked succession of snowy streets where dozens of little boys were hitching sleds behind grocery wagons and automobiles.

"Oh," cried Sally Carrol, "I want to do that! Can we Harry?"

"That's for kids. But we might——"

"It looks like such a circus!" she said regretfully.

Home was a rambling frame house set on a white lap of snow, and there she met a big, gray-haired man of whom she approved, and a lady who was like an egg, and who kissed her—these were Harry's parents. There was a breathless indescribable hour crammed full of self-sentences, hot water, bacon and eggs and confusion; and after that she was alone with Harry in the library, asking him if she dared smoke.

It was a large room with a Madonna over the fireplace and rows upon rows of books in covers of light gold and dark gold and shiny red. All the chairs had little lace squares where one's head should rest, the couch was just comfortable, the books looked as if they had been read—some—and Sally Carrol had an instantaneous vision of the battered old library at home, with her father's huge medical books, and the oil-paintings of her three great-uncles, and the old couch that had been mended up for forty-five years and was still luxurious to dream in. This room struck her as being neither attractive nor particularly otherwise. It was simply a room with a lot of fairly expensive things in it that all looked about fifteen years old.

"What do you think of it up here?" demanded Harry eagerly. "Does it surprise you? Is it what you expected I mean?"

"You are, Harry," she said quietly, and reached out her arms to him.

But after a brief kiss he seemed to extort enthusiasm from her.

"The town, I mean. Do you like it? Can you feel the

pep in the air?"

"Oh, Harry," she laughed, "you'll have to give me time. You can't just fling questions at me."

She puffed at her cigarette with a sigh of contentment.

"One thing I want to ask you," he began rather apologetically; "you Southerners put quite an emphasis on family, and all that—not that it isn't quite all right, but you'll find it a little different here. I mean—you'll notice a lot of things that'll seem to you sort of vulgar display at first, Sally Carrol; but just remember that this is a three-generation town. Everybody has a father, and about half of us have grandfathers. Back of that we don't go."

"Of course," she murmured.

"Our grandfathers, you see, founded the place, and a lot of them had to take some pretty queer jobs while they were doing the founding. For instance there's one woman who at present is about the social model for the town; well, her father was the first public ash man—things like that."

"Why," said Sally Carol, puzzled, "did you s'pose I was goin' to make remarks about people?"

"Not at all," interrupted Harry, "and I'm not apologizing for any one either. It's just that—well, a Southern girl came up here last summer and said some unfortunate things, and—oh, I just thought I'd tell you."

Sally Carrol felt suddenly indignant—as though she had been unjustly spanked—but Harry evidently considered the subject closed, for he went on with a great surge of enthusiasm.

"It's carnival time, you know. First in ten years. And there's an ice palace they're building new that's the first they've had since eighty-five. Built out of blocks of the clearest ice they could find—on a tremendous scale."

She rose and walking to the window pushed aside the heavy Turkish portières and looked out.

"Oh!" she cried suddenly. "There's two little boys makin' a snow man! Harry, do you reckon I can go out an' help 'em?"

"You dream! Come here and kiss me."

She left the window rather reluctantly.

"I don't guess this is a very kissable climate, is it? I mean, it makes you so you don't want to sit round, doesn't it?"

"We're not going to. I've got a vacation for the first week you're here, and there's a dinner-dance to-night."

"Oh, Harry," she confessed, subsiding in a heap, half in his lap, half in the pillows, "I sure do feel confused. I haven't got an idea whether I'll like it or not, an' I don't know what people expect, or anythin'. You'll have to tell me, honey."

"I'll tell you," he said softly, "if you'll just tell me you're glad to be here."

"Glad—just awful glad!" she whispered, insinuating herself into his arms in her own peculiar way. "Where you are is home for me, Harry."

And as she said this she had the feeling for almost the

first time in her life that she was acting a part.

That night, amid the gleaming candles of a dinner-party, where the men seemed to do most of the talking while the girls sat in a haughty and expensive aloofness, even Harry's presence on her left failed to make her feel at home.

"They're a good-looking crowd, don't you think?" he demanded. "Just look round. There's Spud Hubbard, tackle at Princeton last year, and Junie Morton—he and the red-haired fellow next to him were both Yale hockey captains; Junie was in my class. Why, the best athletes in the world come from these States round here. This is a man's country, I tell you. Look at John J. Fishburn!"

"Who's he?" asked Sally Carrol innocently.

"Don't you know?"

"I've heard the name."

"Greatest wheat man in the Northwest, and one of the greatest financiers in the country."

She turned suddenly to a voice on her right.

"I guess they forget to introduce us. My name's Roger Patton."

"My name is Sally Carrol Happer," she said graciously.

"Yes, I know. Harry told me you were coming."

"You a relative?"

"No, I'm a professor."

"Oh," she laughed.

"At the university. You're from the South, aren't you?"

"Yes; Tarleton, Georgia."

She liked him immediately—a reddish-brown mustache under watery blue eyes that had something in them that these other eyes lacked, some quality of appreciation. They exchanged stray sentences through dinner, and she made up her mind to see him again.

After coffee she was introduced to numerous good-looking young men who danced with conscious precision and seemed to take it for granted that she wanted to talk about nothing except Harry.

"Heavens," she thought, "They talk as if my being engaged made me older than they are—as if I'd tell their mothers on them!"

In the South an engaged girl, even a young married woman, expected the same amount of half-affectionate badinage and flattery that would be accorded a débutante, but here all that seemed banned. One young man after getting well started on the subject of Sally Carrol's eyes and, how they had allured him ever since she entered the room, went into a violent convulsion when he found she was visiting the Bellamys—was Harry's fiancée. He seemed to feel as though he had made some risqué and inexcusable blunder, became immediately formal and left her at the first opportunity.

She was rather glad when Roger Patton cut in on her and suggested that they sit out a while.

"Well," he inquired, blinking cheerily, "how's Carmen from the South?"

"Mighty fine. How's—how's Dangerous Dan McGrew?

Sorry, but he's the only Northerner I know much about."

He seemed to enjoy that.

"Of course," he confessed, "as a professor of literature I'm not supposed to have read Dangerous Dan McGrew."

"Are you a native?"

"No, I'm a Philadelphian. Imported from Harvard to teach French. But I've been here ten years."

"Nine years, three hundred an' sixty-four days longer than me."

"Like it here?"

"Uh-huh. Sure do!"

"Really?"

"Well, why not? Don't I look as if I were havin' a good time?"

"I saw you look out the window a minute ago—and shiver."

"Just my imagination," laughed Sally Carroll "I'm used to havin' everythin' quiet outside an' sometimes I look out an' see a flurry of snow an' it's just as if somethin' dead was movin'."

He nodded appreciatively.

"Ever been North before?"

"Spent two Julys in Asheville, North Carolina."

"Nice-looking crowd aren't they?" suggested Patton, indicating the swirling floor.

Sally Carrol started. This had been Harry's remark.

"Sure are! They're—canine."

"What?"

She flushed.

"I'm sorry; that sounded worse than I meant it. You see I always think of people as feline or canine, irrespective of sex."

"Which are you?"

"I'm feline. So are you. So are most Southern men an' most of these girls here."

"What's Harry?"

"Harry's canine distinctly. All the men I've to-night seem to be canine."

"What does canine imply? A certain conscious masculinity as opposed to subtlety?"

"Reckon so. I never analyzed it—only I just look at people an' say 'canine' or 'feline' right off. It's right absurd I guess."

"Not at all. I'm interested. I used to have a theory about these people. I think they're freezing up."

"What?"

"Well, they're growing' like Swedes—Ibsenesque, you know. Very gradually getting gloomy and melancholy. It's these long winters. Ever read Ibsen?"

She shook her head.

"Well, you find in his characters a certain brooding rigidity. They're righteous, narrow, and cheerless, without infinite possibilities for great sorrow or joy."

"Without smiles or tears?"

"Exactly. That's my theory. You see there are thousands of Swedes up here. They come, I imagine, because the climate is very much like their own, and there's been a gradual mingling. There're probably not half a dozen here to-night, but—we've had four Swedish governors. Am I boring you?"

"I'm mighty interested."

"Your future sister-in-law is half Swedish. Personally I like her, but my theory is that Swedes react rather badly on us as a whole. Scandinavians, you know, have the largest suicide rate in the world."

"Why do you live here if it's so depressing?"

"Oh, it doesn't get me. I'm pretty well cloistered, and I suppose books mean more than people to me anyway."

"But writers all speak about the South being tragic. You know—Spanish señoritas, black hair and daggers an' haunting music."

He shook his head.

"No, the Northern races are the tragic races—they don't indulge in the cheering luxury of tears."

Sally Carrol thought of her graveyard. She supposed that that was vaguely what she had meant when she said it didn't depress her.

"The Italians are about the gayest people in the world—but it's a dull subject," he broke off. "Anyway, I want to tell you you're marrying a pretty fine man."

Sally Carrol was moved by an impulse of confidence.

"I know. I'm the sort of person who wants to be taken care of after a certain point, and I feel sure I will be."

"Shall we dance? You know," he continued as they rose,

"it's encouraging to find a girl who knows what she's marrying for. Nine-tenths of them think of it as a sort of walking into a moving-picture sunset."

She laughed and liked him immensely.

Two hours later on the way home she nestled near Harry in the back seat.

"Oh, Harry," she whispered "it's so co-old!"

"But it's warm in here, daring girl."

"But outside it's cold; and oh, that howling wind!"

She buried her face deep in his fur coat and trembled involuntarily as his cold lips kissed the tip of her ear.

IV

The first week of her visit passed in a whirl. She had her promised toboggan-ride at the back of an automobile through a chill January twilight. Swathed in furs she put in a morning tobogganing on the country-club hill; even tried skiing, to sail through the air for a glorious moment and then land in a tangled laughing bundle on a soft snow-drift. She liked all the winter sports, except an afternoon spent snow-shoeing over a glaring plain under pale yellow sunshine, but she soon realized that these things were for children—that she was being humored and that the enjoyment round her was only a reflection of her own.

At first the Bellamy family puzzled her. The men were reliable and she liked them; to Mr. Bellamy especially, with his iron-gray hair and energetic dignity, she took an immediate fancy, once she found that he was born in Kentucky; this made of him a link between the old life and the new. But toward the women she felt a definite hostility. Myra, her future sister-in-law, seemed the essence of spiritless conversationality. Her conversation was so utterly devoid of personality that Sally Carrol, who came from a country where a certain amount of charm and assurance could be taken for granted in the women, was inclined to despise her.

"If those women aren't beautiful," she thought, "they're nothing. They just fade out when you look at them. They're glorified domestics. Men are the centre of every mixed group."

Lastly there was Mrs. Bellamy, whom Sally Carrol detested. The first day's impression of an egg had been confirmed—an egg with a cracked, veiny voice and such an ungracious dumpiness of carriage that Sally Carrol felt that if she once fell she would surely scramble. In addition, Mrs. Bellamy seemed to typify the town in being innately hostile to strangers. She called Sally Carrol "Sally," and could not be persuaded that the double name was anything more than a tedious ridiculous nickname. To Sally Carrol this shortening of her name was presenting her to the public half clothed. She loved "Sally Carrol"; she loathed "Sally." She knew also that Harry's mother disapproved of her bobbed hair; and she had never dared smoke down-stairs after that first day when Mrs. Bellamy had come into the library sniffing violently.

Of all the men she met she preferred Roger Patton, who was a frequent visitor at the house. He never again alluded to the Ibsenesque tendency of the populace, but when he came in one day and found her curled upon the sofa bent over "Peer Gynt" he laughed and told her to forget what he'd said—that it was all rot.

They had been walking homeward between mounds of high-piled snow and under a sun which Sally Carrol scarcely recognized. They passed a little girl done up in gray wool until she resembled a small Teddy bear, and Sally Carrol could not resist a gasp of maternal appreciation.

"Look! Harry!"

"What?"

"That little girl—did you see her face?"

"Yes, why?"

"It was red as a little strawberry. Oh, she was cute!"

"Why, your own face is almost as red as that already! Everybody's healthy here. We're out in the cold as soon as we're old enough to walk. Wonderful climate!"

She looked at him and had to agree. He was mighty healthy-looking; so was his brother. And she had noticed the new red in her own cheeks that very morning.

Suddenly their glances were caught and held, and they stared for a moment at the street-corner ahead of them. A man was standing there, his knees bent, his eyes gazing upward with a tense expression as though he were about to make a leap toward the chilly sky. And then they both exploded into a shout of laughter, for coming closer they discovered it had been a ludicrous momentary illusion produced by the extreme bagginess of the man's trousers.

"Reckon that's one on us," she laughed.

"He must be Southerner, judging by those trousers," suggested Harry mischievously.

"Why, Harry!"

Her surprised look must have irritated him.

"Those damn Southerners!"

Sally Carrol's eyes flashed.

"Don't call 'em that."

"I'm sorry, dear," said Harry, malignantly apologetic, "but you know what I think of them. They're sort of—sort of degenerates—not at all like the old Southerners. They've lived so long down there with all the colored people that they've gotten lazy and shiftless."

"Hush your mouth, Harry!" she cried angrily. "They're not! They may be lazy—anybody would be in that climate—but they're my best friends, an' I don't want to hear 'em criticised in any such sweepin' way. Some of 'em are the finest men in the world."

"Oh, I know. They're all right when they come North to college, but of all the hangdog, ill-dressed, slovenly lot I ever saw, a bunch of small-town Southerners are the worst!"

Sally Carrol was clinching her gloved hands and biting her lip furiously.

"Why," continued Harry, "if there was one in my class at New Haven, and we all thought that at last we'd found the true type of Southern aristocrat, but it turned out that he wasn't an aristocrat at all—just the son of a Northern carpetbagger, who owned about all the cotton round Mobile."

"A Southerner wouldn't talk the way you're talking now," she said evenly.

"They haven't the energy!"

"Or the somethin' else."

"I'm sorry Sally Carrol, but I've heard you say yourself that you'd never marry——"

"That's quite different. I told you I wouldn't want to tie my life to any of the boys that are round Tarleton now, but I never made any sweepin' generalities."

They walked along in silence.

"I probably spread it on a bit thick Sally Carrol. I'm sorry."

She nodded but made no answer. Five minutes later as they stood in the hallway she suddenly threw her arms round him.

"Oh, Harry," she cried, her eyes brimming with tears; "let's get married next week. I'm afraid of having fusses like that. I'm afraid, Harry. It wouldn't be that way if we were married."

But Harry, being in the wrong, was still irritated.

"That'd be idiotic. We decided on March."

The tears in Sally Carrol's eyes faded; her expression

hardened slightly.

"Very well—I suppose I shouldn't have said that."

Harry melted.

"Dear little nut!" he cried. "Come and kiss me and let's forget." That very night at the end of a vaudeville performance the orchestra played "Dixie" and Sally Carrol felt something stronger and more enduring than her tears and smiles of the day brim up inside her. She leaned forward gripping the arms of her chair until her face grew crimson.

"Sort of get you dear?" whispered Harry.

But she did not hear him. To the limited throb of the violins and the inspiring beat of the kettle-drums her own old ghosts were marching by and on into the darkness, and as fifes whistled and sighed in the low encore they seemed so nearly out of sight that she could have waved good-by.

"Away, Away,
Away down South in Dixie!
Away, away,
Away down South in Dixie!"

V

It was a particularly cold night. A sudden thaw had nearly cleared the streets the day before, but now they were traversed again with a powdery wraith of loose snow that travelled in wavy lines before the feet of the wind, and filled the lower air with a fine-particled mist.

There was no sky—only a dark, ominous tent that draped in the tops of the streets and was in reality a vast approaching army of snowflakes—while over it all, chilling away the comfort from the brown-and-green glow of lighted windows and muffling the steady trot of the horse pulling their sleigh, interminably washed the north wind. It was a dismal town after all, she though, dismal.

Sometimes at night it had seemed to her as though no one lived here—they had all gone long ago—leaving lighted houses to be covered in time by tombing heaps of sleet. Oh, if there should be snow on her grave! To be beneath great piles of it all winter long, where even her headstone would be a light shadow against light shadows. Her grave—a grave that should be flower-strewn and washed with sun and rain.

She thought again of those isolated country houses that her train had passed, and of the life there the long winter through—the ceaseless glare through the windows, the crust forming on the soft drifts of snow, finally the slow cheerless melting and the harsh spring of which Roger Patton had told her. Her spring—to lose it forever—with its lilacs and the lazy sweetness it stirred in her heart. She was laying away that spring—afterward she would lay away that sweetness.

With a gradual insistence the storm broke. Sally Carrol felt a film of flakes melt quickly on her eyelashes, and Harry reached over a furry arm and drew down her complicated flannel cap. Then the small flakes came in skirmish-line, and the horse bent his neck patiently as a transparency of white appeared momentarily on his coat.

"Oh, he's cold, Harry," she said quickly.

"Who? The horse? Oh, no, he isn't. He likes it!"

After another ten minutes they turned a corner and came in sight of their destination. On a tall hill outlined in vivid glaring green against the wintry sky stood the ice palace. It was three stories in the air, with battlements and embrasures and narrow icicled windows, and the innumerable electric lights inside made a gorgeous transparency of the great central hall. Sally Carrol clutched Harry's hand under the fur robe.

"It's beautiful!" he cried excitedly. "My golly, it's beautiful, isn't it! They haven't had one here since eighty-five!"

Somehow the notion of there not having been one since eighty-five oppressed her. Ice was a ghost, and this mansion of it was surely peopled by those shades of the eighties, with pale faces and blurred snow-filled hair.

"Come on, dear," said Harry.

She followed him out of the sleigh and waited while he hitched the horse. A party of four—Gordon, Myra, Roger Patton, and another girl—drew up beside them with a mighty jingle of bells. There were quite a crowd already, bundled in fur or sheepskin, shouting and calling to each other as they moved through the snow, which was now so thick that people could scarcely be distinguished a few yards away.

"It's a hundred and seventy feet tall," Harry was saying to a muffled figure beside him as they trudged toward the entrance; "covers six thousand square yards."

She caught snatches of conversation: "One main hall"—"walls twenty to forty inches thick"—"and the ice cave has almost a mile of—"—"this Canuck who built it——"

They found their way inside, and dazed by the magic of the great crystal walls Sally Carrol found herself repeating over and over two lines from "Kubla Khan": "It was a miracle of rare device,

A sunny pleasure-dome with caves of ice!"

In the great glittering cavern with the dark shut out she took a seat on a wooded bench and the evening's oppression lifted. Harry was right—it was beautiful; and her gaze travelled the smooth surface of the walls, the blocks for which had been selected for their purity and dearness to obtain this opalescent, translucent effect.

"Look! Here we go—oh, boy!" cried Harry.

A band in a far corner struck up "Hail, Hail, the Gang's All Here!" which echoed over to them in wild muddled acoustics, and then the lights suddenly went out; silence seemed to flow down the icy sides and sweep over them. Sally Carrol could still see her white breath in the darkness, and a dim row of pale faces over on the other side.

The music eased to a sighing complaint, and from outside drifted in the full-throated remnant chant of the marching clubs. It grew louder like some pæan of a viking tribe traversing an ancient wild; it swelled—they were coming nearer; then a row of torches appeared, and another and another, and keeping time with their moccasined feet a long column of gray-mackinawed figures swept in, snow-shoes slung at their shoulders, torches soaring and flickering as their voice rose along the great walls.

The gray column ended and another followed, the light streaming luridly this time over red toboggan caps and flaming crimson mackinaws, and as they entered they took up the refrain; then came a long platoon of blue and white, of green, of white, of brown and yellow.

"Those white ones are the Wacouta Club," whispered Harry eagerly. "Those are the men you've met round at dances."

The volume of the voices grew; the great cavern was a phantasmagoria of torches waving in great banks of fire, of colors and the rhythm of soft-leather steps. The leading column turned and halted, platoon deploys in front of platoon until the whole procession made a solid flag of flame, and then from thousands of voices burst a mighty shout that filled the air like a crash of thunder, and sent the torches wavering. It was magnificent, it was tremendous! To Sally Carol it was the North offering sacrifice on some mighty altar to the gray pagan God of Snow. As the shout died the band struck up again and there came more singing, and then long reverberating cheers by each club. She sat very quiet listening while the staccato cries rent the stillness; and then she started, for there was a volley of explosion, and great clouds of smoke went up here and there through the cavern—the flash-light photographers at work—and the council was over. With the band at their head the clubs formed in column once more, took up their chant, and began to march out.

"Come on!" shouted Harry. "We want to see the labyrinths down-stairs before they turn the lights off!"

They all rose and started toward the chute—Harry and Sally Carrol in the lead, her little mitten buried in his big fur gantlet. At the bottom of the chute was a long empty room of ice, with the ceiling so low that they had to stoop—and their hands were parted. Before she realized what he intended Harry had darted down one of the half-dozen glittering passages that opened into the room and was only a vague receding blot against the green shimmer.

"Harry!" she called.

"Come on!" he cried back.

She looked round the empty chamber; the rest of the party had evidently decided to go home, were already outside somewhere in the blundering snow. She hesitated and then darted in after Harry.

"Harry!" she shouted.

She had reached a turning-point thirty feet down; she heard a faint muffled answer far to the left, and with a touch of panic fled toward it. She passed another turning, two more yawning alleys.

"Harry!"

No answer. She started to run straight forward, and then turned like lightning and sped back the way she had come, enveloped in a sudden icy terror.

She reached a turn—was it here?—took the left and came to what should have been the outlet into the long, low room, but it was only another glittering passage with darkness at the end. She called again, but the walls gave back a flat, lifeless echo with no reverberations. Retracing her steps she turned another corner, this time following a wide passage. It was like the green lane between the parted water of the Red Sea, like a damp vault connecting empty tombs.

She slipped a little now as she walked, for ice had formed on the bottom of her overshoes; she had to run her gloves along the half-slippery, half-sticky walls to keep her balance.

"Harry!"

Still no answer. The sound she made bounced mockingly down to the end of the passage.

Then on an instant the lights went out, and she was in complete darkness. She gave a small, frightened cry, and sank down into a cold little heap on the ice. She felt her left knee do something as she fell, but she scarcely noticed it as some deep terror far greater than any fear of being lost settled upon her. She was alone with this presence that came out of the North, the dreary loneliness that rose from ice-bound whalers in the Arctic seas, from smokeless, trackless wastes where were strewn the whitened bones of adventure. It was an icy breath of death; it was rolling down low across the land to clutch at her.

With a furious, despairing energy she rose again and started blindly down the darkness. She must get out. She might be lost in here for days, freeze to death and lie embedded in the ice like corpses she had read of, kept perfectly preserved until the melting of a glacier. Harry probably thought she had left with the others—he had gone by now; no one would know until next day. She reached pitifully for the wall. Forty inches thick, they had said—forty inches thick!

On both sides of her along the walls she felt things creeping, damp souls that haunted this palace, this town, this North.

"Oh, send somebody—send somebody!" she cried aloud.

Clark Darrow—he would understand; or Joe Ewing; she couldn't be left here to wander forever—to be frozen, heart, body, and soul. This her—this Sally Carrol! Why, she was a happy thing. She was a happy little girl. She liked warmth and summer and Dixie. These things were foreign—foreign.

"You're not crying," something said aloud. "You'll never cry any more. Your tears would just freeze; all tears freeze up here!"

She sprawled full length on the ice.

"Oh, God!" she faltered.

A long single file of minutes went by, and with a great weariness she felt her eyes dosing. Then some one seemed to sit down near her and take her face in warm, soft hands. She looked up gratefully.

"Why it's Margery Lee," she crooned softly to herself. "I knew you'd come." It really was Margery Lee, and she was just as Sally Carrol had known she would be, with a young, white brow, and wide welcoming eyes, and a hoop-skirt of some soft material that was quite comforting to rest on.

"Margery Lee."

It was getting darker now and darker—all those tombstones ought to be repainted sure enough, only that would spoil 'em, of course. Still, you ought to be able to see 'em.

Then after a succession of moments that went fast and then slow, but seemed to be ultimately resolving themselves into a multitude of blurred rays converging toward a pale-yellow sun, she heard a great cracking noise break her new-found stillness.

It was the sun, it was a light; a torch, and a torch beyond that, and another one, and voices; a face took flesh below the torch, heavy arms raised her and she felt something on her cheek—it felt wet. Some one had seized her and was rubbing her face with snow. How ridiculous—with snow!

"Sally Carrol! Sally Carrol!"

It was Dangerous Dan McGrew; and two other faces she didn't know. "Child, child! We've been looking for you two hours! Harry's half-crazy!"

Things came rushing back into place—the singing, the torches, the great shout of the marching clubs. She squirmed in Patton's arms and gave a long low cry.

"Oh, I want to get out of here! I'm going back home. Take me home"——her voice rose to a scream that sent a chill to Harry's heart as he came racing down the next passage—"to-morrow!" she cried with delirious, unstrained passion—"To-morrow! To-morrow! To-morrow!"

VI

The wealth of golden sunlight poured a quite enervating yet oddly comforting heat over the house where day long it faced the dusty stretch of road. Two birds were making a great to-do in a cool spot found among the branches of a tree next door, and down the street a colored woman was announcing herself melodiously as a purveyor of strawberries. It was April afternoon.

Sally Carrol Happer, resting her chin on her arm, and her arm on an old window-seat, gazed sleepily down over the spangled dust whence the heat waves were rising for the first time this spring. She was watching a very ancient Ford turn a perilous corner and rattle and groan to a jolting stop at the end of the walk. See made no sound and in a minute a strident familiar whistle rent the air. Sally Carrol smiled and blinked.

"Good mawnin'."

A head appeared tortuously from under the car-top below.

"Tain't mawnin', Sally Carrol."

"Sure enough!" she said in affected surprise. "I guess maybe not."

"What you doin'?"

"Eatin' a green peach. 'Spect to die any minute."

Clark twisted himself a last impossible notch to get a view of her face.

"Water's warm as a kettla steam, Sally Carol. Wanta go swimmin'?"

"Hate to move," sighed Sally Carol lazily, "but I reckon so."

The Nightingale and the Rose

Oscar Wilde

"She said that she would dance with me if I brought her red roses," cried the young Student; "but in all my garden there is no red rose."

From her nest in the holm-oak tree the Nightingale heard him, and she looked out through the leaves, and wondered.

"No red rose in all my garden!" he cried, and his beautiful eyes filled with tears. "Ah, on what little things does happiness depend! I have read all that the wise men have written, and all the secrets of philosophy are mine, yet for want of a red rose is my life made wretched." "Here at last is a true lover," said the Nightingale. "Night after night have I sung of him, though I knew him not: night after night have I told his story to the stars, and now I see him. His hair is dark as the hyacinth-blossom, and his lips are red as the rose of his desire; but passion has made his face like pale ivory, and sorrow has set her seal upon his brow." "The Prince gives a ball to-morrow night," murmured the young Student, "and my love will be of the company. If I bring her a red rose she will dance with me till dawn. If I bring her a red rose, I shall hold her in my arms, and she will lean her head upon my shoulder, and her hand will be clasped in mine. But there is no red rose in my garden, so I shall sit lonely, and she will pass me by. She will have no heed of me, and my heart will break." "Here indeed is the true lover," said the Nightingale. "What I sing of, he suffers—what is joy to me, to him is pain. Surely Love is a wonderful thing. It is more precious than emeralds, and dearer than fine opals. Pearls and pomegranates cannot buy it, nor is it set forth in the marketplace. It may not be purchased of the merchants, nor can it be weighed out in the balance for gold." "The musicians will sit in their gallery," said the young Student, "and play upon their stringed instruments, and my love will dance to the sound of the harp and the violin. She will dance so lightly that her feet will not touch the floor, and the courtiers in their gay dresses will throng round her. But with me she will not dance, for I have no red rose to give her"; and he flung himself down on the grass, and buried his face in his hands, and wept.

"Why is he weeping?" asked a little Green Lizard, as he ran past him with his tail in the air.

"Why, indeed?" said a Butterfly, who was fluttering about after a sunbeam.

"Why, indeed?" whispered a Daisy to his neighbour, in a soft, low voice.

"He is weeping for a red rose," said the Nightingale.

"For a red rose?" they cried; "how very ridiculous!" and the little Lizard, who was something of a cynic, laughed outright.

But the Nightingale understood the secret of the Student's sorrow, and she sat silent in the oak-tree, and thought about the mystery of Love.

Suddenly she spread her brown wings for flight, and soared into the air. She passed through the grove like a shadow, and like a shadow she sailed across the garden.

In the centre of the grass-plot was standing a beautiful Rose-tree, and when she saw it she flew over to it, and lit upon a spray.

"Give me a red rose," she cried, "and I will sing you my sweetest song."

But the Tree shook its head.

"My roses are white," it answered; "as white as the foam of the sea, and whiter than the snow upon the mountain. But go to my brother who grows round the old sun-dial, and perhaps he will give you what you want." So the Nightingale flew over to the Rose-tree that was growing round the old sun-dial.

"Give me a red rose," she cried, "and I will sing you my sweetest song."

But the Tree shook its head.

"My roses are yellow," it answered; "as yellow as the hair of the mermaiden who sits upon an amber throne, and yellower than the daffodil that blooms in the meadow before the mower comes with his scythe. But go to my brother who grows beneath the Student's window, and perhaps he will give you what you want." So the Nightingale flew over to the Rose-tree that was growing beneath the Student's window.

"Give me a red rose," she cried, "and I will sing you my sweetest song."

But the Tree shook its head.

"My roses are red," it answered, "as red as the feet of the dove, and redder than the great fans of coral that wave and wave in the ocean-cavern. But the winter has chilled my veins, and the frost has nipped my buds, and the storm has broken my branches, and I shall have no roses at all this year." "One red rose is all I want," cried the Nightingale, "only one red rose! Is there no way by which I can get it?"

"There is a way," answered the Tree; "but it is so terrible that I dare not tell it to you."

"Tell it to me," said the Nightingale, "I am not afraid."

"If you want a red rose," said the Tree, "you must build it out of music by moonlight, and stain it with your own heart's-blood. You must sing to me with your breast against a thorn. All night long you must sing to me, and the thorn must pierce your heart, and your life-blood must flow into my veins, and become mine." "Death is a great price to pay for a red rose," cried the Nightingale, "and Life is very dear to all. It is pleasant to sit in the green wood, and to watch the Sun in his chariot of gold, and the Moon in her chariot of pearl. Sweet is the scent of the hawthorn, and sweet are the bluebells that hide in the valley, and the heather that blows on the hill. Yet Love is better than Life, and what is the heart of a bird compared to the heart of a man?" So she spread her brown wings for flight, and soared into the air. She swept over the garden like a shadow, and like a shadow she sailed through the grove.

The young Student was still lying on the grass, where she had left him, and the tears were not yet dry in his beautiful eyes.

"Be happy," cried the Nightingale, "be happy; you shall have your red rose. I will build it out of music by moonlight, and stain it with my own heart's-blood. All that I ask of you in return is that you will be a true lover, for Love is wiser than Philosophy, though she is wise, and mightier than Power, though he is mighty. Flame-coloured are his wings, and coloured like flame is his body. His lips are sweet as honey, and his breath is like frankincense." The Student looked up from the grass, and listened, but he could not understand what the Nightingale was saying to him, for he only knew the things that are written down in books.

But the Oak-tree understood, and felt sad, for he was very fond of the little Nightingale who had built her nest in his branches.

"Sing me one last song," he whispered; "I shall feel very lonely when you are gone."

So the Nightingale sang to the Oak-tree, and her voice was like water bubbling from a silver jar.

When she had finished her song the Student got up, and pulled a note-book and a lead-pencil out of his pocket.

"She has form," he said to himself, as he walked away through the grove—"that cannot be denied to her; but has she got feeling? I am afraid not. In fact, she is like most artists; she is all style, without any sincerity. She would not sacrifice herself for others. She thinks merely of music, and everybody knows that the arts are selfish. Still, it must be admitted that she has some beautiful notes in her voice. What a pity it is that they do not mean anything, or do any practical good." And he went into his room, and lay down on his little pallet-bed, and began to think of his love; and, after a time, he fell asleep.

And when the Moon shone in the heavens the Nightingale flew to the Rose-tree, and set her breast against the thorn. All night long she sang with her breast against the thorn, and the cold crystal Moon leaned down and listened. All night long she sang, and the thorn went deeper and deeper into her breast, and her life-blood ebbed away from her.

She sang first of the birth of love in the heart of a boy and a girl. And on the top-most spray of the Rose-tree there blossomed a marvellous rose, petal following petal, as song followed song. Pale was it, at first, as the mist that hangs over the river—pale as the feet of the morning, and silver as the wings of the dawn. As the shadow of a rose in a mirror of silver, as the shadow of a rose in a water-pool, so was the rose that blossomed on the topmost spray of the Tree.

But the Tree cried to the Nightingale to press closer against the thorn. "Press closer, little Nightingale," cried the Tree, "or the Day will come before the rose is finished." So the Nightingale pressed closer against the thorn, and louder and louder grew her song, for she sang of the birth of passion in the soul of a man and a maid.

And a delicate flush of pink came into the leaves of the rose, like the flush in the face of the bridegroom when he kisses the lips of the bride. But the thorn had not yet reached her heart, so the rose's heart remained white, for only a Nightingale's heart's-blood can crimson the heart of a rose.

And the Tree cried to the Nightingale to press closer against the thorn. "Press closer, little Nightingale," cried the Tree, "or the Day will come before the rose is finished." So the Nightingale pressed closer against the thorn, and the thorn touched her heart, and a fierce pang of pain shot through her. Bitter, bitter was the pain, and wilder and wilder grew her song, for she sang of the Love that is perfected by Death, of the Love that dies not in the tomb.

And the marvellous rose became crimson, like the rose of the eastern sky. Crimson was the girdle of petals, and crimson as a ruby was the heart.

But the Nightingale's voice grew fainter, and her little wings began to beat, and a film came over her eyes. Fainter and fainter grew her song, and she felt something choking her in her throat.

Then she gave one last burst of music. The white Moon heard it, and she forgot the dawn, and lingered on in the sky. The red rose heard it, and it trembled all over with ecstasy, and opened its petals to the cold morning air. Echo bore it to her purple cavern in the hills, and woke the sleeping shepherds from their dreams. It floated through the reeds of the river, and they carried its message to the sea.

"Look, look!" cried the Tree, "the rose is finished now"; but the Nightingale made no answer, for she was lying dead in the long grass, with the thorn in her heart.

And at noon the Student opened his window and looked out.

"Why, what a wonderful piece of luck!" he cried; "here is a red rose! I have never seen any rose like it in all my life. It is so beautiful that I am sure it has a long Latin name"; and he leaned down and plucked it.

Then he put on his hat, and ran up to the Professor's house with the rose in his hand.

The daughter of the Professor was sitting in the doorway winding blue silk on a reel, and her little dog was lying at her feet.

"You said that you would dance with me if I brought you a red rose," cried the Student. "Here is the reddest rose in all the world. You will wear it to-night next your heart, and as we dance together it will tell you how I love you." But the girl frowned.

"I am afraid it will not go with my dress," she answered;

"and, besides, the Chamberlain's nephew has sent me some real jewels, and everybody knows that jewels cost far more than flowers." "Well, upon my word, you are very ungrateful," said the Student angrily; and he threw the rose into the street, where it fell into the gutter, and a cart-wheel went over it.

"Ungrateful!" said the girl. "I tell you what, you are very rude; and, after all, who are you? Only a Student. Why, I don't believe you have even got silver buckles to your shoes as the Chamberlain's nephew has"; and she got up from her chair and went into the house.

"What a silly thing Love is," said the Student as he walked away. "It is not half as useful as Logic, for it does not prove anything, and it is always telling one of things that are not going to happen, and making one believe things that are not true. In fact, it is quite unpractical, and, as in this age to be practical is everything, I shall go back to Philosophy and study Metaphysics." So he returned to his room and pulled out a great dusty book, and began to read.

Macbeth

William Shakespeare

When Duncan the Meek reigned king of Scotland, there lived a great thane, or lord, called Macbeth. This Macbeth was a near kinsman to the king, and in great esteem at court for his velour and conduct in the wars; an example of which he had lately given, in defeating a rebel army assisted by the troops of Norway in terrible numbers.

The two Scottish generals, Macbeth and Banquo, returning victorious from this great battle, their way lay over a blasted heath, where they were stopped by the strange appearance of three figures like women, except that they had beards, and their withered skins and wild attire made them look not like any earthly creatures. Macbeth first addressed them, when they, seemingly offended, laid each one her choppy finger upon her skinny lips, in token of silence; and the first of them saluted Macbeth with the title of thane of Glamis. The general was not a little startled to find himself known by such creatures; but how much more, when the second of them followed up that salute by giving him the title of thane of Cawdor, to which honour he had no pretensions; and again the third bid him 'All hail! king that shalt be hereafter!' Such a prophetic greeting might well amaze him, who knew that while the king's sons lived he could not hope to succeed to the throne. Then turning to Banquo, they pronounced him, in a sort of riddling terms, to be lesser than Macbeth and greater! not so happy, but much happier! and prophesied that though he should never reign, yet his sons after him should be kings in Scotland. They then turned into air, and vanished: by which the generals knew them to be the weird sisters, or witches.

While they stood pondering on the strangeness of this adventure, there arrived certain messengers from the king, who were empowered by him to confer upon Macbeth the dignity of thane of Cawdor: an event so miraculously corresponding with the prediction of the witches astonished Macbeth, and he stood wrapped in amazement, unable to make reply to the messengers; and in that point of time swelling hopes arose in his mind that the prediction of the third witch might in like manner have its accomplishment, and that he should one day reign king in Scotland.

Turning to Banquo, he said: 'Do you not hope that your children shall be kings, when what the witches promised to me has so wonderfully come to pass?' 'That hope,' answered the general, 'might enkindle you to aim at the throne; but oftentimes these ministers of darkness tell us truths in little things, to betray us into deeds of greatest consequence.'

But the wicked suggestions of the witches had sunk too deep into the mind of Macbeth to allow him to attend to the warnings of the good Banquo. From that time he bent all his thoughts how to compass the throne of Scotland.

Macbeth had a wife, to whom he communicated the strange prediction of the weird sisters, and its partial accomplishment. She was a bad, ambitious woman, and so as her husband and herself could arrive at greatness, she cared not much by what means. She spurred on the reluctant purpose of Macbeth, who felt compunction at the thoughts of blood, and did not cease to represent the murder of the king as a step absolutely necessary to the fulfilment of the flattering prophecy.

It happened at this time that the king, who out of his royal condescension would oftentimes visit his principal nobility upon gracious terms, came to Macbeth's house, attended by his two sons, Malcolm and Donalbain, and a numerous train of thanes and attendants, the more to honour Macbeth for the triumphal success of his wars.

The castle of Macbeth was pleasantly situated, and the air about it was sweet and wholesome, which appeared by the nests which the martlet, or swallow, had built under all the jutting friezes and buttresses of the building, wherever it found a place of advantage; for where those birds most breed and haunt, the air is observed to be delicate. The king entered well-pleased with the place, and not less so with the attentions and respect of his honoured hostess, lady Macbeth, who had the art of covering treacherous purposes with smiles; and could look like the innocent flower, while she was indeed the serpent under it.

The king being tired with his journey, went early to bed, and in his state-room two grooms of his chamber (as was the custom) slept beside him. He had been unusually pleased with his reception, and had made presents before he retired to his principal officers; and among the rest, had sent a rich diamond to lady Macbeth, greeting her by the name of his most kind hostess.

Now was the middle of night, when over half the world nature seems dead, and wicked dreams abuse men's minds asleep, and none but the wolf and the murderer is abroad. This was the time when lady Macbeth waked to plot the murder of the king. She would not have undertaken a deed so abhorrent to her sex, but that she feared her husband's nature, that it was too full of the milk of human kindness, to do a contrived murder. She knew him to be ambitious, but withal to be scrupulous, and not yet prepared for that height of crime which commonly in the end accompanies inordinate ambition. She had won him to consent to the murder, but she doubted his resolution; and she feared that the natural tenderness of his disposition (more humane than her own) would come between, and defeat the purpose. So with her own hands armed with a dagger, she approached the king's bed; having taken care to ply the grooms of his chamber so with wine, that they slept intoxicated, and careless of their charge. There lay Duncan in a sound sleep after the fatigues of his journey, and as she viewed him earnestly, there was something in his face, as he slept, which resembled her own father; and she had not the courage to proceed.

She returned to confer with her husband. His resolution had begun to stagger. He considered that there were strong reasons against the deed. In the first place, he was not only a subject, but a near kinsman to the king; and he had been his host and entertainer that day, whose duty, by the laws of hospitality, it was to shut the door against his murderers, not bear the knife himself. Then he considered how just and merciful a king this Duncan had been, how clear of offence to his subjects, how loving to his nobility, and in particular to him; that such kings are the peculiar care of Heaven, and their subjects doubly bound to revenge their deaths. Besides, by the favours of the king, Macbeth stood high in the opinion of all sorts of men, and how would those honours be stained by the reputation of so foul a murder!

In these conflicts of the mind lady Macbeth found her husband inclining to the better part, and resolving to proceed no further. But she being a woman not easily shaken from her evil purpose, began to pour in at his ears words which infused a portion of her own spirit into his mind, assigning reason upon reason why he should not shrink from what he had undertaken, how easy the deed was; how soon it would be over; and how the action of one short night would give to all their nights and days to come sovereign sway and royalty! Then she threw contempt on his change of purpose, and accused him of fickleness and cowardice; and declared that she had given suck, and knew how tender it was to love the babe 'that milked her; but she would, while it was smiling in her face, have plucked it from her breast, and dashed its brains out, if she had so sworn to do it, as he had sworn to perform that murder. Then she added, how practicable it was to lay the guilt of the deed upon the drunken sleepy grooms. And with the velour of her tongue she so chastised his sluggish resolutions, that he once more summoned up courage to the bloody business.

So, taking the dagger in his hand, he softly stole in the dark to the room where Duncan lay; and as he went, he thought he saw another dagger in the air, with the handle towards him, and on the blade and at the point of it drops of blood; but when he tried to grasp at it, it was nothing but air, a mere phantasm proceeding from his own hot and oppressed brain and the business he had in hand.

Getting rid of this fear, he entered the king's room, whom he despatched with one stroke of his dagger. Just as he had done the murder, one of the grooms, who slept in the chamber, laughed in his sleep, and the other cried: 'Murder,' which woke them both, but they said a short prayer; one of them said: 'God bless us!' and the other answered 'Amen'; and addressed themselves to sleep again. Macbeth, who stood listening to them, tried to say 'Amen,' when the fellow said 'God bless us!' but, though he had most need of a blessing, the word stuck in his throat, and he could not pronounce it.

Again he thought he heard a voice which cried: 'Sleep no more: Macbeth cloth murder sleep, the innocent sleep, that nourishes life.' Still it cried: 'Sleep no more,' to all the house. 'Glamis hath murdered sleep, and therefore Cawdor shall sleep no more. Macbeth shall sleep no more.'

With such horrible imaginations Macbeth returned to his listening wife, who began to think he had failed of his purpose, and that the deed was somehow frustrated. He came in so distracted a state, that she reproached him with his want of firmness, and sent him to wash his hands of the blood which stained them, while she took his dagger, with purpose to stain the cheeks of the grooms with blood, to make it seem their guilt.

Morning came, and with it the discovery of the murder, which could not be concealed; and though Macbeth and his lady made great show of grief, and the proofs against the grooms (the dagger being produced against them and their faces smeared with blood) were sufficiently strong, yet the entire suspicion fell upon Macbeth, whose inducements to such a deed were so much more forcible than such poor silly grooms could be supposed to have; and Duncan's two sons fled. Malcolm, the eldest, sought for refuge in the English court; and the youngest, Donalbain, made his escape to Ireland.

The king's sons, who should have succeeded him, having thus vacated the throne, Macbeth as next heir was crowned king, and thus the prediction of the weird sisters was literally accomplished.

Though placed so high, Macbeth and his queen could not forget the prophecy of the weird sisters, that, though Macbeth should be king, yet not his children, but the children of Banquo, should be kings after him. The thought of this, and that they had defiled their hands with blood, and done so great crimes, only to place the posterity of Banquo upon the throne, so rankled within them, that they determined to put to death both Banquo and his son, to make void the predictions of the weird sisters, which in their own case had been so remarkably brought to pass.

For this purpose they made a great supper, to which they invited all the chief thanes; and, among the rest, with marks of particular respect, Banquo and his son Fleance were invited. The way by which Banquo was to pass to the palace at night was beset by murderers appointed by Macbeth, who stabbed Banquo; but in the scuffle Fleance escaped. From that Fleance descended a race of monarchs who afterwards filled the Scottish throne, ending with James the Sixth of Scotland and the First of England, under whom the two crowns of England and Scotland were united.

At supper, the queen, whose manners were in the highest degree affable and royal, played the hostess with a gracefulness and attention which conciliated every one present, and Macbeth discoursed freely with his thanes and nobles, saying, that all that was honourable in the country was under his roof, if he had but his good friend Banquo present, whom yet he hoped he should rather have to chide for neglect, than to lament for any mischance. Just at these words the ghost of Banquo, whom he had caused to be murdered, entered the room and placed himself on the chair which Macbeth was about to occupy. Though Macbeth was a bold man, and one that could have faced the devil without trembling, at this horrible sight his cheeks turned white with fear, and he stood quite unmanned with his eyes fixed upon the ghost. His queen and all the nobles, who saw nothing, but perceived him gazing (as they thought) upon an empty chair, took it for a fit of distraction; and she reproached him, whispering that it was but the same fancy which made him see the dagger in the air, when he was about to kill Duncan. But Macbeth continued to see the ghost, and gave no heed to all they could say, while he addressed it with distracted words, yet so significant, that his queen, fearing the dreadful secret would be disclosed, in great haste dismissed the guests, excusing the infirmity of Macbeth as a disorder he was often troubled with.

To such dreadful fancies Macbeth was subject. His

queen and he had their sleeps afflicted with terrible dreams, and the blood of Banquo troubled them not more than the escape of Fleance, whom now they looked upon as father to a line of kings who should keep their posterity out of the throne. With these miserable thoughts they found no peace, and Macbeth determined once more to seek out the weird sisters, and know from them the worst.

He sought them in a cave upon the heath, where they, who knew by foresight of his coming, were engaged in preparing their dreadful charms, by which they conjured up infernal spirits to reveal to them futurity. Their horrid ingredients were toads, bats, and serpents, the eye of a newt, and the tongue of a dog, the leg of a lizard, and the wing of the night-owl, the scale of a dragon, the tooth of a wolf, the maw of the ravenous salt-sea shark, the mummy of a witch, the root of the poisonous hemlock (this to have effect must be digged in the dark), the gall of a goat, and the liver of a Jew, with slips of the yew tree that roots itself in graves, and the finger of a dead child: all these were set on to boil in a great kettle, or cauldron, which, as fast as it grew too hot, was cooled with a baboon's blood: to these they poured in the blood of a sow that had eaten her young, and they threw into the flame the grease that had sweaten from a murderer's gibbet. By these charms they bound the infernal spirits to answer their questions.

It was demanded of Macbeth, whether he would have

his doubts resolved by them, or by their masters, the spirits. He, nothing daunted by the dreadful ceremonies which he saw, boldly answered: 'Where are they? let me see them.' And they called the spirits, which were three. And the first arose in the likeness of an armed head, and he called Macbeth by name, and bid him beware of the thane of Fife; for which caution Macbeth thanked him; for Macbeth had entertained a jealousy of Macduff, the thane of Fife.

And the second spirit arose in the likeness of a bloody child, and he called Macbeth by name, and bid him have no fear, but laugh to scorn the power of man, for none of woman born should have power to hurt him; and he advised him to be bloody, bold, and resolute. 'Then live, Macduff! cried the king; 'what need I fear of thee? but yet I will make assurance doubly sure. Thou shalt not live; that I may tell pale-hearted Fear it lies, and sleep in spite of thunder.'

That spirit being dismissed, a third arose in the form of a child crowned, with a tree in his hand. He called Macbeth by name, and comforted him against conspiracies, saying, that he should never be vanquished, until the wood of Birnam to Dunsinane Hill should come against him. 'Sweet bodements! good!' cried Macbeth; 'who can unfix the forest, and move it from its earth-bound roots? I see I shall live the usual period of man's life, and not be cut off by a violent death. But my heart throbs to know one thing. Tell me, if your art can tell so much, if Banquo's issue shall ever reign in this kingdom?' Here the cauldron sank into the ground, and a noise of music was heard, and eight shadows, like kings, passed by Macbeth, and Banquo last, who bore a glass which showed the figures of many more, and Banquo all bloody smiled upon Macbeth, and pointed to them; by which Macbeth knew that these were the posterity of Banquo, who should reign after him in Scotland; and the witches, with a sound of soft music, and with dancing, making a show of duty and welcome to Macbeth, vanished. And from this time the thoughts of Macbeth were all bloody and dreadful.

The first thing he heard when he got out of the witches' cave, was that Macduff, thane of Fife, had fled to England, to join the army which was forming against him under Malcolm, the eldest son of the late king, with intent to displace Macbeth, and set Malcolm, the right heir, upon the throne. Macbeth, stung with rage, set upon the castle of Macduff, and put his wife and children, whom the thane had left behind, to the sword, and extended the slaughter to all who claimed the least relationship to Macduff.

These and such-like deeds alienated the minds of all his chief nobility from him. Such as could, fled to join with Malcolm and Macduff, who were now approaching with a powerful army, which they had raised in England; and the rest secretly wished success to their arms, though for fear of Macbeth they could take no active part. His recruits went on slowly. Everybody hated the tyrant; nobody loved or honoured him; but all suspected him, and he began to envy the condition of Duncan, whom he had murdered, who slept soundly in his grave, against whom treason had done its worst: steel nor poison, domestic malice nor foreign levies, could hurt him any longer.

While these things were acting, the queen, who had been the sole partner in his wickedness, in whose bosom he could sometimes seek a momentary repose from those terrible dreams which afflicted them both nightly, died, it is supposed, by her own hands, unable to bear the remorse of guilt, and public hate; by which event he was left alone, without a soul to love or care for him, or a friend to whom he could confide his wicked purposes.

He grew careless of life, and wished for death, but the near approach of Malcolm's army roused in him what remained of his ancient courage, and he determined to die (as he expressed it) 'with armour on his back.' Besides this, the hollow promises of the witches had filled him with a false confidence, and he remembered the sayings of the spirits, that none of woman born was to hurt him, and that he was never to be vanquished till Birnam wood should come to Dunsinane, which he thought could never be. So he shut himself up in his castle, whose impregnable strength was such as defied a siege: here he sullenly waited the approach of Malcolm. When, upon a day, there came a messenger to him, pale and shaking with fear, almost unable to report that which he had seen; for he averred, that as he stood upon his watch on the hill, he looked towards Birnam, and to his thinking the wood began to move! 'Liar and slave!' cried Macbeth: 'if thou speakest false, thou shalt hang alive upon the next tree, till famine end thee. If thy tale be true, I care not if thou cost as much by me': for Macbeth now began to faint in resolution, and to doubt the equivocal speeches of the spirits. He was not to fear till Birnam wood should come to Dunsinane; and now a wood did move! 'However,' said he, 'if this which he avouches be true, let us arm and out. There is no flying hence, nor staying here. I begin to be weary of the sun, and wish my life at an end.' With these desperate speeches he sallied forth upon the besiegers, who had now come up to the castle.

The strange appearance which had given the messenger an idea of a wood moving is easily solved. When the besieging army marched through the wood of Birnam, Malcolm, like a skilful general, instructed his soldiers to hew down every one a bough and bear it before him, by way of concealing the true numbers of his host. This marching of the soldiers with boughs had at a distance the appearance which had frightened the messenger. Thus were the words of the spirit brought to pass, in a sense different from that in which Macbeth had understood them, and one great hold of his confidence was gone.

And now a severe skirmishing took place, in which Macbeth, though feebly supported by those who called themselves his friends, but in reality hated the tyrant and inclined to the party of Malcolm and Macduff, yet fought with the extreme of rage and velour, cutting to pieces all who were opposed to him, till he came to where Macduff was fighting. Seeing Macduff, and remembering the caution of the spirit who had counselled him to avoid Macduff, above all men, he would have turned, but Macduff, who had been seeking him through the whole fight, opposed his turning, and a fierce contest ensued; Macduff giving him many foul reproaches for the murder of his wife and children. Macbeth, whose soul was charged enough with blood of that family already, would still have declined the combat: but Macduff still urged him to it, calling him tyrant, murderer, hell-hound, and villain.

Then Macbeth remembered the words of the spirit, how none of woman born should hurt him; and smiling confidently he said to Macduff: 'Thou losest thy labour, Macduff. As easily thou mayest impress the air with thy sword, as make me vulnerable. I bear a charmed life, which must not yield to one of woman born.'

'Despair thy charm,' said Macduff, 'and let that lying spirit whom thou hast served, tell thee, that Macduff was never born of woman, never as the ordinary manner of men is to be born, but was untimely taken from his mother.'

'Accursed be the tongue which tells me so,' said the trembling Macbeth, who felt his last hold of confidence give way; 'and let never man in future believe the lying equivocations of witches and juggling spirits, who deceive us in words which have double senses, and while they keep their promise literally, disappoint our hopes with a different meaning. I will not fight with thee.'

'Then live!' said the scornful Macduff; 'we will have a show of thee, as men show monsters, and a painted board, on which shall be written: 'Here men may see the tyrant!''

'Never,' said Macbeth, whose courage returned with despair; 'I will not live to kiss the ground before young Malcolm's feet, and to be baited with the curses of the rabble. Though Birnam wood be come to Dunsinane, and thou opposed to me, who west never born of woman, yet will I try the last.' With these frantic words he threw himself upon Macduff, who, after a severe struggle, in the end overcame him, and cutting off his head, made a present of it to the young and lawful king, Malcolm; who took upon him the government which, by the machinations of the usurper, he had so long been deprived of, and ascended the throne of Duncan the Meek, amid the acclamations of the nobles and the people.

The Red-Headed League

Arthur Conan Doyle

I had called upon my friend, Mr. Sherlock Holmes, one day in the autumn of last year and found him in deep conversation with a very stout, florid-faced, elderly gentleman with fiery red hair. With an apology for my intrusion, I was about to withdraw when Holmes pulled me abruptly into the room and closed the door behind me.

"You could not possibly have come at a better time, my dear Watson," he said cordially.

"I was afraid that you were engaged."

"So I am. Very much so."

"Then I can wait in the next room."

"Not at all. This gentleman, Mr. Wilson, has been my partner and helper in many of my most successful cases, and I have no doubt that he will be of the utmost use to me in yours also."

The stout gentleman half rose from his chair and gave a bob of greeting, with a quick little questioning glance from his small fat-encircled eyes.

"Try the settee," said Holmes, relapsing into his armchair and putting his fingertips together, as was his custom when in judicial moods. "I know, my dear Watson, that you share my love of all that is bizarre and outside the conventions and humdrum routine of everyday life. You have shown your relish for it by the enthusiasm which has prompted you to chronicle, and, if you will excuse my saying so, somewhat to embellish so many of my own little adventures." "Your cases have indeed been of the greatest interest to me," I observed.

"You will remember that I remarked the other day, just before we went into the very simple problem presented by Miss Mary Sutherland, that for strange effects and extraordinary combinations we must go to life itself, which is always far more daring than any effort of the imagination." "A proposition which I took the liberty of doubting."

"You did, Doctor, but none the less you must come round to my view, for otherwise I shall keep on piling fact upon fact on you until your reason breaks down under them and acknowledges me to be right. Now, Mr. Jabez Wilson here has been good enough to call upon me this morning, and to begin a narrative which promises to be one of the most singular which I have listened to for some time. You have heard me remark that the strangest and most unique things are very often connected not with the larger but with the smaller crimes, and occasionally, indeed, where there is room for doubt whether any positive crime has been committed. As far as I have heard, it is impossible for me to say whether the present case is an instance of crime or not, but the course of events is certainly among the most singular that I have ever listened to. Perhaps, Mr. Wilson, you would have the great kindness to recommence your narrative. I ask you not merely because my friend Dr. Watson has not heard the opening part but also because the peculiar nature of the story makes me anxious to have every possible detail from your lips. As a rule, when I have heard some slight indication of the course of events, I am able to guide myself by the thousands of other similar cases which occur to my memory. In the present instance I am forced to admit that the facts are, to the best of my belief, unique." The portly client puffed out his chest with an appearance of some little pride and pulled a dirty and wrinkled newspaper from the inside pocket of his greatcoat. As he glanced down the advertisement column, with his head thrust forward and the paper flattened out upon his knee, I took a good look at the man and endeavoured, after the fashion of my companion, to read the indications which might be presented by his dress or appearance.

I did not gain very much, however, by my inspection. Our visitor bore every mark of being an average commonplace British tradesman, obese, pompous, and slow. He wore rather baggy grey shepherd's check trousers, a not over-clean black frock-coat, unbuttoned in the front, and a drab waistcoat with a heavy brassy Albert chain, and a square pierced bit of metal dangling down as an ornament. A frayed top-hat and a faded brown overcoat with a wrinkled velvet collar lay upon a chair beside him. Altogether, look as I would, there was nothing remarkable about the man save his blazing red head, and the expression of extreme chagrin and discontent upon his features.

Sherlock Holmes' quick eye took in my occupation, and he shook his head with a smile as he noticed my questioning glances. "Beyond the obvious facts that he has at some time done manual labour, that he takes snuff, that he is a Freemason, that he has been in China, and that he has done a considerable amount of writing lately, I can deduce nothing else." Mr. Jabez Wilson started up in his chair, with his forefinger upon the paper, but his eyes upon my companion.

"How, in the name of good-fortune, did you know all that, Mr. Holmes?" he asked. "How did you know, for example, that I did manual labour. It's as true as gospel, for I began as a ship's carpenter." "Your hands, my dear sir. Your right hand is quite a size larger than your left. You have worked with it, and the muscles are more developed."

"Well, the snuff, then, and the Freemasonry?"

"I won't insult your intelligence by telling you how I read that, especially as, rather against the strict rules of your order, you use an arc-and-compass breastpin."

"Ah, of course, I forgot that. But the writing?"

"What else can be indicated by that right cuff so very shiny for five inches, and the left one with the smooth patch near the elbow where you rest it upon the desk?"

"Well, but China?"

"The fish that you have tattooed immediately above your right wrist could only have been done in China. I have made a small study of tattoo marks and have even contributed to the literature of the subject. That trick of staining the fishes' scales of a delicate pink is quite peculiar to China. When, in addition, I see a Chinese coin hanging from your watch-chain, the matter becomes even more simple." Mr. Jabez Wilson laughed heavily. "Well, I never!" said he. "I thought at first that you had done something clever, but I see that there was nothing in it after all."

"I begin to think, Watson," said Holmes, "that I make a mistake in explaining. 'Omne ignotum pro magnifico,' you know, and my poor little reputation, such as it is, will suffer shipwreck if I am so candid. Can you not find the advertisement, Mr. Wilson?" "Yes, I have got it now," he answered with his thick red finger planted halfway down the column. "Here it is. This is what began it all. You just read it for yourself, sir."

I took the paper from him and read as follows:

"TO THE RED-HEADED LEAGUE: On account of the bequest of the late Ezekiah Hopkins, of Lebanon, Pennsylvania, U.S.A., there is now another vacancy open which entitles a member of the League to a salary of £ 4 a week for purely nominal services. All red-headed men who are sound in body and mind and above the age of twenty-one years, are eligible. Apply in person on Monday, at eleven o'clock, to Duncan Ross, at the offices of the League, 7 Pope's Court, Fleet Street." "What on earth does this mean?" I ejaculated after I had twice read over the extraordinary announcement.

Holmes chuckled and wriggled in his chair, as was his habit when in high spirits. "It is a little off the beaten track, isn't it?" said he. "And now, Mr. Wilson, off you go at scratch and tell us all about yourself, your household, and the effect which this advertisement had upon your fortunes. You will first make a note, Doctor, of the paper and the date." "It is The Morning Chronicle of April 27, 1890. Just two months ago."

"Very good. Now, Mr. Wilson?"

"Well, it is just as I have been telling you, Mr. Sherlock Holmes," said Jabez Wilson, mopping his forehead; "I have a small pawnbroker's business at Coburg Square, near the City. It's not a very large affair, and of late years it has not done more than just give me a living. I used to be able to keep two assistants, but now I only keep one; and I would have a job to pay him but that he is willing to come for half wages so as to learn the business." "What is the name of this obliging youth?" asked Sherlock Holmes.

"His name is Vincent Spaulding, and he's not such a youth, either. It's hard to say his age. I should not wish a smarter assistant, Mr. Holmes; and I know very well that he could better himself and earn twice what I am able to give him. But, after all, if he is satisfied, why should I put ideas in his head?" "Why, indeed? You seem most fortunate in having an employé who comes under the full market price. It is not a common experience among employers in this age. I don't know that your assistant is not as remarkable as your advertisement."

"Oh, he has his faults, too," said Mr. Wilson. "Never was such a fellow for photography. Snapping away with a camera when he ought to be improving his mind, and then diving down into the cellar like a rabbit into its hole to develop his pictures. That is his main fault, but on the whole he's a good worker. There's no vice in him." "He is still with you, I presume?"

"Yes, sir. He and a girl of fourteen, who does a bit of simple cooking and keeps the place clean—that's all I have in the house, for I am a widower and never had any family. We live very quietly, sir, the three of us; and we keep a roof over our heads and pay our debts, if we do nothing more.

"The first thing that put us out was that advertisement. Spaulding, he came down into the office just this day eight weeks, with this very paper in his hand, and he says:

"'I wish to the Lord, Mr. Wilson, that I was a red-headed man.'

"'Why that?' I asks.

"'Why,' says he, 'here's another vacancy on the League of the Red-headed Men. It's worth quite a little fortune to any man who gets it, and I understand that there are more vacancies than there are men, so that the trustees are at their wits' end what to do with the money. If my hair would only change colour, here's a nice little crib all ready for me to step into.' "'Why, what is it, then?' I asked. You see, Mr. Holmes, I am a very stay-at-home man, and as my business came to me instead of my having to go to it, I was often weeks on end without putting my foot over the door-mat. In that way I didn't know much of what was going on outside, and I was always glad of a bit of news.

"'Have you never heard of the League of the Red-headed Men?' he asked with his eyes open.

"'Never.'

"'Why, I wonder at that, for you are eligible yourself for one of the vacancies.'

"'And what are they worth?' I asked.

"'Oh, merely a couple of hundred a year, but the work is slight, and it need not interfere very much with one's other occupations.'

"Well, you can easily think that that made me prick up my ears, for the business has not been over good for some years, and an extra couple of hundred would have been very handy.

"'Tell me all about it,' said I.

"'Well,' said he, showing me the advertisement, 'you can see for yourself that the League has a vacancy, and there is the address where you should apply for particulars. As far as I can make out, the League was founded by an American millionaire, Ezekiah Hopkins, who was very peculiar in his ways. He was himself red-headed, and he had a great sympathy for all red-headed men; so, when he died, it was found that he had left his enormous fortune in the hands of trustees, with instructions to apply the interest to the providing of easy berths to men whose hair is of that colour. From all I hear it is splendid pay and very little to do.' "'But,' said I, 'there would be millions of red-headed men who would apply.'

"'Not so many as you might think,' he answered. 'You see it is really confined to Londoners, and to grown men. This American had started from London when he was young, and he wanted to do the old town a good turn. Then, again, I have heard it is no use your applying if your hair is light red, or dark red, or anything but real bright, blazing, fiery red. Now, if you cared to apply, Mr. Wilson, you would just walk in; but perhaps it would hardly be worth your while to put yourself out of the way for the sake of a few hundred pounds.' "Now, it is a fact, gentlemen, as you may see for yourselves, that my hair is of a very full and rich tint, so that it seemed to me that if there was to be any competition in the matter I stood as good a chance as any man that I had ever met. Vincent Spaulding seemed to know so much about it that I thought he might prove useful, so I just ordered him to put up the shutters for the day and to come right away with me. He was very willing to have a holiday, so we shut the business up and started off for the address that was given us in the advertisement.

"I never hope to see such a sight as that again, Mr. Holmes. From north, south, east, and west every man who had a shade of red in his hair had tramped into the city to answer the advertisement. Fleet Street was choked with red-headed folk, and Pope's Court looked like a coster's orange barrow. I should not have thought there were so many in the whole country as were brought together by that single advertisement. Every shade of colour they were—straw, lemon, orange, brick, Irish-setter, liver, clay; but, as Spaulding said, there were not many who had the real vivid flame-coloured tint. When I saw how many were waiting, I would have given it up in despair; but Spaulding would not hear of it. How he did it I could not imagine, but he pushed and pulled and butted until he got me through the crowd, and right up to the steps which led to the office. There was a double stream upon the stair, some going up in hope, and some coming back dejected; but we wedged in as well as we could and soon found ourselves in the office."

"Your experience has been a most entertaining one," remarked Holmes as his client paused and refreshed his memory with a huge pinch of snuff. "Pray continue your very interesting statement."

"There was nothing in the office but a couple of wooden chairs and a deal table, behind which sat a small man with a head that was even redder than mine. He said a few words to each candidate as he came up, and then he always managed to find some fault in them which would disqualify them. Getting a vacancy did not seem to be such a very easy matter, after all. However, when our turn came the little man was much more favourable to me than to any of the others, and he closed the door as we entered, so that he might have a private word with us.

"'This is Mr. Jabez Wilson,' said my assistant, 'and he is willing to fill a vacancy in the League.'

"'And he is admirably suited for it,' the other answered. 'He has every requirement. I cannot recall when I have seen anything so fine.' He took a step backward, cocked his head on one side, and gazed at my hair until I felt quite bashful. Then suddenly he plunged forward, wrung my hand, and congratulated me warmly on my success.

"'It would be injustice to hesitate,' said he. 'You will, however, I am sure, excuse me for taking an obvious precaution.' With that he seized my hair in both his hands, and tugged until I yelled with the pain. 'There is water in your eyes,' said he as he released me. 'I perceive that all is as it should be. But we have to be careful, for we have twice been deceived by wigs and once by paint. I could tell you tales of cobbler's wax which would disgust you with human nature.' He stepped over to the window and shouted through it at the top of his voice that the vacancy was filled. A groan of disappointment came up from below, and the folk all trooped away in different directions until there was not a red-head to be seen except my own and that of the manager.

"'My name,' said he, 'is Mr. Duncan Ross, and I am myself one of the pensioners upon the fund left by our noble benefactor. Are you a married man, Mr. Wilson? Have you a family?'

"I answered that I had not.

"His face fell immediately.

"'Dear me!' he said gravely, 'that is very serious indeed! I am sorry to hear you say that. The fund was, of course, for the propagation and spread of the red-heads as well as for their maintenance. It is exceedingly unfortunate that you should be a bachelor.' "My face lengthened at this, Mr. Holmes, for I thought that I was not to have the vacancy after all; but after thinking it over for a few minutes he said that it would be all right.

"'In the case of another,' said he, 'the objection might be fatal, but we must stretch a point in favour of a man with such a head of hair as yours. When shall you be able to enter upon your new duties?' "'Well, it is a little awkward, for I have a business already,' said I.

"'Oh, never mind about that, Mr. Wilson!' said Vincent Spaulding. 'I should be able to look after that for you.'

"'What would be the hours?' I asked.

"'Ten to two.'

"Now a pawnbroker's business is mostly done of an evening, Mr. Holmes, especially Thursday and Friday evening, which is just before pay-day; so it would suit me very well to earn a little in the mornings. Besides, I knew that my assistant was a good man, and that he would see to anything that turned up.

"'That would suit me very well,' said I. 'And the pay?'

"'Is £ 4 a week.'

"'And the work?'

"'Is purely nominal.'

"'What do you call purely nominal?'

"'Well, you have to be in the office, or at least in the building, the whole time. If you leave, you forfeit your whole position forever. The will is very clear upon that point. You don't comply with the conditions if you budge from the office during that time.' "'It's only four hours a day, and I should not think of leaving,' said I.

"'No excuse will avail,' said Mr. Duncan Ross; 'neither sickness nor business nor anything else. There you must stay, or you lose your billet.'

"'And the work?'

"'Is to copy out the Encyclopædia Britannica. There is the first volume of it in that press. You must find your own ink, pens, and blotting-paper, but we provide this table and chair. Will you be ready to-morrow?' "'Certainly,' I answered.

"'Then, good-bye, Mr. Jabez Wilson, and let me congratulate you once more on the important position which you have been fortunate enough to gain.' He bowed me out of the room and I went home with my assistant, hardly knowing what to say or do, I was so pleased at my own good fortune.

"Well, I thought over the matter all day, and by evening I was in low spirits again; for I had quite persuaded myself that the whole affair must be some great hoax or fraud, though what its object might be I could not imagine. It seemed altogether past belief that anyone could make such a will, or that they would pay such a sum for doing anything so simple as copying out the Encyclopædia Britannica. Vincent Spaulding did what he could to cheer me up, but by bedtime I had reasoned myself out of the whole thing. However, in the morning I determined to have a look at it anyhow, so I bought a penny bottle of ink, and with a quill-pen, and seven sheets of foolscap paper, I started off for Pope's Court.

"Well, to my surprise and delight, everything was as right as possible. The table was set out ready for me, and Mr. Duncan Ross was there to see that I got fairly to work. He started me off upon the letter A, and then he left me; but he would drop in from time to time to see that all was right with me. At two o'clock he bade me good-day, complimented me upon the amount that I had written, and locked the door of the office after me.

"This went on day after day, Mr. Holmes, and on Saturday the manager came in and planked down four golden sovereigns for my week's work. It was the same next week, and the same the week after. Every morning I was there at ten, and every afternoon I left at two. By degrees Mr. Duncan Ross took to coming in only once of a morning, and then, after a time, he did not come in at all. Still, of course, I never dared to leave the room for an instant, for I was not sure when he might come, and the billet was such a good one, and suited me so well, that I would not risk the loss of it.

"Eight weeks passed away like this, and I had written about Abbots and Archery and Armour and Architecture and Attica, and hoped with diligence that I might get on to the B's before very long. It cost me something in foolscap, and I had pretty nearly filled a shelf with my writings. And then suddenly the whole business came to an end." "To an end?"

"Yes, sir. And no later than this morning. I went to my work as usual at ten o'clock, but the door was shut and locked, with a little square of cardboard hammered on to the middle of the panel with a tack. Here it is, and you can read for yourself." He held up a piece of white cardboard about the size of a sheet of note-paper. It read in this fashion:

"THE RED-HEADED LEAGUE IS DISSOLVED. October 9, 1890."

Sherlock Holmes and I surveyed this curt announcement and the rueful face behind it, until the comical side of the affair so completely overtopped every other consideration that we both burst out into a roar of laughter.

"I cannot see that there is anything very funny," cried our client, flushing up to the roots of his flaming head. "If you can do nothing better than laugh at me, I can go elsewhere."

"No, no," cried Holmes, shoving him back into the chair from which he had half risen. "I really wouldn't miss your case for the world. It is most refreshingly unusual. But there is, if you will excuse my saying so, something just a little funny about it. Pray what steps did you take when you found the card upon the door?" "I was staggered, sir. I did not know what to do. Then I called at the offices round, but none of them seemed to know anything about it. Finally, I went to the landlord, who is an accountant living on the ground floor, and I asked him if he could tell me what had become of the Red-headed League. He said that he had never heard of any such body. Then I asked him who Mr. Duncan Ross was. He answered that the name was new to him.

"'Well,' said I, 'the gentleman at No. 4.'

"'What, the red-headed man?'

"'Yes.'

"'Oh,' said he, 'his name was William Morris. He was a solicitor and was using my room as a temporary convenience until his new premises were ready. He moved out yesterday.'

"'Where could I find him?'

"'Oh, at his new offices. He did tell me the address. Yes, 17 King Edward Street, near St. Paul's.'

"I started off, Mr. Holmes, but when I got to that address it was a manufactory of artificial knee-caps, and no one in it had ever heard of either Mr. William Morris or Mr. Duncan Ross."

"And what did you do then?" asked Holmes.

"I went home to Saxe-Coburg Square, and I took the advice of my assistant. But he could not help me in any way. He could only say that if I waited I should hear by post. But that was not quite good enough, Mr. Holmes. I did not wish to lose such a place without a struggle, so, as I had heard that you were good enough to give advice to poor folk who were in need of it, I came right away to you." "And you did very wisely," said Holmes. "Your case is an exceedingly remarkable one, and I shall be happy to look into it. From what you have told me I think that it is possible that graver issues hang from it than might at first sight appear." "Grave enough!" said Mr. Jabez Wilson. "Why, I have lost four pound a week."

"As far as you are personally concerned," remarked Holmes, "I do not see that you have any grievance against this extraordinary league. On the contrary, you are, as I understand, richer by some £ 30, to say nothing of the minute knowledge which you have gained on every subject which comes under the letter A. You have lost nothing by them." "No, sir. But I want to find out about them, and who they are, and what their object was in playing this prank—if it was a prank—upon me. It was a pretty expensive joke for them, for it cost them two and thirty pounds." "We shall endeavour to clear up these points for you. And, first, one or two questions, Mr. Wilson. This assistant of yours who first called your attention to the advertisement—how long had he been with you?" "About a month then."

"How did he come?"

"In answer to an advertisement."

"Was he the only applicant?"

"No, I had a dozen."

"Why did you pick him?"

"Because he was handy and would come cheap."

"At half wages, in fact."

"Yes."

"What is he like, this Vincent Spaulding?"

"Small, stout-built, very quick in his ways, no hair on his face, though he's not short of thirty. Has a white splash of acid upon his forehead."

Holmes sat up in his chair in considerable excitement. "I thought as much," said he. "Have you ever observed that his ears are pierced for earrings?"

"Yes, sir. He told me that a gipsy had done it for him when he was a lad."

"Hum!" said Holmes, sinking back in deep thought. "He is still with you?"

"Oh, yes, sir; I have only just left him."

"And has your business been attended to in your absence?"

"Nothing to complain of, sir. There's never very much to do of a morning."

"That will do, Mr. Wilson. I shall be happy to give you an opinion upon the subject in the course of a day or two. To-day is Saturday, and I hope that by Monday we may come to a conclusion."

"Well, Watson," said Holmes when our visitor had left us, "what do you make of it all?"

"I make nothing of it," I answered frankly. "It is a most mysterious business."

"As a rule," said Holmes, "the more bizarre a thing is the less mysterious it proves to be. It is your commonplace, featureless crimes which are really puzzling, just as a commonplace face is the most difficult to identify. But I must be prompt over this matter."

"What are you going to do, then?" I asked.

"To smoke," he answered. "It is quite a three pipe problem, and I beg that you won't speak to me for fifty minutes." He curled himself up in his chair, with his thin knees drawn up to his hawk-like nose, and there he sat with his eyes closed and his black clay pipe thrusting out like the bill of some strange bird. I had come to the conclusion that he had dropped asleep, and indeed was nodding myself, when he suddenly sprang out of his chair with the gesture of a man who has made up his mind and put his pipe down upon the mantelpiece.

"Sarasate plays at the St. James's Hall this afternoon," he remarked. "What do you think, Watson? Could your patients spare you for a few hours?"

"I have nothing to do to-day. My practice is never very absorbing."

"Then put on your hat and come. I am going through

the City first, and we can have some lunch on the way. I observe that there is a good deal of German music on the programme, which is rather more to my taste than Italian or French. It is introspective, and I want to introspect. Come along!" We travelled by the Underground as far as Aldersgate; and a short walk took us to Saxe-Coburg Square, the scene of the singular story which we had listened to in the morning. It was a poky, little, shabby-genteel place, where four lines of dingy two-storied brick houses looked out into a small railed-in enclosure, where a lawn of weedy grass and a few clumps of faded laurel bushes made a hard fight against a smoke-laden and uncongenial atmosphere. Three gilt balls and a brown board with "JABEZ WILSON" in white letters, upon a corner house, announced the place where our red-headed client carried on his business. Sherlock Holmes stopped in front of it with his head on one side and looked it all over, with his eyes shining brightly between puckered lids. Then he walked slowly up the street, and then down again to the corner, still looking keenly at the houses. Finally he returned to the pawnbroker's, and, having thumped vigorously upon the pavement with his stick two or three times, he went up to the door and knocked. It was instantly opened by a bright-looking, clean-shaven young fellow, who asked him to step in.

"Thank you," said Holmes, "I only wished to ask you how you would go from here to the Strand."

"Third right, fourth left," answered the assistant promptly, closing the door.

"Smart fellow, that," observed Holmes as we walked away. "He is, in my judgment, the fourth smartest man in London, and for daring I am not sure that he has not a claim to be third. I have known something of him before." "Evidently," said I, "Mr. Wilson's assistant counts for a good deal in this mystery of the Red-headed League. I am sure that you inquired your way merely in order that you might see him."

"Not him."

"What then?"

"The knees of his trousers."

"And what did you see?"

"What I expected to see."

"Why did you beat the pavement?"

"My dear doctor, this is a time for observation, not for talk. We are spies in an enemy's country. We know something of Saxe-Coburg Square. Let us now explore the parts which lie behind it."

The road in which we found ourselves as we turned round the corner from the retired Saxe-Coburg Square presented as great a contrast to it as the front of a picture does to the back. It was one of the main arteries which conveyed the traffic of the City to the north and west. The roadway was blocked with the immense stream of commerce flowing in a double tide inward and outward, while the footpaths were black with the hurrying swarm of pedestrians. It was difficult to realise as we looked at the line of fine shops and stately business premises that they really abutted on the other side upon the faded and stagnant square which we had just quitted.

"Let me see," said Holmes, standing at the corner and glancing along the line, "I should like just to remember the order of the houses here. It is a hobby of mine to have an exact knowledge of London. There is Mortimer's, the tobacconist, the little newspaper shop, the Coburg branch of the City and Suburban Bank, the Vegetarian Restaurant, and McFarlane's carriage-building depot. That carries us right on to the other block. And now, Doctor, we've done our work, so it's time we had some play. A sandwich and a cup of coffee, and then off to violin-land, where all is sweetness and delicacy and harmony, and there are no red-headed clients to vex us with their conundrums." My friend was an enthusiastic musician, being himself not only a very capable performer but a composer of no ordinary merit. All the afternoon he sat in the stalls wrapped in the most perfect happiness, gently waving his long, thin fingers in time to the music, while his gently smiling face and his languid, dreamy eyes were as unlike those of Holmes the sleuth-hound, Holmes the relentless, keen-witted, ready-handed criminal agent, as it was possible to conceive. In his singular character the dual nature alternately asserted itself, and his extreme exactness and astuteness represented, as I have often thought, the reaction against the poetic and contemplative mood which occasionally predominated in him. The swing of his nature took him from extreme languor to devouring energy; and, as I knew well, he was never so truly formidable as when, for days on end, he had been lounging in his armchair amid his improvisations and his black-letter editions. Then it was that the lust of the chase would suddenly come upon him, and that his brilliant reasoning power would rise to the level of intuition, until those who were unacquainted with his methods would look askance at him as on a man whose knowledge was not that of other mortals. When I saw him that afternoon so enwrapped in the music at St. James's Hall I felt that an evil time might be coming upon those whom he had set himself to hunt down.

"You want to go home, no doubt, Doctor," he remarked as we emerged.

"Yes, it would be as well."

"And I have some business to do which will take some hours. This business at Coburg Square is serious."

"Why serious?"

"A considerable crime is in contemplation. I have every reason to believe that we shall be in time to stop it. But to-day being Saturday rather complicates matters. I shall want your help to-night."

"At what time?"

"Ten will be early enough."

"I shall be at Baker Street at ten."

"Very well. And, I say, Doctor, there may be some little danger, so kindly put your army revolver in your pocket." He waved his hand, turned on his heel, and disappeared in an instant among the crowd.

I trust that I am not more dense than my neighbours, but I was always oppressed with a sense of my own stupidity in my dealings with Sherlock Holmes. Here I had heard what he had heard, I had seen what he had seen, and yet from his words it was evident that he saw clearly not only what had happened but what was about to happen, while to me the whole business was still confused and grotesque. As I drove home to my house in Kensington I thought over it all, from the extraordinary story of the red-headed copier of the Encyclopædia down to the visit to Saxe-Coburg Square, and the ominous words with which he had parted from me. What was this nocturnal expedition, and why should I go armed? Where were we going, and what were we to do? I had the hint from Holmes that this smooth-faced pawnbroker's assistant was a formidable man—a man who might play a deep game. I tried to puzzle it out, but gave it up in despair and set the matter aside until night should bring an explanation.

It was a quarter-past nine when I started from home and made my way across the Park, and so through Oxford Street to Baker Street. Two hansoms were standing at the door, and as I entered the passage I heard the sound of voices from above. On entering his room, I found Holmes in animated conversation with two men, one of whom I recognised as Peter Jones, the official police agent, while the other was a long, thin, sad-faced man, with a very shiny hat and oppressively respectable frock-coat.

"Ha! Our party is complete," said Holmes, buttoning up his pea-jacket and taking his heavy hunting crop from the rack. "Watson, I think you know Mr. Jones, of Scotland Yard? Let me introduce you to Mr. Merryweather, who is to be our companion in to-night's adventure." "We're hunting in couples again, Doctor, you see," said Jones in his consequential way. "Our friend here is a wonderful man for starting a chase. All he wants is an old dog to help him to do the running down." "I hope a wild goose may not prove to be the end of our chase," observed Mr. Merryweather gloomily.

"You may place considerable confidence in Mr. Holmes, sir," said the police agent loftily. "He has his own little methods, which are, if he won't mind my saying so, just a little too theoretical and fantastic, but he has the makings of a detective in him. It is not too much to say that once or twice, as in that business of the Sholto murder and the Agra treasure, he has been more nearly correct than the official force." "Oh, if you say so, Mr. Jones, it is all right," said the stranger with deference. "Still, I confess that I miss my rubber. It is the first Saturday night for seven-and-twenty years that I have not had my rubber." "I think you will find," said Sherlock Holmes, "that you will play for a higher stake to-night than you have ever done yet, and that the play will be more exciting. For you, Mr. Merryweather, the stake will be some £ 30,000; and for you, Jones, it will be the man upon whom you wish to lay your hands." "John Clay, the murderer, thief, smasher, and forger. He's a young man, Mr. Merryweather, but he is at the head of his profession, and I would rather have my bracelets on him than on any criminal in London. He's a remarkable man, is young John Clay. His grandfather was a royal duke, and he himself has been to Eton and Oxford. His brain is as cunning as his fingers, and though we meet signs of him at every turn, we never know where to find the man himself. He'll crack a crib in Scotland one week, and be raising money to build an orphanage in Cornwall the next. I've been on his track for years and have never set eyes on him yet." "I hope that I may have the pleasure of introducing you to-night. I've had one or two little turns also with Mr. John Clay, and I agree with you that he is at the head of his profession. It is past ten, however, and quite time that we started. If you two will take the first hansom, Watson and I will follow in the second." Sherlock Holmes was not very communicative during the long drive and lay back in the cab humming the tunes which he had heard in the afternoon. We rattled through an endless labyrinth of gas-lit streets until we emerged into Farrington Street.

"We are close there now," my friend remarked. "This fellow Merryweather is a bank director, and personally interested in the matter. I thought it as well to have Jones with us also. He is not a bad fellow, though an absolute imbecile in his profession. He has one positive virtue. He is as brave as a bulldog and as tenacious as a lobster if he gets his claws upon anyone. Here we are, and they are waiting for us." We had reached the same crowded thoroughfare in which we had found ourselves in the morning. Our cabs were dismissed, and, following the guidance of Mr. Merryweather, we passed down a narrow passage and through a side door, which he opened for us. Within there was a small corridor, which ended in a very massive iron gate. This also was opened, and led down a flight of winding stone steps, which terminated at another formidable gate. Mr. Merryweather stopped to light a lantern, and then conducted us down a dark, earth-smelling passage, and so, after opening a third door, into a huge vault or cellar, which was piled all round with crates and massive boxes.

"You are not very vulnerable from above," Holmes remarked as he held up the lantern and gazed about him.

"Nor from below," said Mr. Merryweather, striking his stick upon the flags which lined the floor. "Why, dear me, it sounds quite hollow!" he remarked, looking up in surprise.

"I must really ask you to be a little more quiet!" said

Holmes severely. "You have already imperilled the whole success of our expedition. Might I beg that you would have the goodness to sit down upon one of those boxes, and not to interfere?" The solemn Mr. Merryweather perched himself upon a crate, with a very injured expression upon his face, while Holmes fell upon his knees upon the floor and, with the lantern and a magnifying lens, began to examine minutely the cracks between the stones. A few seconds sufficed to satisfy him, for he sprang to his feet again and put his glass in his pocket.

"We have at least an hour before us," he remarked, "for they can hardly take any steps until the good pawnbroker is safely in bed. Then they will not lose a minute, for the sooner they do their work the longer time they will have for their escape. We are at present, Doctor—as no doubt you have divined—in the cellar of the City branch of one of the principal London banks. Mr. Merryweather is the chairman of directors, and he will explain to you that there are reasons why the more daring criminals of London should take a considerable interest in this cellar at present." "It is our French gold," whispered the director. "We have had several warnings that an attempt might be made upon it."

"Your French gold?"

"Yes. We had occasion some months ago to strengthen our resources and borrowed for that purpose 30,000 napoleons from the Bank of France. It has become known that we have never had occasion to unpack the money, and that it is still lying in our cellar. The crate upon which I sit contains 2,000 napoleons packed between layers of lead foil. Our reserve of bullion is much larger at present than is usually kept in a single branch office, and the directors have had misgivings upon the subject." "Which were very well justified," observed Holmes. "And now it is time that we arranged our little plans. I expect that within an hour matters will come to a head. In the meantime Mr. Merryweather, we must put the screen over that dark lantern." "And sit in the dark?"

"I am afraid so. I had brought a pack of cards in my pocket, and I thought that, as we were a partie carrée, you might have your rubber after all. But I see that the enemy's preparations have gone so far that we cannot risk the presence of a light. And, first of all, we must choose our positions. These are daring men, and though we shall take them at a disadvantage, they may do us some harm unless we are careful. I shall stand behind this crate, and do you conceal yourselves behind those. Then, when I flash a light upon them, close in swiftly. If they fire, Watson, have no compunction about shooting them down." I placed my revolver, cocked, upon the top of the wooden case behind which I crouched. Holmes shot the slide across the front of his lantern and left us in pitch darkness—such an absolute darkness as I have never before experienced. The smell of hot metal remained to assure us that the light was still there, ready to flash out at a moment's notice. To me, with my nerves worked up to a pitch of expectancy, there was something depressing and subduing in the sudden gloom, and in the cold dank air of the vault.

"They have but one retreat," whispered Holmes. "That is back through the house into Saxe-Coburg Square. I hope that you have done what I asked you, Jones?"

"I have an inspector and two officers waiting at the front door."

"Then we have stopped all the holes. And now we must be silent and wait."

What a time it seemed! From comparing notes afterwards it was but an hour and a quarter, yet it appeared to me that the night must have almost gone, and the dawn be breaking above us. My limbs were weary and stiff, for I feared to change my position; yet my nerves were worked up to the highest pitch of tension, and my hearing was so acute that I could not only hear the gentle breathing of my companions, but I could distinguish the deeper, heavier in-breath of the bulky Jones from the thin, sighing note of the bank director. From my position I could look over the case in the direction of the floor. Suddenly my eyes caught the glint of a light.

At first it was but a lurid spark upon the stone pavement. Then it lengthened out until it became a yellow line, and then, without any warning or sound, a gash seemed to open and a hand appeared, a white, almost womanly hand, which felt about in the centre of the little area of light. For a minute or more the hand, with its writhing fingers, protruded out of the floor. Then it was withdrawn as suddenly as it appeared, and all was dark again save the single lurid spark which marked a chink between the stones.

Its disappearance, however, was but momentary. With a rending, tearing sound, one of the broad, white stones turned over upon its side and left a square, gaping hole, through which streamed the light of a lantern. Over the edge there peeped a clean-cut, boyish face, which looked keenly about it, and then, with a hand on either side of the aperture, drew itself shoulder-high and waist-high, until one knee rested upon the edge. In another instant he stood at the side of the hole and was hauling after him a companion, lithe and small like himself, with a pale face and a shock of very red hair.

"It's all clear," he whispered. "Have you the chisel and the bags? Great Scott! Jump, Archie, jump, and I'll swing for it!"

Sherlock Holmes had sprung out and seized the intruder by the collar. The other dived down the hole, and I heard the sound of rending cloth as Jones clutched at his skirts. The light flashed upon the barrel of a revolver, but Holmes' hunting crop came down on the man's wrist, and the pistol clinked upon the stone floor.

"It's no use, John Clay," said Holmes blandly. "You have

no chance at all."

"So I see," the other answered with the utmost coolness. "I fancy that my pal is all right, though I see you have got his coat-tails."

"There are three men waiting for him at the door," said Holmes.

"Oh, indeed! You seem to have done the thing very completely. I must compliment you."

"And I you," Holmes answered. "Your red-headed idea was very new and effective."

"You'll see your pal again presently," said Jones. "He's quicker at climbing down holes than I am. Just hold out while I fix the derbies."

"I beg that you will not touch me with your filthy hands," remarked our prisoner as the handcuffs clattered upon his wrists. "You may not be aware that I have royal blood in my veins. Have the goodness, also, when you address me always to say 'sir' and 'please.'" "All right," said Jones with a stare and a snigger. "Well, would you please, sir, march upstairs, where we can get a cab to carry your Highness to the police-station?"

"That is better," said John Clay serenely. He made a sweeping bow to the three of us and walked quietly off in the custody of the detective.

"Really, Mr. Holmes," said Mr. Merryweather as we followed them from the cellar, "I do not know how the bank can thank you or repay you. There is no doubt that you have detected and defeated in the most complete manner one of the most determined attempts at bank robbery that have ever come within my experience." "I have had one or two little scores of my own to settle with Mr. John Clay," said Holmes. "I have been at some small expense over this matter, which I shall expect the bank to refund, but beyond that I am amply repaid by having had an experience which is in many ways unique, and by hearing the very remarkable narrative of the Red-headed League." "You see, Watson," he explained in the early hours of the morning as we sat over a glass of whisky and soda in Baker Street, "it was perfectly obvious from the first that the only possible object of this rather fantastic business of the advertisement of the League, and the copying of the Encyclopædia, must be to get this not over-bright pawnbroker out of the way for a number of hours every day. It was a curious way of managing it, but, really, it would be difficult to suggest a better. The method was no doubt suggested to Clay's ingenious mind by the colour of his accomplice's hair. The £ 4 a week was a lure which must draw him, and what was it to them, who were playing for thousands? They put in the advertisement, one rogue has the temporary office, the other rogue incites the man to apply for it, and together they manage to secure his absence every morning in the week. From the time that I heard of the assistant having come for half wages, it was obvious to me that he had some strong motive for securing the situation." "But how could you guess what the motive was?"

"Had there been women in the house, I should have suspected a mere vulgar intrigue. That, however, was out of the question. The man's business was a small one, and there was nothing in his house which could account for such elaborate preparations, and such an expenditure as they were at. It must, then, be something out of the house. What could it be? I thought of the assistant's fondness for photography, and his trick of vanishing into the cellar. The cellar! There was the end of this tangled clue. Then I made inquiries as to this mysterious assistant and found that I had to deal with one of the coolest and most daring criminals in London. He was doing something in the cellar—something which took many hours a day for months on end. What could it be, once more? I could think of nothing save that he was running a tunnel to some other building.

"So far I had got when we went to visit the scene of action. I surprised you by beating upon the pavement with my stick. I was ascertaining whether the cellar stretched out in front or behind. It was not in front. Then I rang the bell, and, as I hoped, the assistant answered it. We have had some skirmishes, but we had never set eyes upon each other before. I hardly looked at his face. His knees were what I wished to see. You must yourself have remarked how worn, wrinkled, and stained they were. They spoke of those hours of burrowing. The only remaining point was what they were burrowing for. I walked round the corner, saw the City and Suburban

Bank abutted on our friend's premises, and felt that I had solved my problem. When you drove home after the concert I called upon Scotland Yard and upon the chairman of the bank directors, with the result that you have seen." "And how could you tell that they would make their attempt to-night?" I asked.

"Well, when they closed their League offices that was a sign that they cared no longer about Mr. Jabez Wilson's presence—in other words, that they had completed their tunnel. But it was essential that they should use it soon, as it might be discovered, or the bullion might be removed. Saturday would suit them better than any other day, as it would give them two days for their escape. For all these reasons I expected them to come to-night." "You reasoned it out beautifully," I exclaimed in unfeigned admiration. "It is so long a chain, and yet every link rings true."

"It saved me from ennui," he answered, yawning. "Alas! I already feel it closing in upon me. My life is spent in one long effort to escape from the commonplaces of existence. These little problems help me to do so." "And you are a benefactor of the race," said I.

He shrugged his shoulders. "Well, perhaps, after all, it is of some little use," he remarked. "'L'homme c'est rien—l'œuvre c'est tout,' as Gustave Flaubert wrote to George Sand."

An Adventure on Island Rock

Lucy Maud Montgomery

"Who was the man I saw talking to you in the hayfield?" asked Aunt Kate, as Uncle Richard came to dinner.

"Bob Marks," said Uncle Richard briefly. "I've sold Laddie to him."

Ernest Hughes, the twelve-year-old orphan boy whom Uncle "boarded and kept" for the chores he did, suddenly stopped eating.

"Oh, Mr. Lawson, you're not going to sell Laddie?" he cried chokily.

Uncle Richard stared at him. Never before, in the five years that Ernest had lived with him, had the quiet little fellow spoken without being spoken to, much less ventured to protest against anything Uncle Richard might do.

"Certainly I am," answered the latter curtly. "Bob offered me twenty dollars for the dog, and he's coming after him next week."

"Oh, Mr. Lawson," said Ernest, rising to his feet, his small, freckled face crimson. "Oh, don't sell Laddie! Please, Mr. Lawson, don't sell him!"

"What nonsense is this?" said Uncle Richard sharply. He was a man who brooked no opposition from anybody, and who never changed his mind when it was once made up.

"Don't sell Laddie!" pleaded Ernest miserably. "He is the only friend I've got. I can't live if Laddie goes away. Oh, don't sell him, Mr. Lawson!"

"Sit down and hold your tongue," said Uncle Richard sternly. "The dog is mine, and I shall do with him as I think fit. He is sold, and that is all there is about it. Go on with your dinner."

But Ernest for the first time did not obey. He snatched his cap from the back of his chair, dashed it down over his eyes, and ran from the kitchen with a sob choking his breath. Uncle Richard looked angry, but Aunt Kate hastened to soothe him.

"Don't be vexed with the boy, Richard," she said. "You know he is very fond of Laddie. He's had to do with him ever since he was a pup, and no doubt he feels badly at the thought of losing him. I'm rather sorry myself that you have sold the dog."

"Well, he is sold and there's an end of it. I don't say but that the dog is a good dog. But he is of no use to us, and twenty dollars will come in mighty handy just now. He's worth that to Bob, for he is a good watch dog, so we've both made a fair bargain."

Nothing more was said about Ernest or Laddie. I had taken no part in the discussion, for I felt no great interest in the matter. Laddie was a nice dog; Ernest was a quiet, inoffensive little fellow, five years younger than myself; that was all I thought about either of them.

I was spending my vacation at Uncle Richard's farm on

the Nova Scotian Bay of Fundy shore. I was a great favourite with Uncle Richard, partly because he had been much attached to my mother, his only sister, partly because of my strong resemblance to his only son, who had died several years before. Uncle Richard was a stern, undemonstrative man, but I knew that he entertained a deep and real affection for me, and I always enjoyed my vacation sojourns at his place.

"What are you going to do this afternoon, Ned?" he asked, after the disturbance caused by Ernest's outbreak had quieted down.

"I think I'll row out to Island Rock," I replied. "I want to take some views of the shore from it."

Uncle Richard nodded. He was much interested in my new camera.

"If you're on it about four o'clock, you'll get a fine view of the 'Hole in the Wall' when the sun begins to shine on the water through it," he said. "I've often thought it would make a handsome picture."

"After I've finished taking the pictures, I think I'll go down shore to Uncle Adam's and stay all night," I said. "Jim's dark room is more convenient than mine, and he has some pictures he is going to develop tonight, too."

I started for the shore about two o'clock. Ernest was sitting on the woodpile as I passed through the yard, with his arms about Laddie's neck and his face buried in Laddie's curly hair. Laddie was a handsome and intelligent black-and-white Newfoundland, with a magnificent coat. He and Ernest were great chums. I felt sorry for the boy who was to lose his pet.

"Don't take it so hard, Ern," I said, trying to comfort him. "Uncle will likely get another pup."

"I don't want any other pup!" Ernest blurted out. "Oh, Ned, won't you try and coax your uncle not to sell him? Perhaps he'd listen to you."

I shook my head. I knew Uncle Richard too well to hope that.

"Not in this case, Ern," I said. "He would say it did not concern me, and you know nothing moves him when he determines on a thing. You'll have to reconcile yourself to losing Laddie, I'm afraid."

Ernest's tow-coloured head went down on Laddie's neck again, and I, deciding that there was no use in saying anything more, proceeded towards the shore, which was about a mile from Uncle Richard's house. The beach along his farm and for several farms along shore was a lonely, untenanted one, for the fisher-folk all lived two miles further down, at Rowley's Cove. About three hundred yards from the shore was the peculiar formation known as Island Rock. This was a large rock that stood abruptly up out of the water. Below, about the usual water-line, it was seamed and fissured, but its summit rose up in a narrow, flat-topped peak. At low tide twenty feet of it was above water, but at high tide it was six feet and often more under water.

I pushed Uncle Richard's small flat down the rough path

and rowed out to Island Rock. Arriving there, I thrust the painter deep into a narrow cleft. This was the usual way of mooring it, and no doubt of its safety occurred to me.

I scrambled up the rock and around to the eastern end, where there was a broader space for standing and from which some capital views could be obtained. The sea about the rock was calm, but there was quite a swell on and an off-shore breeze was blowing. There were no boats visible. The tide was low, leaving bare the curious caves and headlands along shore, and I secured a number of excellent snapshots. It was now three o'clock. I must wait another hour yet before I could get the best view of the "Hole in the Wall"—a huge, arch-like opening through a jutting headland to the west of me. I went around to look at it, when I saw a sight that made me stop short in dismay. This was nothing less than the flat, drifting outward around the point. The swell and suction of the water around the rock must have pulled her loose —and I was a prisoner! At first my only feeling was one of annoyance. Then a thought flashed into my mind that made me dizzy with fear. The tide would be high that night. If I could not escape from Island Rock I would inevitably be drowned.

I sat down limply on a ledge and tried to look matters fairly in the face. I could not swim; calls for help could not reach anybody; my only hope lay in the chance of somebody passing down the shore or of some boat appearing.

I looked at my watch. It was a quarter past three. The tide would begin to turn about five, but it would be at least ten before the rock would be covered. I had, then, little more than six hours to live unless rescued.

The flat was by this time out of sight around the point. I hoped that the sight of an empty flat drifting down shore might attract someone's attention and lead to investigation. That seemed to be my only hope. No alarm would be felt at Uncle Richard's because of my non-appearance. They would suppose I had gone to Uncle Adam's.

I have heard of time seeming long to a person in my predicament, but to me it seemed fairly to fly, for every moment decreased my chance of rescue. I determined I would not give way to cowardly fear, so, with a murmured prayer for help, I set myself to the task of waiting for death as bravely as possible. At intervals I shouted as loudly as I could and, when the sun came to the proper angle for the best view of the "Hole in the Wall," I took the picture. It afterwards turned out to be a great success, but I have never been able to look at it without a shudder.

At five the tide began to come in. Very, very slowly the water rose around Island Rock. Up, up, up it came, while I watched it with fascinated eyes, feeling like a rat in a trap. The sun fell lower and lower; at eight o'clock the moon rose large and bright; at nine it was a lovely night, dear, calm, bright as day, and the water was swishing over the highest ledge of the rock. With some difficulty I climbed to the top and sat there to await the end. I had no longer any hope of rescue but, by a great effort, I preserved self-control. If I had to die, I would at least face death staunchly. But when I thought of my mother at home, it tasked all my energies to keep from breaking down utterly.

Suddenly I heard a whistle. Never was sound so sweet. I stood up and peered eagerly shoreward. Coming around the "Hole in the Wall" headland, on top of the cliffs, I saw a boy and a dog. I sent a wild halloo ringing shoreward.

The boy started, stopped and looked out towards Island Rock. The next moment he hailed me. It was Ernest's voice, and it was Laddie who was barking beside him.

"Ernest," I shouted wildly, "run for help—quick! quick! The tide will be over the rock in half an hour! Hurry, or you will be too late!"

Instead of starting off at full speed, as I expected him to do, Ernest stood still for a moment, and then began to pick his steps down a narrow path over the cliff, followed by Laddie.

"Ernest," I shouted frantically, "what are you doing? Why don't you go for help?"

Ernest had by this time reached a narrow ledge of rock just above the water-line. I noticed that he was carrying something over his arm.

"It would take too long," he shouted. "By the time I got

to the Cove and a boat could row back here, you'd be drowned. Laddie and I will save you. Is there anything there you can tie a rope to? I've a coil of rope here that I think will be long enough to reach you. I've been down to the Cove and Alec Martin sent it up to your uncle."

I looked about me; a smooth, round hole had been worn clean through a thin part of the apex of the rock.

"I could fasten the rope if I had it!" I called. "But how can you get it to me?"

For answer Ernest tied a bit of driftwood to the rope and put it into Laddie's mouth. The next minute the dog was swimming out to me. As soon as he came close I caught the rope. It was just long enough to stretch from shore to rock, allowing for a couple of hitches which Ernest gave around a small boulder on the ledge. I tied my camera case on my head by means of some string I found in my pocket, then I slipped into the water and, holding to the rope, went hand over hand to the shore with Laddie swimming beside me. Ernest held on to the shoreward end of the rope like grim death, a task that was no light one for his small arms. When I finally scrambled up beside him, his face was dripping with perspiration and he trembled like a leaf.

"Ern, you are a brick!" I exclaimed. "You've saved my life!"

"No, it was Laddie," said Ernest, refusing to take any credit at all.

We hurried home and arrived at Uncle Richard's about

ten, just as they were going to bed. When Uncle Richard heard what had happened, he turned very pale, and murmured, "Thank God!" Aunt Kate got me out of my wet clothes as quickly as possible, put me away to bed in hot blankets and dosed me with ginger tea. I slept like a top and felt none the worse for my experience the next morning.

At the breakfast table Uncle Richard scarcely spoke. But, just as we finished, he said abruptly to Ernest, "I'm not going to sell Laddie. You and the dog saved Ned's life between you, and no dog who helped do that is ever going to be sold by me. Henceforth he belongs to you. I give him to you for your very own."

"Oh, Mr. Lawson!" said Ernest, with shining eyes.

I never saw a boy look so happy. As for Laddie, who was sitting beside him with his shaggy head on Ernest's knee, I really believe the dog understood, too. The look in his eyes was almost human. Uncle Richard leaned over and patted him.

"Good dog!" he said. "Good dog!"

Young Goodman Brown

Nathaniel Hawthorne

Young Goodman Brown came forth at sunset into the street at Salem village; but put his head back, after crossing the threshold, to exchange a parting kiss with his young wife. And Faith, as the wife was aptly named, thrust her own pretty head into the street, letting the wind play with the pink ribbons of her cap while she called to Goodman Brown.

"Dearest heart," whispered she, softly and rather sadly, when her lips were close to his ear, "prithee put off your journey until sunrise and sleep in your own bed to-night. A lone woman is troubled with such dreams and such thoughts that she's afeard of herself sometimes. Pray tarry with me this night, dear husband, of all nights in the year."

"My love and my Faith," replied young Goodman Brown, "of all nights in the year, this one night must I tarry away from thee. My journey, as thou callest it, forth and back again, must needs be done 'twixt now and sunrise. What, my sweet, pretty wife, dost thou doubt me already, and we but three months married?"

"Then God bless you!" said Faith, with the pink ribbons; "and may you find all well when you come back."

"Amen!" cried Goodman Brown. "Say thy prayers, dear Faith, and go to bed at dusk, and no harm will come to thee."

So they parted; and the young man pursued his way until, being about to turn the corner by the meeting-house, he looked back and saw the head of Faith still peeping after him with a melancholy air, in spite of her pink ribbons.

"Poor little Faith!" thought he, for his heart smote him. "What a wretch am I to leave her on such an errand! She talks of dreams, too. Methought as she spoke there was trouble in her face, as if a dream had warned her what work is to be done tonight. But no, no; 't would kill her to think it. Well, she's a blessed angel on earth; and after this one night I'll cling to her skirts and follow her to heaven."

With this excellent resolve for the future, Goodman Brown felt himself justified in making more haste on his present evil purpose. He had taken a dreary road, darkened by all the gloomiest trees of the forest, which barely stood aside to let the narrow path creep through, and closed immediately behind. It was all as lonely as could be; and there is this peculiarity in such a solitude, that the traveller knows not who may be concealed by the innumerable trunks and the thick boughs overhead; so that with lonely footsteps he may yet be passing through an unseen multitude.

"There may be a devilish Indian behind every tree," said Goodman Brown to himself; and he glanced fearfully behind him as he added, "What if the devil himself should be at my very elbow!"

His head being turned back, he passed a crook of the road, and, looking forward again, beheld the figure of a man, in grave and decent attire, seated at the foot of an old tree. He arose at Goodman Brown's approach and walked onward side by side with him.

"You are late, Goodman Brown," said he. "The clock of the Old South was striking as I came through Boston, and that is full fifteen minutes agone."

"Faith kept me back a while," replied the young man, with a tremor in his voice, caused by the sudden appearance of his companion, though not wholly unexpected.

It was now deep dusk in the forest, and deepest in that part of it where these two were journeying. As nearly as could be discerned, the second traveller was about fifty years old, apparently in the same rank of life as Goodman Brown, and bearing a considerable resemblance to him, though perhaps more in expression than features. Still they might have been taken for father and son. And yet, though the elder person was as simply clad as the younger, and as simple in manner too, he had an indescribable air of one who knew the world, and who would not have felt abashed at the governor's dinner table or in King William's court, were it possible that his affairs should call him thither. But the only thing about him that could be fixed upon as remarkable was his staff, which bore the likeness of a great black snake, so curiously wrought that it might almost be seen to twist and wriggle itself like a living serpent. This, of course, must have been an ocular deception, assisted by the uncertain light.

"Come, Goodman Brown," cried his fellow-traveller, "this is a dull pace for the beginning of a journey. Take my staff, if you are so soon weary."

"Friend," said the other, exchanging his slow pace for a full stop, "having kept covenant by meeting thee here, it is my purpose now to return whence I came. I have scruples touching the matter thou wot'st of."

"Sayest thou so?" replied he of the serpent, smiling apart. "Let us walk on, nevertheless, reasoning as we go; and if I convince thee not thou shalt turn back. We are but a little way in the forest yet."

"Too far! too far!" exclaimed the goodman, unconsciously resuming his walk. "My father never went into the woods on such an errand, nor his father before him. We have been a race of honest men and good Christians since the days of the martyrs; and shall I be the first of the name of Brown that ever took this path and kept—"

"Such company, thou wouldst say," observed the elder person, interpreting his pause. "Well said, Goodman Brown! I have been as well acquainted with your family as with ever a one among the Puritans; and that's no trifle to say. I helped your grandfather, the constable, when he lashed the Quaker woman so smartly through the streets of Salem; and it was I that brought your father a pitch-pine knot, kindled at my own hearth, to set fire to an Indian village, in King Philip's war. They were my good friends, both; and many a pleasant walk have we had along this path, and returned merrily after midnight. I would fain be friends with you for their sake."

"If it be as thou sayest," replied Goodman Brown, "I marvel they never spoke of these matters; or, verily, I marvel not, seeing that the least rumor of the sort would have driven them from New England. We are a people of prayer, and good works to boot, and abide no such wickedness."

"Wickedness or not," said the traveller with the twisted staff, "I have a very general acquaintance here in New England. The deacons of many a church have drunk the communion wine with me; the selectmen of divers towns make me their chairman; and a majority of the Great and General Court are firm supporters of my interest. The governor and I, too—But these are state secrets."

"Can this be so?" cried Goodman Brown, with a stare of amazement at his undisturbed companion. "Howbeit, I have nothing to do with the governor and council; they have their own ways, and are no rule for a simple husbandman like me. But, were I to go on with thee, how should I meet the eye of that good old man, our minister, at Salem village? Oh, his voice would make me tremble both Sabbath day and lecture day."

Thus far the elder traveller had listened with due gravity; but now burst into a fit of irrepressible mirth, shaking himself so violently that his snake-like staff actually seemed to wriggle in sympathy.

"Ha! ha! ha!" shouted he again and again; then composing himself, "Well, go on, Goodman Brown, go on; but, prithee, don't kill me with laughing."

"Well, then, to end the matter at once," said Goodman Brown, considerably nettled, "there is my wife, Faith. It would break her dear little heart; and I'd rather break my own."

"Nay, if that be the case," answered the other, "e'en go thy ways, Goodman Brown. I would not for twenty old women like the one hobbling before us that Faith should come to any harm."

As he spoke he pointed his staff at a female figure on the path, in whom Goodman Brown recognized a very pious and exemplary dame, who had taught him his catechism in youth, and was still his moral and spiritual adviser, jointly with the minister and Deacon Gookin.

"A marvel, truly, that Goody Cloyse should be so far in the wilderness at nightfall," said he. "But with your leave, friend, I shall take a cut through the woods until we have left this Christian woman behind. Being a stranger to you, she might ask whom I was consorting with and whither I was going."

"Be it so," said his fellow-traveller. "Betake you to the woods, and let me keep the path."

Accordingly the young man turned aside, but took care to watch his companion, who advanced softly along the road until he had come within a staff's length of the old dame. She, meanwhile, was making the best of her way, with singular speed for so aged a woman, and mumbling some indistinct words—a prayer, doubtless—as she went. The traveller put forth his staff and touched her withered neck with what seemed the serpent's tail.

"The devil!" screamed the pious old lady.

"Then Goody Cloyse knows her old friend?" observed the traveller, confronting her and leaning on his writhing stick.

"Ah, forsooth, and is it your worship indeed?" cried the good dame. "Yea, truly is it, and in the very image of my old gossip, Goodman Brown, the grandfather of the silly fellow that now is. But—would your worship believe it?—my broomstick hath strangely disappeared, stolen, as I suspect, by that unhanged witch, Goody Cory, and that, too, when I was all anointed with the juice of smallage, and cinquefoil, and wolf's bane."

"Mingled with fine wheat and the fat of a new-born babe," said the shape of old Goodman Brown.

"Ah, your worship knows the recipe," cried the old lady, cackling aloud. "So, as I was saying, being all ready for the meeting, and no horse to ride on, I made up my mind to foot it; for they tell me there is a nice young man to be taken into communion to-night. But now your good worship will lend me your arm, and we shall be there in a twinkling."

"That can hardly be," answered her friend. "I may not spare you my arm, Goody Cloyse; but here is my staff, if you will."

So saying, he threw it down at her feet, where, perhaps, it assumed life, being one of the rods which its owner had formerly lent to the Egyptian magi. Of this fact, however, Goodman Brown could not take cognizance. He had cast up his eyes in astonishment, and, looking down again, beheld neither Goody Cloyse nor the serpentine staff, but his fellow-traveller alone, who waited for him as calmly as if nothing had happened.

"That old woman taught me my catechism," said the young man; and there was a world of meaning in this simple comment.

They continued to walk onward, while the elder traveller exhorted his companion to make good speed and persevere in the path, discoursing so aptly that his arguments seemed rather to spring up in the bosom of his auditor than to be suggested by himself. As they went, he plucked a branch of maple to serve for a walking stick, and began to strip it of the twigs and little boughs, which were wet with evening dew. The moment his fingers touched them they became strangely withered and dried up as with a week's sunshine. Thus the pair proceeded, at a good free pace, until suddenly, in a gloomy hollow of the road, Goodman Brown sat himself down on the stump of a tree and refused to go any farther.

"Friend," said he, stubbornly, "my mind is made up. Not another step will I budge on this errand. What if a wretched old woman do choose to go to the devil when I thought she was going to heaven: is that any reason why I should quit my dear Faith and go after her?"

"You will think better of this by and by," said his acquaintance, composedly. "Sit here and rest yourself a while; and when you feel like moving again, there is my staff to help you along."

Without more words, he threw his companion the maple stick, and was as speedily out of sight as if he had vanished into the deepening gloom. The young man sat a few moments by the roadside, applauding himself greatly, and thinking with how clear a conscience he should meet the minister in his morning walk, nor shrink from the eye of good old Deacon Gookin. And what calm sleep would be his that very night, which was to have been spent so wickedly, but so purely and sweetly now, in the arms of Faith! Amidst these pleasant and praiseworthy meditations, Goodman Brown heard the tramp of horses along the road, and deemed it advisable to conceal himself within the verge of the forest, conscious of the guilty purpose that had brought him thither, though now so happily turned from it.

On came the hoof tramps and the voices of the riders, two grave old voices, conversing soberly as they drew near. These mingled sounds appeared to pass along the road, within a few yards of the young man's hiding-place; but, owing doubtless to the depth of the gloom at that particular spot, neither the travellers nor their steeds were visible. Though their figures brushed the small boughs by the wayside, it could not be seen that they intercepted, even for a moment, the faint gleam from the strip of bright sky athwart which they must have passed. Goodman Brown alternately crouched and stood on tiptoe, pulling aside the branches and thrusting forth his head as far as he durst without discerning so much as a shadow. It vexed him the more, because he could have sworn, were such a thing possible, that he recognized the voices of the minister and Deacon Gookin, jogging along quietly, as they were wont to do, when bound to some ordination or ecclesiastical council. While yet within hearing, one of the riders stopped to pluck a switch.

"Of the two, reverend sir," said the voice like the deacon's, "I had rather miss an ordination dinner than to-night's meeting. They tell me that some of our community are to be here from Falmouth and beyond, and others from Connecticut and Rhode Island, besides several of the Indian powwows, who, after their fashion, know almost as much deviltry as the best of us. Moreover, there is a goodly young woman to be taken into communion."

"Mighty well, Deacon Gookin!" replied the solemn old tones of the minister. "Spur up, or we shall be late.

Nothing can be done, you know, until I get on the ground."

The hoofs clattered again; and the voices, talking so strangely in the empty air, passed on through the forest, where no church had ever been gathered or solitary Christian prayed. Whither, then, could these holy men be journeying so deep into the heathen wilderness? Young Goodman Brown caught hold of a tree for support, being ready to sink down on the ground, faint and overburdened with the heavy sickness of his heart. He looked up to the sky, doubting whether there really was a heaven above him. Yet there was the blue arch, and the stars brightening in it.

"With heaven above and Faith below, I will yet stand firm against the devil!" cried Goodman Brown.

While he still gazed upward into the deep arch of the firmament and had lifted his hands to pray, a cloud, though no wind was stirring, hurried across the zenith and hid the brightening stars. The blue sky was still visible, except directly overhead, where this black mass of cloud was sweeping swiftly northward. Aloft in the air, as if from the depths of the cloud, came a confused and doubtful sound of voices. Once the listener fancied that he could distinguish the accents of towns-people of his own, men and women, both pious and ungodly, many of whom he had met at the communion table, and had seen others rioting at the tavern. The next moment, so indistinct were the sounds, he doubted whether he had heard aught but the murmur of the old forest, whispering without a wind. Then came a stronger swell of those familiar tones, heard daily in the sunshine at Salem village, but never until now from a cloud of night There was one voice of a young woman, uttering lamentations, yet with an uncertain sorrow, and entreating for some favor, which, perhaps, it would grieve her to obtain; and all the unseen multitude, both saints and sinners, seemed to encourage her onward.

"Faith!" shouted Goodman Brown, in a voice of agony and desperation; and the echoes of the forest mocked him, crying, "Faith! Faith!" as if bewildered wretches were seeking her all through the wilderness.

The cry of grief, rage, and terror was yet piercing the night, when the unhappy husband held his breath for a response. There was a scream, drowned immediately in a louder murmur of voices, fading into far-off laughter, as the dark cloud swept away, leaving the clear and silent sky above Goodman Brown. But something fluttered lightly down through the air and caught on the branch of a tree. The young man seized it, and beheld a pink ribbon.

"My Faith is gone!" cried he, after one stupefied moment. "There is no good on earth; and sin is but a name. Come, devil; for to thee is this world given."

And, maddened with despair, so that he laughed loud and long, did Goodman Brown grasp his staff and set forth again, at such a rate that he seemed to fly along the forest path rather than to walk or run. The road grew wilder and drearier and more faintly traced, and vanished at length, leaving him in the heart of the dark wilderness, still rushing onward with the instinct that guides mortal man to evil. The whole forest was peopled with frightful sounds—the creaking of the trees, the howling of wild beasts, and the yell of Indians; while sometimes the wind tolled like a distant church bell, and sometimes gave a broad roar around the traveller, as if all Nature were laughing him to scorn. But he was himself the chief horror of the scene, and shrank not from its other horrors.

"Ha! ha! ha!" roared Goodman Brown when the wind laughed at him.

"Let us hear which will laugh loudest. Think not to frighten me with your deviltry. Come witch, come wizard, come Indian powwow, come devil himself, and here comes Goodman Brown. You may as well fear him as he fear you."

In truth, all through the haunted forest there could be nothing more frightful than the figure of Goodman Brown. On he flew among the black pines, brandishing his staff with frenzied gestures, now giving vent to an inspiration of horrid blasphemy, and now shouting forth such laughter as set all the echoes of the forest laughing like demons around him. The fiend in his own shape is less hideous than when he rages in the breast of man. Thus sped the demoniac on his course, until, quivering among the trees, he saw a red light before him, as when the felled trunks and branches of a clearing have been set on fire, and throw up their lurid blaze against the sky, at the hour of midnight. He paused, in a lull of the tempest that had driven him onward, and heard the swell of what seemed a hymn, rolling solemnly from a distance with the weight of many voices. He knew the tune; it was a familiar one in the choir of the village meeting-house. The verse died heavily away, and was lengthened by a chorus, not of human voices, but of all the sounds of the benighted wilderness pealing in awful harmony together. Goodman Brown cried out, and his cry was lost to his own ear by its unison with the cry of the desert.

In the interval of silence he stole forward until the light glared full upon his eyes. At one extremity of an open space, hemmed in by the dark wall of the forest, arose a rock, bearing some rude, natural resemblance either to an altar or a pulpit, and surrounded by four blazing pines, their tops aflame, their stems untouched, like candles at an evening meeting. The mass of foliage that had overgrown the summit of the rock was all on fire, blazing high into the night and fitfully illuminating the whole field. Each pendent twig and leafy festoon was in a blaze. As the red light arose and fell, a numerous congregation alternately shone forth, then disappeared in shadow, and again grew, as it were, out of the darkness, peopling the heart of the solitary woods at once.

"A grave and dark-clad company," quoth Goodman Brown.

In truth they were such. Among them, quivering to and fro between gloom and splendor, appeared faces that would be seen next day at the council board of the province, and others which, Sabbath after Sabbath, looked devoutly heavenward, and benignantly over the crowded pews, from the holiest pulpits in the land. Some affirm that the lady of the governor was there. At least there were high dames well known to her, and wives of honored husbands, and widows, a great multitude, and ancient maidens, all of excellent repute, and fair young girls, who trembled lest their mothers should espy them. Either the sudden gleams of light flashing over the obscure field bedazzled Goodman Brown, or he recognized a score of the church members of Salem village famous for their especial sanctity. Good old Deacon Gookin had arrived, and waited at the skirts of that venerable saint, his revered pastor. But, irreverently consorting with these grave, reputable, and pious people, these elders of the church, these chaste dames and dewy virgins, there were men of dissolute lives and women of spotted fame, wretches given over to all mean and filthy vice, and suspected even of horrid crimes. It was strange to see that the good shrank not from the wicked, nor were the sinners abashed by the saints. Scattered also among their pale-faced enemies were the Indian priests, or powwows, who had often scared their native forest with more hideous incantations than any known to English witchcraft.

"But where is Faith?" thought Goodman Brown; and, as hope came into his heart, he trembled.

Another verse of the hymn arose, a slow and mournful strain, such as the pious love, but joined to words which expressed all that our nature can conceive of sin, and darkly hinted at far more. Unfathomable to mere mortals is the lore of fiends. Verse after verse was sung; and still the chorus of the desert swelled between like the deepest tone of a mighty organ; and with the final peal of that dreadful anthem there came a sound, as if the roaring wind, the rushing streams, the howling beasts, and every other voice of the unconcerted wilderness were mingling and according with the voice of guilty man in homage to the prince of all. The four blazing pines threw up a loftier flame, and obscurely discovered shapes and visages of horror on the smoke wreaths above the impious assembly. At the same moment the fire on the rock shot redly forth and formed a glowing arch above its base, where now appeared a figure. With reverence be it spoken, the figure bore no slight similitude, both in garb and manner, to some grave divine of the New England churches.

"Bring forth the converts!" cried a voice that echoed through the field and rolled into the forest.

At the word, Goodman Brown stepped forth from the shadow of the trees and approached the congregation, with whom he felt a loathful brotherhood by the sympathy of all that was wicked in his heart. He could have well-nigh sworn that the shape of his own dead father beckoned him to advance, looking downward from a smoke wreath, while a woman, with dim features of despair, threw out her hand to warn him back. Was it his mother? But he had no power to retreat one step, nor to resist, even in thought, when the minister and good old Deacon Gookin seized his arms and led him to the blazing rock. Thither came also the slender form of a veiled female, led between Goody Cloyse, that pious teacher of the catechism, and Martha Carrier, who had received the devil's promise to be queen of hell. A rampant hag was she. And there stood the proselytes beneath the canopy of fire.

"Welcome, my children," said the dark figure, "to the communion of your race. Ye have found thus young your nature and your destiny. My children, look behind you!"

They turned; and flashing forth, as it were, in a sheet of flame, the fiend worshippers were seen; the smile of welcome gleamed darkly on every visage.

"There," resumed the sable form, "are all whom ye have reverenced from youth. Ye deemed them holier than yourselves, and shrank from your own sin, contrasting it with their lives of righteousness and prayerful aspirations heavenward. Yet here are they all in my worshipping assembly. This night it shall be granted you to know their secret deeds: how hoary-bearded elders of the church have whispered wanton words to the young maids of their households; how many a woman, eager for widows' weeds, has given her husband a drink at bedtime and let him sleep his last sleep in her bosom; how beardless youths have made haste to inherit their fathers' wealth; and how fair damsels—blush not, sweet ones—have dug little graves in the garden, and bidden me, the sole guest to an infant's funeral. By the sympathy of your human hearts for sin ye shall scent out all the places—whether in church, bedchamber, street, field, or forest—where crime has been committed, and shall exult to behold the whole earth one stain of guilt, one mighty blood spot. Far more than this. It shall be yours to penetrate, in every bosom, the deep mystery of sin, the fountain of all wicked arts, and which inexhaustibly supplies more evil impulses than human power—than my power at its utmost—can make manifest in deeds. And now, my children, look upon each other."

They did so; and, by the blaze of the hell-kindled torches, the wretched man beheld his Faith, and the wife her husband, trembling before that unhallowed altar.

"Lo, there ye stand, my children," said the figure, in a deep and solemn tone, almost sad with its despairing awfulness, as if his once angelic nature could yet mourn for our miserable race. "Depending upon one another's hearts, ye had still hoped that virtue were not all a dream. Now are ye undeceived. Evil is the nature of mankind. Evil must be your only happiness. Welcome again, my children, to the communion of your race."

"Welcome," repeated the fiend worshippers, in one cry of despair and triumph.

And there they stood, the only pair, as it seemed, who were yet hesitating on the verge of wickedness in this dark world. A basin was hollowed, naturally, in the rock. Did it contain water, reddened by the lurid light? or was it blood? or, perchance, a liquid flame? Herein did the shape of evil dip his hand and prepare to lay the mark of baptism upon their foreheads, that they might be partakers of the mystery of sin, more conscious of the secret guilt of others, both in deed and thought, than they could now be of their own. The husband cast one look at his pale wife, and Faith at him. What polluted wretches would the next glance show them to each other, shuddering alike at what they disclosed and what they saw!

"Faith! Faith!" cried the husband, "look up to heaven, and resist the wicked one."

Whether Faith obeyed he knew not. Hardly had he spoken when he found himself amid calm night and solitude, listening to a roar of the wind which died heavily away through the forest. He staggered against the rock, and felt it chill and damp; while a hanging twig, that had been all on fire, besprinkled his cheek with the coldest dew.

The next morning young Goodman Brown came slowly into the street of Salem village, staring around him like a bewildered man. The good old minister was taking a walk along the graveyard to get an appetite for breakfast and meditate his sermon, and bestowed a blessing, as he passed, on Goodman Brown. He shrank from the venerable saint as if to avoid an anathema. Old Deacon Gookin was at domestic worship, and the holy words of his prayer were heard through the open window. "What God doth the wizard pray to?" quoth Goodman Brown. Goody Cloyse, that excellent old Christian, stood in the early sunshine at her own lattice, catechizing a little girl who had brought her a pint of morning's milk. Goodman Brown snatched away the child as from the grasp of the fiend himself. Turning the corner by the meeting-house, he spied the head of Faith, with the pink ribbons, gazing anxiously forth, and bursting into such joy at sight of him that she skipped along the street and almost kissed her husband before the whole village. But Goodman Brown looked sternly and sadly into her face, and passed on without a greeting.

Had Goodman Brown fallen asleep in the forest and only dreamed a wild dream of a witch-meeting?

Be it so if you will; but, alas! it was a dream of evil omen for young Goodman Brown. A stern, a sad, a darkly meditative, a distrustful, if not a desperate man did he become from the night of that fearful dream. On the Sabbath day, when the congregation were singing a holy psalm, he could not listen because an anthem of sin rushed loudly upon his ear and drowned all the blessed strain. When the minister spoke from the pulpit with power and fervid eloquence, and, with his hand on the open Bible, of the sacred truths of our religion, and of saint-like lives and triumphant deaths, and of future bliss or misery unutterable, then did Goodman Brown turn pale, dreading lest the roof should thunder down upon the gray blasphemer and his hearers. Often, waking suddenly at midnight, he shrank from the bosom of Faith; and at morning or eventide, when the family knelt down at prayer, he scowled and muttered to himself, and gazed sternly at his wife, and turned away. And when he had lived long, and was borne to his grave a hoary corpse, followed by Faith, an aged woman, and children and grandchildren, a goodly procession, besides neighbors not a few, they carved no hopeful verse upon his tombstone, for his dying hour was gloom.

The Garden-Party

Katherine Mansfield

And after all the weather was ideal. They could not have had a more perfect day for a garden-party if they had ordered it. Windless, warm, the sky without a cloud. Only the blue was veiled with a haze of light gold, as it is sometimes in early summer. The gardener had been up since dawn, mowing the lawns and sweeping them, until the grass and the dark flat rosettes where the daisy plants had been seemed to shine. As for the roses, you could not help feeling they understood that roses are the only flowers that impress people at garden-parties; the only flowers that everybody is certain of knowing. Hundreds, yes, literally hundreds, had come out in a single night; the green bushes bowed down as though they had been visited by archangels.

Breakfast was not yet over before the men came to put up the marquee.

"Where do you want the marquee put, mother?"

"My dear child, it's no use asking me. I'm determined to leave everything to you children this year. Forget I am your mother. Treat me as an honoured guest." But Meg could not possibly go and supervise the men. She had washed her hair before breakfast, and she sat drinking her coffee in a green turban, with a dark wet curl stamped on each cheek. Jose, the butterfly, always came down in a silk petticoat and a kimono jacket.

"You'll have to go, Laura; you're the artistic one."

Away Laura flew, still holding her piece of bread-and-butter. It's so delicious to have an excuse for eating out of doors, and besides, she loved having to arrange things; she always felt she could do it so much better than anybody else.

Four men in their shirt-sleeves stood grouped together on the garden path. They carried staves covered with rolls of canvas, and they had big tool-bags slung on their backs. They looked impressive. Laura wished now that she had not got the bread-and-butter, but there was nowhere to put it, and she couldn't possibly throw it away. She blushed and tried to look severe and even a little bit short-sighted as she came up to them.

"Good morning," she said, copying her mother's voice. But that sounded so fearfully affected that she was ashamed, and stammered like a little girl, "Oh—er—have you come—is it about the marquee?" "That's right, miss," said the tallest of the men, a lanky, freckled fellow, and he shifted his tool-bag, knocked back his straw hat and smiled down at her. "That's about it." His smile was so easy, so friendly that Laura recovered. What nice eyes he had, small, but such a dark blue! And now she looked at the others, they were smiling too. "Cheer up, we won't bite," their smile seemed to say. How very nice workmen were! And what a beautiful morning! She mustn't mention the morning; she must be business-like. The marquee.

"Well, what about the lily-lawn? Would that do?"

And she pointed to the lily-lawn with the hand that didn't hold the bread-and-butter. They turned, they stared in the direction. A little fat chap thrust out his under-lip, and the tall fellow frowned.

"I don't fancy it," said he. "Not conspicuous enough. You see, with a thing like a marquee," and he turned to Laura in his easy way, "you want to put it somewhere where it'll give you a bang slap in the eye, if you follow me." Laura's upbringing made her wonder for a moment whether it was quite respectful of a workman to talk to her of bangs slap in the eye. But she did quite follow him.

"A corner of the tennis-court," she suggested. "But the band's going to be in one corner."

"H'm, going to have a band, are you?" said another of the workmen. He was pale. He had a haggard look as his dark eyes scanned the tennis-court. What was he thinking?

"Only a very small band," said Laura gently. Perhaps he wouldn't mind so much if the band was quite small. But the tall fellow interrupted.

"Look here, miss, that's the place. Against those trees. Over there. That'll do fine."

Against the karakas. Then the karaka-trees would be hidden. And they were so lovely, with their broad, gleaming leaves, and their clusters of yellow fruit. They were like trees you imagined growing on a desert island, proud, solitary, lifting their leaves and fruits to the sun in a kind of silent splendour. Must they be hidden by a marquee?

They must. Already the men had shouldered their staves and were making for the place. Only the tall fellow was left. He bent down, pinched a sprig of lavender, put his thumb and forefinger to his nose and snuffed up the smell. When Laura saw that gesture she forgot all about the karakas in her wonder at him caring for things like that—caring for the smell of lavender. How many men that she knew would have done such a thing? Oh, how extraordinarily nice workmen were, she thought. Why couldn't she have workmen for her friends rather than the silly boys she danced with and who came to Sunday night supper? She would get on much better with men like these.

It's all the fault, she decided, as the tall fellow drew something on the back of an envelope, something that was to be looped up or left to hang, of these absurd class distinctions. Well, for her part, she didn't feel them. Not a bit, not an atom.... And now there came the chock-chock of wooden hammers. Some one whistled, some one sang out, "Are you right there, matey?" "Matey!" The friendliness of it, the—the—Just to prove how happy she was, just to show the tall fellow how at home she felt, and how she despised stupid conventions, Laura took a big bite of her bread-and-butter as she stared at the little drawing. She felt just like a work-girl.

"Laura, Laura, where are you? Telephone, Laura!" a voice cried from the house.

"Coming!" Away she skimmed, over the lawn, up the path, up the steps, across the veranda, and into the porch. In the hall her father and Laurie were brushing their hats ready to go to the office.

"I say, Laura," said Laurie very fast, "you might just give a squiz at my coat before this afternoon. See if it wants pressing."

"I will," said she. Suddenly she couldn't stop herself. She ran at Laurie and gave him a small, quick squeeze. "Oh, I do love parties, don't you?" gasped Laura.

"Ra-ther," said Laurie's warm, boyish voice, and he squeezed his sister too, and gave her a gentle push. "Dash off to the telephone, old girl." The telephone. "Yes, yes; oh yes. Kitty? Good morning, dear. Come to lunch? Do, dear. Delighted of course. It will only be a very scratch meal—just the sandwich crusts and broken meringue-shells and what's left over. Yes, isn't it a perfect morning? Your white? Oh, I certainly should. One moment—hold the line. Mother's calling." And Laura sat back. "What, mother? Can't hear." Mrs. Sheridan's voice floated down the stairs. "Tell her to wear that sweet hat she had on last Sunday."

"Mother says you're to wear that sweet hat you had on last Sunday. Good. One o'clock. Bye-bye."

Laura put back the receiver, flung her arms over her head, took a deep breath, stretched and let them fall.

"Huh," she sighed, and the moment after the sigh she sat up quickly. She was still, listening. All the doors in the house seemed to be open. The house was alive with soft, quick steps and running voices. The green baize door that led to the kitchen regions swung open and shut with a muffled thud. And now there came a long, chuckling absurd sound. It was the heavy piano being moved on its stiff castors. But the air! If you stopped to notice, was the air always like this? Little faint winds were playing chase, in at the tops of the windows, out at the doors. And there were two tiny spots of sun, one on the inkpot, one on a silver photograph frame, playing too. Darling little spots. Especially the one on the inkpot lid. It was quite warm. A warm little silver star. She could have kissed it.

The front door bell pealed, and there sounded the rustle of Sadie's print skirt on the stairs. A man's voice murmured; Sadie answered, careless, "I'm sure I don't know. Wait. I'll ask Mrs Sheridan." "What is it, Sadie?" Laura came into the hall.

"It's the florist, Miss Laura."

It was, indeed. There, just inside the door, stood a wide, shallow tray full of pots of pink lilies. No other kind. Nothing but lilies—canna lilies, big pink flowers, wide open, radiant, almost frighteningly alive on bright crimson stems.

"O-oh, Sadie!" said Laura, and the sound was like a little moan. She crouched down as if to warm herself at that blaze of lilies; she felt they were in her fingers, on her lips, growing in her breast.

"It's some mistake," she said faintly. "Nobody ever ordered so many. Sadie, go and find mother."

But at that moment Mrs. Sheridan joined them.

"It's quite right," she said calmly. "Yes, I ordered them. Aren't they lovely?" She pressed Laura's arm. "I was passing the shop yesterday, and I saw them in the window. And I suddenly thought for once in my life I shall have enough canna lilies. The garden-party will be a good excuse." "But I thought you said you didn't mean to interfere," said Laura. Sadie had gone. The florist's man was still outside at his van. She put her arm round her mother's neck and gently, very gently, she bit her mother's ear.

"My darling child, you wouldn't like a logical mother, would you? Don't do that. Here's the man."

He carried more lilies still, another whole tray.

"Bank them up, just inside the door, on both sides of the porch, please," said Mrs. Sheridan. "Don't you agree, Laura?"

"Oh, I do, mother."

In the drawing-room Meg, Jose and good little Hans had at last succeeded in moving the piano.

"Now, if we put this chesterfield against the wall and move everything out of the room except the chairs, don't you think?"

"Quite."

"Hans, move these tables into the smoking-room, and bring a sweeper to take these marks off the carpet and—one moment, Hans—" Jose loved giving orders to the servants, and they loved obeying her. She always made them feel they were taking part in some drama. "Tell mother and Miss Laura to come here at once." "Very good, Miss Jose."

She turned to Meg. "I want to hear what the piano sounds like, just in case I'm asked to sing this afternoon. Let's try over 'This life is Weary.'" Pom! Ta-ta-ta Tee-ta! The piano burst out so passionately that Jose's face changed. She clasped her hands. She looked mournfully and enigmatically at her mother and Laura as they came in.

This Life is Wee-ary,
A Tear—a Sigh.
A Love that Chan-ges,
This Life is Wee-ary,
A Tear—a Sigh.
A Love that Chan-ges,
And then. . . Good-bye!

But at the word "Good-bye," and although the piano sounded more desperate than ever, her face broke into a brilliant, dreadfully unsympathetic smile.

"Aren't I in good voice, mummy?" she beamed.

This Life is Wee-ary,
Hope comes to Die.
A Dream—a Wa-kening.

But now Sadie interrupted them. "What is it, Sadie?"

"If you please, m'm, cook says have you got the flags for the sandwiches?"

"The flags for the sandwiches, Sadie?" echoed Mrs. Sheridan dreamily. And the children knew by her face that she hadn't got them. "Let me see." And she said to Sadie firmly, "Tell cook I'll let her have them in ten minutes." Sadie went.

"Now, Laura," said her mother quickly, "come with me into the smoking-room. I've got the names somewhere on the back of an envelope. You'll have to write them out for me. Meg, go upstairs this minute and take that wet thing off your head. Jose, run and finish dressing this instant. Do you hear me, children, or shall I have to tell your father when he comes home to-night? And—and, Jose, pacify cook if you do go into the kitchen, will you? I'm terrified of her this morning." The envelope was found at last behind the dining-room clock, though how it had got there Mrs. Sheridan could not imagine.

"One of you children must have stolen it out of my bag, because I remember vividly—cream-cheese and lemon-curd. Have you done that?"

"Yes."

"Egg and—" Mrs. Sheridan held the envelope away from her. "It looks like mice. It can't be mice, can it?"

"Olive, pet," said Laura, looking over her shoulder.

"Yes, of course, olive. What a horrible combination it sounds. Egg and olive."

They were finished at last, and Laura took them off to the kitchen. She found Jose there pacifying the cook, who did not look at all terrifying.

"I have never seen such exquisite sandwiches," said Jose's rapturous voice. "How many kinds did you say there were, cook? Fifteen?"

"Fifteen, Miss Jose."

"Well, cook, I congratulate you."

Cook swept up crusts with the long sandwich knife, and smiled broadly.

"Godber's has come," announced Sadie, issuing out of the pantry. She had seen the man pass the window.

That meant the cream puffs had come. Godber's were famous for their cream puffs. Nobody ever thought of making them at home.

"Bring them in and put them on the table, my girl," ordered cook.

Sadie brought them in and went back to the door. Of course Laura and Jose were far too grown-up to really care about such things. All the same, they couldn't help agreeing that the puffs looked very attractive. Very. Cook began arranging them, shaking off the extra icing sugar.

"Don't they carry one back to all one's parties?" said Laura.

"I suppose they do," said practical Jose, who never liked to be carried back. "They look beautifully light and feathery, I must say."

"Have one each, my dears," said cook in her

comfortable voice. "Yer ma won't know."

Oh, impossible. Fancy cream puffs so soon after breakfast. The very idea made one shudder. All the same, two minutes later Jose and Laura were licking their fingers with that absorbed inward look that only comes from whipped cream.

"Let's go into the garden, out by the back way," suggested Laura. "I want to see how the men are getting on with the marquee. They're such awfully nice men." But the back door was blocked by cook, Sadie, Godber's man and Hans.

Something had happened.

"Tuk-tuk-tuk," clucked cook like an agitated hen. Sadie had her hand clapped to her cheek as though she had toothache. Hans's face was screwed up in the effort to understand. Only Godber's man seemed to be enjoying himself; it was his story.

"What's the matter? What's happened?"

"There's been a horrible accident," said Cook. "A man killed."

"A man killed! Where? How? When?"

But Godber's man wasn't going to have his story snatched from under his very nose.

"Know those little cottages just below here, miss?" Know them? Of course, she knew them. "Well, there's a young chap living there, name of Scott, a carter. His horse shied at a traction-engine, corner of Hawke Street this morning, and he was thrown out on the back of his head. Killed." "Dead!" Laura stared at Godber's man.

"Dead when they picked him up," said Godber's man with relish. "They were taking the body home as I come up here." And he said to the cook, "He's left a wife and five little ones." "Jose, come here." Laura caught hold of her sister's sleeve and dragged her through the kitchen to the other side of the green baize door. There she paused and leaned against it. "Jose!" she said, horrified, "however are we going to stop everything?" "Stop everything, Laura!" cried Jose in astonishment. "What do you mean?"

"Stop the garden-party, of course." Why did Jose pretend?

But Jose was still more amazed. "Stop the garden-party? My dear Laura, don't be so absurd. Of course we can't do anything of the kind. Nobody expects us to. Don't be so extravagant." "But we can't possibly have a garden-party with a man dead just outside the front gate."

That really was extravagant, for the little cottages were in a lane to themselves at the very bottom of a steep rise that led up to the house. A broad road ran between. True, they were far too near. They were the greatest possible eyesore, and they had no right to be in that neighbourhood at all. They were little mean dwellings painted a chocolate brown. In the garden patches there was nothing but cabbage stalks, sick hens and tomato cans. The very smoke coming out of their chimneys was poverty-stricken. Little rags and shreds of smoke, so unlike the great silvery plumes that uncurled from the Sheridans' chimneys. Washerwomen lived in the lane and sweeps and a cobbler, and a man whose house-front was studded all over with minute bird-cages. Children swarmed. When the Sheridans were little they were forbidden to set foot there because of the revolting language and of what they might catch. But since they were grown up, Laura and Laurie on their prowls sometimes walked through. It was disgusting and sordid. They came out with a shudder. But still one must go everywhere; one must see everything. So through they went.

"And just think of what the band would sound like to that poor woman," said Laura.

"Oh, Laura!" Jose began to be seriously annoyed. "If you're going to stop a band playing every time some one has an accident, you'll lead a very strenuous life. I'm every bit as sorry about it as you. I feel just as sympathetic." Her eyes hardened. She looked at her sister just as she used to when they were little and fighting together. "You won't bring a drunken workman back to life by being sentimental," she said softly.

"Drunk! Who said he was drunk?" Laura turned furiously on Jose. She said, just as they had used to say on those occasions, "I'm going straight up to tell mother." "Do, dear," cooed Jose.

"Mother, can I come into your room?" Laura turned the big glass door-knob.

"Of course, child. Why, what's the matter? What's given you such a colour?" And Mrs. Sheridan turned round from her dressing-table. She was trying on a new hat.

"Mother, a man's been killed," began Laura.

"Not in the garden?" interrupted her mother.

"No, no!"

"Oh, what a fright you gave me!" Mrs. Sheridan sighed with relief, and took off the big hat and held it on her knees.

"But listen, mother," said Laura. Breathless, half-choking, she told the dreadful story. "Of course, we can't have our party, can we?" she pleaded. "The band and everybody arriving. They'd hear us, mother; they're nearly neighbours!" To Laura's astonishment her mother behaved just like Jose; it was harder to bear because she seemed amused. She refused to take Laura seriously.

"But, my dear child, use your common sense. It's only by accident we've heard of it. If some one had died there normally—and I can't understand how they keep alive in those poky little holes—we should still be having our party, shouldn't we?" Laura had to say "yes" to that, but she felt it was all wrong. She sat down on her mother's sofa and pinched the cushion frill.

"Mother, isn't it terribly heartless of us?" she asked.

"Darling!" Mrs. Sheridan got up and came over to her, carrying the hat. Before Laura could stop her she had popped it on. "My child!" said her mother, "the hat is yours. It's made for you. It's much too young for me. I have never seen you look such a picture. Look at yourself!" And she held up her hand-mirror.

"But, mother," Laura began again. She couldn't look at herself; she turned aside.

This time Mrs. Sheridan lost patience just as Jose had done.

"You are being very absurd, Laura," she said coldly. "People like that don't expect sacrifices from us. And it's not very sympathetic to spoil everybody's enjoyment as you're doing now." "I don't understand," said Laura, and she walked quickly out of the room into her own bedroom. There, quite by chance, the first thing she saw was this charming girl in the mirror, in her black hat trimmed with gold daisies, and a long black velvet ribbon. Never had she imagined she could look like that. Is mother right? she thought. And now she hoped her mother was right. Am I being extravagant? Perhaps it was extravagant. Just for a moment she had another glimpse of that poor woman and those little children, and the body being carried into the house. But it all seemed blurred, unreal, like a picture in the newspaper. I'll remember it again after the party's over, she decided. And somehow that seemed quite the best plan....

Lunch was over by half-past one. By half-past two they were all ready for the fray. The green-coated band had arrived and was established in a corner of the tennis-court.

"My dear!" trilled Kitty Maitland, "aren't they too like

frogs for words? You ought to have arranged them round the pond with the conductor in the middle on a leaf."

Laurie arrived and hailed them on his way to dress. At the sight of him Laura remembered the accident again. She wanted to tell him. If Laurie agreed with the others, then it was bound to be all right. And she followed him into the hall.

"Laurie!"

"Hallo!" He was half-way upstairs, but when he turned round and saw Laura he suddenly puffed out his cheeks and goggled his eyes at her. "My word, Laura! You do look stunning," said Laurie. "What an absolutely topping hat!" Laura said faintly "Is it?" and smiled up at Laurie, and didn't tell him after all.

Soon after that people began coming in streams. The band struck up; the hired waiters ran from the house to the marquee. Wherever you looked there were couples strolling, bending to the flowers, greeting, moving on over the lawn. They were like bright birds that had alighted in the Sheridans' garden for this one afternoon, on their way to—where? Ah, what happiness it is to be with people who all are happy, to press hands, press cheeks, smile into eyes.

"Darling Laura, how well you look!"

"What a becoming hat, child!"

"Laura, you look quite Spanish. I've never seen you look so striking."

And Laura, glowing, answered softly, "Have you had tea?

Won't you have an ice? The passion-fruit ices really are rather special." She ran to her father and begged him. "Daddy darling, can't the band have something to drink?" And the perfect afternoon slowly ripened, slowly faded, slowly its petals closed.

"Never a more delightful garden-party...." "The greatest success...." "Quite the most...."

Laura helped her mother with the good-byes. They stood side by side in the porch till it was all over.

"All over, all over, thank heaven," said Mrs. Sheridan. "Round up the others, Laura. Let's go and have some fresh coffee. I'm exhausted. Yes, it's been very successful. But oh, these parties, these parties! Why will you children insist on giving parties!" And they all of them sat down in the deserted marquee.

"Have a sandwich, daddy dear. I wrote the flag."

"Thanks." Mr. Sheridan took a bite and the sandwich was gone. He took another. "I suppose you didn't hear of a beastly accident that happened to-day?" he said.

"My dear," said Mrs. Sheridan, holding up her hand, "we did. It nearly ruined the party. Laura insisted we should put it off."

"Oh, mother!" Laura didn't want to be teased about it.

"It was a horrible affair all the same," said Mr. Sheridan. "The chap was married too. Lived just below in the lane, and leaves a wife and half a dozen kiddies, so they say." An awkward little silence fell. Mrs. Sheridan fidgeted with her cup. Really, it was very tactless of father....

Suddenly she looked up. There on the table were all those sandwiches, cakes, puffs, all uneaten, all going to be wasted. She had one of her brilliant ideas.

"I know," she said. "Let's make up a basket. Let's send that poor creature some of this perfectly good food. At any rate, it will be the greatest treat for the children. Don't you agree? And she's sure to have neighbours calling in and so on. What a point to have it all ready prepared. Laura!" She jumped up. "Get me the big basket out of the stairs cupboard." "But, mother, do you really think it's a good idea?" said Laura.

Again, how curious, she seemed to be different from them all. To take scraps from their party. Would the poor woman really like that?

"Of course! What's the matter with you to-day? An hour or two ago you were insisting on us being sympathetic, and now—"

Oh well! Laura ran for the basket. It was filled, it was heaped by her mother.

"Take it yourself, darling," said she. "Run down just as you are. No, wait, take the arum lilies too. People of that class are so impressed by arum lilies." "The stems will ruin her lace frock," said practical Jose.

So they would. Just in time. "Only the basket, then. And, Laura!"—her mother followed her out of the marquee—"don't on any account—" "What mother?"

No, better not put such ideas into the child's head! "Nothing! Run along."

It was just growing dusky as Laura shut their garden gates. A big dog ran by like a shadow. The road gleamed white, and down below in the hollow the little cottages were in deep shade. How quiet it seemed after the afternoon. Here she was going down the hill to somewhere where a man lay dead, and she couldn't realize it. Why couldn't she? She stopped a minute. And it seemed to her that kisses, voices, tinkling spoons, laughter, the smell of crushed grass were somehow inside her. She had no room for anything else. How strange! She looked up at the pale sky, and all she thought was, "Yes, it was the most successful party." Now the broad road was crossed. The lane began, smoky and dark. Women in shawls and men's tweed caps hurried by. Men hung over the palings; the children played in the doorways. A low hum came from the mean little cottages. In some of them there was a flicker of light, and a shadow, crab-like, moved across the window. Laura bent her head and hurried on. She wished now she had put on a coat. How her frock shone! And the big hat with the velvet streamer—if only it was another hat! Were the people looking at her? They must be. It was a mistake to have come; she knew all along it was a mistake. Should she go back even now?

No, too late. This was the house. It must be. A dark knot of people stood outside. Beside the gate an old, old woman with a crutch sat in a chair, watching. She had her feet on a newspaper. The voices stopped as Laura drew near. The group parted. It was as though she was expected, as though they had known she was coming here.

Laura was terribly nervous. Tossing the velvet ribbon over her shoulder, she said to a woman standing by, "Is this Mrs. Scott's house?" and the woman, smiling queerly, said, "It is, my lass." Oh, to be away from this! She actually said, "Help me, God," as she walked up the tiny path and knocked. To be away from those staring eyes, or to be covered up in anything, one of those women's shawls even. I'll just leave the basket and go, she decided. I shan't even wait for it to be emptied.

Then the door opened. A little woman in black showed in the gloom.

Laura said, "Are you Mrs. Scott?" But to her horror the woman answered, "Walk in please, miss," and she was shut in the passage.

"No," said Laura, "I don't want to come in. I only want to leave this basket. Mother sent—"

The little woman in the gloomy passage seemed not to have heard her. "Step this way, please, miss," she said in an oily voice, and Laura followed her.

She found herself in a wretched little low kitchen, lighted by a smoky lamp. There was a woman sitting before the fire.

"Em," said the little creature who had let her in. "Em! It's a young lady." She turned to Laura. She said meaningly, "I'm 'er sister, miss. You'll excuse 'er, won't you?" "Oh, but of course!" said Laura. "Please, please don't disturb her. I—I only want to leave—"

But at that moment the woman at the fire turned round. Her face, puffed up, red, with swollen eyes and swollen lips, looked terrible. She seemed as though she couldn't understand why Laura was there. What did it mean? Why was this stranger standing in the kitchen with a basket? What was it all about? And the poor face puckered up again.

"All right, my dear," said the other. "I'll thenk the young lady."

And again she began, "You'll excuse her, miss, I'm sure," and her face, swollen too, tried an oily smile.

Laura only wanted to get out, to get away. She was back in the passage. The door opened. She walked straight through into the bedroom, where the dead man was lying.

"You'd like a look at 'im, wouldn't you?" said Em's sister, and she brushed past Laura over to the bed. "Don't be afraid, my lass,"—and now her voice sounded fond and sly, and fondly she drew down the sheet—"'e looks a picture. There's nothing to show. Come along, my dear." Laura came.

There lay a young man, fast asleep—sleeping so soundly, so deeply, that he was far, far away from them both. Oh, so remote, so peaceful. He was dreaming. Never wake him up again. His head was sunk in the pillow, his eyes were closed; they were blind under the closed eyelids. He was given up to his dream. What did garden-parties and baskets and lace frocks matter to him? He was far from all those things. He was wonderful, beautiful. While they were laughing and while the band was playing, this marvel had come to the lane. Happy... happy.... All is well, said that sleeping face. This is just as it should be. I am content.

But all the same you had to cry, and she couldn't go out of the room without saying something to him. Laura gave a loud childish sob.

"Forgive my hat," she said.

And this time she didn't wait for Em's sister. She found her way out of the door, down the path, past all those dark people. At the corner of the lane she met Laurie.

He stepped out of the shadow. "Is that you, Laura?"

"Yes."

"Mother was getting anxious. Was it all right?"

"Yes, quite. Oh, Laurie!" She took his arm, she pressed up against him.

"I say, you're not crying, are you?" asked her brother.

Laura shook her head. She was.

Laurie put his arm round her shoulder. "Don't cry," he said in his warm, loving voice. "Was it awful?"

"No," sobbed Laura. "It was simply marvellous. But Laurie—" She stopped, she looked at her brother. "Isn't life," she stammered, "isn't life—" But what life was she couldn't explain. No matter. He quite understood.

"Isn't it, darling?" said Laurie.

The Star

H. G. Wells

It was on the first day of the New Year that the announcement was made, almost simultaneously from three observatories, that the motion of the planet Neptune, the outermost of all the planets that wheel about the sun, had become very erratic. Ogilvy had already called attention to a suspected retardation in its velocity in December. Such a piece of news was scarcely calculated to interest a world the greater portion of whose inhabitants were unaware of the existence of the planet Neptune, nor outside the astronomical profession did the subsequent discovery of a faint remote speck of light in the region of the perturbed planet cause any very great excitement. Scientific people, however, found the intelligence remarkable enough, even before it became known that the new body was rapidly growing larger and brighter, that its motion was quite different from the orderly progress of the planets, and that the deflection of Neptune and its satellite was becoming now of an unprecedented kind.

Few people without a training in science can realise the huge isolation of the solar system. The sun with its specks of planets, its dust of planetoids, and its impalpable comets, swims in a vacant immensity that almost defeats the imagination. Beyond the orbit of

Neptune there is space, vacant so far as human observation has penetrated, without warmth or light or sound, blank emptiness, for twenty million times a million miles. That is the smallest estimate of the distance to be traversed before the very nearest of the stars is attained. And, saving a few comets more unsubstantial than the thinnest flame, no matter had ever to human knowledge crossed this gulf of space, until early in the twentieth century this strange wanderer appeared. A vast mass of matter it was, bulky, heavy, rushing without warning out of the black mystery of the sky into the radiance of the sun. By the second day it was clearly visible to any decent instrument, as a speck with a barely sensible diameter, in the constellation Leo near Regulus. In a little while an opera glass could attain it.

On the third day of the new year the newspaper readers of two hemispheres were made aware for the first time of the real importance of this unusual apparition in the heavens. "A Planetary Collision," one London paper headed the news, and proclaimed Duchaine's opinion that this strange new planet would probably collide with Neptune. The leader writers enlarged upon the topic; so that in most of the capitals of the world, on January 3rd, there was an expectation, however vague of some imminent phenomenon in the sky; and as the night followed the sunset round the globe, thousands of men turned their eyes skyward to see—the old familiar stars just as they had always been.

Until it was dawn in London and Pollux setting and the stars overhead grown pale. The Winter's dawn it was, a sickly filtering accumulation of daylight, and the light of gas and candles shone yellow in the windows to show where people were astir. But the yawning policeman saw the thing, the busy crowds in the markets stopped agape, workmen going to their work betimes, milkmen, the drivers of news-carts, dissipation going home jaded and pale, homeless wanderers, sentinels on their beats, and in the country, labourers trudging afield, poachers slinking home, all over the dusky quickening country it could be seen—and out at sea by seamen watching for the day—a great white star, come suddenly into the westward sky!

Brighter it was than any star in our skies; brighter than the evening star at its brightest. It still glowed out white and large, no mere twinkling spot of light, but a small round clear shining disc, an hour after the day had come. And where science has not reached, men stared and feared, telling one another of the wars and pestilences that are foreshadowed by these fiery signs in the Heavens. Sturdy Boers, dusky Hottentots, Gold Coast Negroes, Frenchmen, Spaniards, Portuguese, stood in the warmth of the sunrise watching the setting of this strange new star.

And in a hundred observatories there had been suppressed excitement, rising almost to shouting pitch, as the two remote bodies had rushed together; and a hurrying to and fro, to gather photographic apparatus and spectroscope, and this appliance and that, to record this novel astonishing sight, the destruction of a world. For it was a world, a sister planet of our earth, far greater than our earth indeed, that had so suddenly flashed into flaming death. Neptune it was, had been struck, fairly and squarely, by the strange planet from outer space and the heat of the concussion had incontinently turned two solid globes into one vast mass of incandescence. Round the world that day, two hours before the dawn, went the pallid great white star, fading only as it sank westward and the sun mounted above it. Everywhere men marvelled at it, but of all those who saw it none could have marvelled more than those sailors, habitual watchers of the stars, who far away at sea had heard nothing of its advent and saw it now rise like a pigmy moon and climb zenithward and hang overhead and sink westward with the passing of the night.

And when next it rose over Europe everywhere were crowds of watchers on hilly slopes, on house-roofs, in open spaces, staring eastward for the rising of the great new star. It rose with a white glow in front of it, like the glare of a white fire, and those who had seen it come into existence the night before cried out at the sight of it. "It is larger," they cried. "It is brighter!" And, indeed the moon a quarter full and sinking in the west was in its apparent size beyond comparison, but scarcely in all its breadth had it as much brightness now as the little circle of the strange new star.

"It is brighter!" cried the people clustering in the streets. But in the dim observatories the watchers held their breath and peered at one another. "It is nearer," they said. "Nearer!"

And voice after voice repeated, "It is nearer," and the clicking telegraph took that up, and it trembled along telephone wires, and in a thousand cities grimy compositors fingered the type. "It is nearer." Men writing in offices, struck with a strange realisation, flung down their pens, men talking in a thousand places suddenly came upon a grotesque possibility in those words, "It is nearer." It hurried along wakening streets, it was shouted down the frost-stilled ways of quiet villages; men who had read these things from the throbbing tape stood in yellow-lit doorways shouting the news to the passersby. "It is nearer." Pretty women, flushed and glittering, heard the news told jestingly between the dances, and feigned an intelligent interest they did not feel. "Nearer! Indeed. How curious! How very, very clever people must be to find out things like that!" Lonely tramps faring through the wintry night murmured those words to comfort themselves—looking skyward. "It has need to be nearer, for the night's as cold as charity. Don't seem much warmth from it if it is nearer, all the same."

"What is a new star to me?" cried the weeping woman kneeling beside her dead.

The schoolboy, rising early for his examination work,

puzzled it out for himself—with the great white star shining broad and bright through the frost-flowers of his window. "Centrifugal, centripetal," he said, with his chin on his fist. "Stop a planet in its flight, rob it of its centrifugal force, what then? Centripetal has it, and down it falls into the sun! And this—!

"Do we come in the way? I wonder—"

The light of that day went the way of its brethren, and with the later watches of the frosty darkness rose the strange star again. And it was now so bright that the waxing moon seemed but a pale yellow ghost of itself, hanging huge in the sunset. In a South African City a great man had married, and the streets were alight to welcome his return with his bride. "Even the skies have illuminated," said the flatterer. Under Capricorn, two negro lovers, daring the wild beasts and evil spirits, for love of one another, crouched together in a cane brake where the fire-flies hovered. "That is our star," they whispered, and felt strangely comforted by the sweet brilliance of its light.

The master mathematician sat in his private room and pushed the papers from him. His calculations were already finished. In a small white phial there still remained a little of the drug that had kept him awake and active for four long nights. Each day, serene, explicit, patient as ever, he had given his lecture to his students, and then had come back at once to this momentous calculation. His face was grave, a little drawn and hectic from his drugged activity. For some time he seemed lost in thought. Then he went to the window, and the blind went up with a click. Half way up the sky, over the clustering roofs, chimneys and steeples of the city, hung the star.

He looked at it as one might look into the eyes of a brave enemy. "You may kill me," he said after a silence. "But I can hold you—and all the universe for that matter —in the grip of this little brain. I would not change. Even now."

He looked at the little phial. "There will be no need of sleep again," he said. The next day at noon—punctual to the minute, he entered his lecture theatre, put his hat on the end of the table as his habit was, and carefully selected a large piece of chalk. It was a joke among his students that he could not lecture without that piece of chalk to fumble in his fingers, and once he had been stricken to impotence by their hiding his supply. He came and looked under his grey eyebrows at the rising tiers of young fresh faces, and spoke with his accustomed studied commonness of phrasing. "Circumstances have arisen—circumstances beyond my control," he said and paused, "which will debar me from completing the course I had designed. It would seem, gentlemen, if I may put the thing clearly and briefly, that —Man has lived in vain." The students glanced at one another. Had they heard aright? Mad? Raised eyebrows and grinning lips there were, but one or two faces remained intent upon his calm grey-fringed face. "It will be interesting," he was saying, "to devote this morning to an exposition, so far as I can make it clear to you, of the calculations that have led me to this conclusion. Let us assume—"

He turned towards the blackboard, meditating a diagram in the way that was usual to him. "What was that about 'lived in vain?'" whispered one student to another. "Listen," said the other, nodding towards the lecturer.

And presently they began to understand.

That night the star rose later, for its proper eastward motion had carried it some way across Leo towards Virgo, and its brightness was so great that the sky became a luminous blue as it rose, and every star was hidden in its turn, save only Jupiter near the zenith, Capella, Aldebaran, Sirius and the pointers of the Bear. It was very white and beautiful. In many parts of the world that night a pallid halo encircled it about. It was perceptibly larger; in the clear refractive sky of the tropics it seemed as if it were nearly a quarter the size of the moon. The frost was still on the ground in England, but the world was as brightly lit as if it were midsummer moonlight. One could see to read quite ordinary print by that cold clear light, and in the cities the lamps burnt yellow and wan.

And everywhere the world was awake that night, and throughout Christendom a sombre murmur hung in the keen air over the country side like the belling of bees in the heather, and this murmurous tumult grew to a clangour in the cities. It was the tolling of the bells in a million belfry towers and steeples, summoning the people to sleep no more, to sin no more, but to gather in their churches and pray. And overhead, growing larger and brighter as the earth rolled on its way and the night passed, rose the dazzling star.

And the streets and houses were alight in all the cities, the shipyards glared, and whatever roads led to high country were lit and crowded all night long. And in all the seas about the civilised lands, ships with throbbing engines, and ships with bellying sails, crowded with men and living creatures, were standing out to ocean and the north. For already the warning of the master mathematician had been telegraphed all over the world, and translated into a hundred tongues. The new planet and Neptune, locked in a fiery embrace, were whirling headlong, ever faster and faster towards the sun. Already every second this blazing mass flew a hundred miles, and every second its terrific velocity increased. As it flew now, indeed, it must pass a hundred million of miles wide of the earth and scarcely affect it. But near its destined path, as yet only slightly perturbed, spun the mighty planet Jupiter and his moons sweeping splendid round the sun. Every moment now the attraction between the fiery star and the greatest of the planets grew stronger. And the result of that attraction? Inevitably Jupiter would be deflected from its orbit into an elliptical path, and the burning star, swung by his attraction wide of its sunward rush, would "describe a curved path" and perhaps collide with, and certainly pass very close to, our earth. "Earthquakes, volcanic outbreaks, cyclones, sea waves, floods, and a steady rise in temperature to I know not what limit"—so prophesied the master mathematician.

And overhead, to carry out his words, lonely and cold and livid, blazed the star of the coming doom.

To many who stared at it that night until their eyes ached, it seemed that it was visibly approaching. And that night, too, the weather changed, and the frost that had gripped all Central Europe and France and England softened towards a thaw.

But you must not imagine because I have spoken of people praying through the night and people going aboard ships and people fleeing toward mountainous country that the whole world was already in a terror because of the star. As a matter of fact, use and wont still ruled the world, and save for the talk of idle moments and the splendour of the night, nine human beings out of ten were still busy at their common occupations. In all the cities the shops, save one here and there, opened and closed at their proper hours, the doctor and the undertaker plied their trades, the workers gathered in the factories, soldiers drilled, scholars studied, lovers sought one another, thieves lurked and fled, politicians planned their schemes. The presses of the newspapers roared through the night, and many a priest of this church and that would not open his holy building to further what he considered a foolish panic. The newspapers insisted on the lesson of the year 1000—for then, too, people had anticipated the end. The star was no star—mere gas—a comet; and were it a star it could not possibly strike the earth. There was no precedent for such a thing. Common sense was sturdy everywhere, scornful, jesting, a little inclined to persecute the obdurate fearful. That night, at seven-fifteen by Greenwich time, the star would be at its nearest to Jupiter. Then the world would see the turn things would take. The master mathematician's grim warnings were treated by many as so much mere elaborate self-advertisement. Common sense at last, a little heated by argument, signified its unalterable convictions by going to bed. So, too, barbarism and savagery, already tired of the novelty, went about their nightly business, and save for a howling dog here and there, the beast world left the star unheeded.

And yet, when at last the watchers in the European States saw the star rise, an hour later it is true, but no larger than it had been the night before, there were still plenty awake to laugh at the master mathematician—to take the danger as if it had passed.

But hereafter the laughter ceased. The star grew—it grew with a terrible steadiness hour after hour, a little larger each hour, a little nearer the midnight zenith, and brighter and brighter, until it had turned night into a second day. Had it come straight to the earth instead of in a curved path, had it lost no velocity to Jupiter, it must have leapt the intervening gulf in a day, but as it was it took five days altogether to come by our planet. The next night it had become a third the size of the moon before it set to English eyes, and the thaw was assured. It rose over America near the size of the moon, but blinding white to look at, and hot; and a breath of hot wind blew now with its rising and gathering strength, and in Virginia, and Brazil, and down the St. Lawrence valley, it shone intermittently through a driving reek of thunder-clouds, flickering violet lightning, and hail unprecedented. In Manitoba was a thaw and devastating floods. And upon all the mountains of the earth the snow and ice began to melt that night, and all the rivers coming out of high country flowed thick and turbid, and soon—in their upper reaches—with swirling trees and the bodies of beasts and men. They rose steadily, steadily in the ghostly brilliance, and came trickling over their banks at last, behind the flying population of their valleys.

And along the coast of Argentina and up the South Atlantic the tides were higher than had ever been in the memory of man, and the storms drove the waters in many cases scores of miles inland, drowning whole cities. And so great grew the heat during the night that the rising of the sun was like the coming of a shadow. The earthquakes began and grew until all down America from the Arctic Circle to Cape Horn, hillsides were sliding, fissures were opening, and houses and walls crumbling to destruction. The whole side of Cotopaxi slipped out in one vast convulsion, and a tumult of lava poured out so high and broad and swift and liquid that in one day it reached the sea.

So the star, with the wan moon in its wake, marched across the Pacific, trailed the thunderstorms like the hem of a robe, and the growing tidal wave that toiled behind it, frothing and eager, poured over island and island and swept them clear of men. Until that wave came at last—in a blinding light and with the breath of a furnace, swift and terrible it came—a wall of water, fifty feet high, roaring hungrily, upon the long coasts of Asia, and swept inland across the plains of China. For a space the star, hotter now and larger and brighter than the sun in its strength, showed with pitiless brilliance the wide and populous country; towns and villages with their pagodas and trees, roads, wide cultivated fields, millions of sleepless people staring in helpless terror at the incandescent sky; and then, low and growing, came the murmur of the flood. And thus it was with millions of men that night—a flight nowhither, with limbs heavy with heat and breath fierce and scant, and the flood like a wall swift and white behind. And then death.

China was lit glowing white, but over Japan and Java and all the islands of Eastern Asia the great star was a ball of dull red fire because of the steam and smoke and ashes the volcanoes were spouting forth to salute its coming. Above was the lava, hot gases and ash, and below the seething floods, and the whole earth swayed and rumbled with the earthquake shocks. Soon the immemorial snows of Thibet and the Himalaya were melting and pouring down by ten million deepening converging channels upon the plains of Burmah and Hindostan. The tangled summits of the Indian jungles were aflame in a thousand places, and below the hurrying waters around the stems were dark objects that still struggled feebly and reflected the blood-red tongues of fire. And in a rudderless confusion a multitude of men and women fled down the broad river-ways to that one last hope of men—the open sea.

Larger grew the star, and larger, hotter, and brighter with a terrible swiftness now. The tropical ocean had lost its phosphorescence, and the whirling steam rose in ghostly wreaths from the black waves that plunged incessantly, speckled with storm-tossed ships.

And then came a wonder. It seemed to those who in Europe watched for the rising of the star that the world must have ceased its rotation. In a thousand open spaces of down and upland the people who had fled thither from the floods and the falling houses and sliding slopes of hill watched for that rising in vain. Hour followed hour through a terrible suspense, and the star rose not. Once again men set their eyes upon the old constellations they had counted lost to them forever. In England it was hot and clear overhead, though the ground quivered perpetually, but in the tropics, Sirius and Capella and Aldebaran showed through a veil of steam. And when at last the great star rose near ten hours late, the sun rose close upon it, and in the centre of its white heart was a disc of black.

Over Asia it was the star had begun to fall behind the movement of the sky, and then suddenly, as it hung over India, its light had been veiled. All the plain of India from the mouth of the Indus to the mouths of the Ganges was a shallow waste of shining water that night, out of which rose temples and palaces, mounds and hills, black with people. Every minaret was a clustering mass of people, who fell one by one into the turbid waters, as heat and terror overcame them. The whole land seemed a-wailing and suddenly there swept a shadow across that furnace of despair, and a breath of cold wind, and a gathering of clouds, out of the cooling air. Men looking up, near blinded, at the star, saw that a black disc was creeping across the light. It was the moon, coming between the star and the earth. And even as men cried to God at this respite, out of the East with a strange inexplicable swiftness sprang the sun. And then star, sun and moon rushed together across the heavens.

So it was that presently, to the European watchers, star and sun rose close upon each other, drove headlong for a space and then slower, and at last came to rest, star and sun merged into one glare of flame at the zenith of the sky. The moon no longer eclipsed the star but was lost to sight in the brilliance of the sky. And though those who were still alive regarded it for the most part with that dull stupidity that hunger, fatigue, heat and despair engender, there were still men who could perceive the meaning of these signs. Star and earth had been at their nearest, had swung about one another, and the star had passed. Already it was receding, swifter and swifter, in the last stage of its headlong journey downward into the sun.

And then the clouds gathered, blotting out the vision of the sky, the thunder and lightning wove a garment round the world; all over the earth was such a downpour of rain as men had never before seen, and where the volcanoes flared red against the cloud canopy there descended torrents of mud. Everywhere the waters were pouring off the land, leaving mud-silted ruins, and the earth littered like a storm-worn beach with all that had floated, and the dead bodies of the men and brutes, its children. For days the water streamed off the land, sweeping away soil and trees and houses in the way, and piling huge dykes and scooping out Titanic gullies over the country side. Those were the days of darkness that followed the star and the heat. All through them, and for many weeks and months, the earthquakes continued.

But the star had passed, and men, hunger-driven and gathering courage only slowly, might creep back to their ruined cities, buried granaries, and sodden fields. Such few ships as had escaped the storms of that time came stunned and shattered and sounding their way cautiously through the new marks and shoals of once familiar ports. And as the storms subsided men perceived that everywhere the days were hotter than of yore, and the sun larger, and the moon, shrunk to a third of its former size, took now fourscore days between its new and new.

But of the new brotherhood that grew presently among men, of the saving of laws and books and machines, of the strange change that had come over Iceland and Greenland and the shores of Baffin's Bay, so that the sailors coming there presently found them green and gracious, and could scarce believe their eyes, this story does not tell. Nor of the movement of mankind now that the earth was hotter, northward and southward towards the poles of the earth. It concerns itself only with the coming and the passing of the Star.

The Martian astronomers—for there are astronomers on Mars, although they are very different beings from men—were naturally profoundly interested by these things. They saw them from their own standpoint of course. "Considering the mass and temperature of the missile that was flung through our solar system into the sun," one wrote, "it is astonishing what a little damage the earth, which it missed so narrowly, has sustained. All the familiar continental markings and the masses of the seas remain intact, and indeed the only difference seems to be a shrinkage of the white discoloration (supposed to be frozen water) round either pole." Which only shows how small the vastest of human catastrophes may seem, at a distance of a few million miles.

A Novel in Nine Letters

Fyodor Dostoevsky

I

(FROM PYOTR IVANITCH TO IVAN PETROVITCH)

DEAR SIR AND MOST PRECIOUS FRIEND, IVAN PETROVITCH,

For the last two days I have been, I may say, in pursuit of you, my friend, having to talk over most urgent business with you, and I cannot come across you anywhere. Yesterday, while we were at Semyon Alexeyitch's, my wife made a very good joke about you, saying that Tatyana Petrovna and you were a pair of birds always on the wing. You have not been married three months and you already neglect your domestic hearth. We all laughed heartily--from our genuine kindly feeling for you, of course--but, joking apart, my precious friend, you have given me a lot of trouble. Semyon Alexeyitch said to me that you might be going to the ball at the Social Union's club!

Leaving my wife with Semyon Alexeyitch's good lady, I flew off to the Social Union. It was funny and tragic! Fancy my position! Me at the ball--and alone, without my wife! Ivan Andreyitch meeting me in the porter's lodge and seeing me alone, at once concluded (the rascal!) that I had a passion for dances, and taking me by the arm, wanted to drag me off by force to a dancing class, saying that it was too crowded at the Social Union, that an ardent spirit had not room to turn, and that his head ached from the patchouli and mignonette. I found neither you, nor Tatyana Petrovna. Ivan Andreyitch vowed and declared that you would be at _Woe from Wit_, at the Alexandrinsky theatre.

I flew off to the Alexandrinsky theatre: you were not there either. This morning I expected to find you at Tchistoganov's--no sign of you there.

Tchistoganov sent to the Perepalkins'--the same thing there. In fact, I am quite worn out; you can judge how much trouble I have taken! Now I am writing to you (there is nothing else I can do). My business is by no means a literary one (you understand me?); it would be better to meet face to face, it is extremely necessary to discuss something with you and as quickly as possible, and so I beg you to come to us to-day with Tatyana Petrovna to tea and for a chat in the evening. My Anna Mihalovna will be extremely pleased to see you. You will truly, as they say, oblige me to my dying day. By the way, my precious friend--since I have taken up my pen I'll go into all I have against you--I have a slight complaint I must make; in fact, I must reproach you, my worthy friend, for an apparently very innocent little trick which you have played at my expense.... You are a rascal, a man without conscience. About the middle of last month, you brought into my house an acquaintance of yours, Yevgeny Nikolaitch; you vouched for him by your friendly and, for me, of course, sacred recommendation; I rejoiced at the opportunity of receiving the young man with open arms, and when I did so I put my head in a noose. A noose it hardly is, but it has turned out a pretty business. I have not time now to explain, and indeed it is an awkward thing to do in writing, only a very humble request to you, my malicious friend: could you not somehow very delicately, in passing, drop a hint into the young man's ear that there are a great many houses in the metropolis besides ours? It's more than I can stand, my dear fellow! We fall at your feet, as our friend Semyonovitch says. I will tell you all about it when we meet. I don't mean to say that the young man has sinned against good manners, or is lacking in spiritual qualities, or is not up to the mark in some other way. On the contrary, he is an amiable and pleasant fellow; but wait, we shall meet; meanwhile if you see him, for goodness' sake whisper a hint to him, my good friend. I would do it myself, but you know what I am, I simply can't, and that's all about it. You introduced him. But I will explain myself more fully this evening, anyway. Now good-bye. I remain, etc.

P.S.--My little boy has been ailing for the last week, and gets worse and worse every day; he is cutting his poor little teeth. My wife is nursing him all the time, and is depressed, poor thing. Be sure to come, you will give us real pleasure, my precious friend.

II
(FROM IVAN PETROVITCH TO PYOTR IVANITCH)

DEAR SIR, PYOTR IVANITCH!

I got your letter yesterday, I read it and was perplexed. You looked for me, goodness knows where, and I was simply at home. Till ten o'clock I was expecting Ivan Ivanitch Tolokonov. At once on getting your letter I set out with my wife, I went to the expense of taking a cab, and reached your house about half-past six. You were not at home, but we were met by your wife. I waited to see you till half-past ten, I could not stay later. I set off with my wife, went to the expense of a cab again, saw her home, and went on myself to the Perepalkins', thinking I might meet you there, but again I was out in my reckoning. When I get home I did not sleep all night, I felt uneasy; in the morning I drove round to you three times, at nine, at ten and at eleven; three times I went to the expense of a cab, and again you left me in the lurch.

I read your letter and was amazed. You write about Yevgeny Nikolaitch, beg me to whisper some hint, and do not tell me what about. I commend your caution, but all letters are not alike, and I don't give documents of importance to my wife for curl-papers. I am puzzled, in fact, to know with what motive you wrote all this to me. However, if it comes to that, why should I meddle in the matter? I don't poke my nose into other people's business. You can be not at home to him; I only see that I must have a brief and decisive explanation with you, and, moreover, time is passing.

And I am in straits and don't know what to do if you are going to neglect the terms of our agreement. A journey for nothing; a journey costs something, too, and my wife's whining for me to get her a velvet mantle of the latest fashion. About Yevgeny Nikolaitch I hasten to mention that when I was at Pavel Semyonovitch Perepalkin's yesterday I made inquiries without loss of time. He has five hundred serfs in the province of Yaroslav, and he has expectations from his grandmother of an estate of three hundred serfs near Moscow. How much money he has I cannot tell; I think you ought to know that better. I beg you once for all to appoint a place where I can meet you. You met Ivan Andreyitch yesterday, and you write that he told you that I was at the Alexandrinsky theatre with my wife. I write, that he is a liar, and it shows how little he is to be trusted in such cases, that only the day before yesterday he did his grandmother out of eight hundred roubles. I have the honour to remain, etc.

P.S.--My wife is going to have a baby; she is nervous about it and feels depressed at times. At the theatre they sometimes have fire-arms going off and sham thunderstorms. And so for fear of a shock to my wife's nerves I do not take her to the theatre. I have no great partiality for the theatre myself.

III
(FROM PYOTR IVANITCH TO IVAN PETROVITCH)

MY PRECIOUS FRIEND, IVAN PETROVITCH,

I am to blame, to blame, a thousand times to blame, but I hasten to defend myself. Between five and six yesterday, just as we were talking of you with the warmest affection, a messenger from Uncle Stepan Alexeyitch galloped up with the news that my aunt was very bad. Being afraid of alarming my wife, I did not say a word of this to her, but on the pretext of other urgent business I drove off to my aunt's house. I found her almost dying. Just at five o'clock she had had a stroke, the third she has had in the last two years. Karl Fyodoritch, their family doctor, told us that she might not live through the night. You can judge of my position, dearest friend. We were on our legs all night in grief and anxiety. It was not till morning that, utterly exhausted and overcome by moral and physical weakness, I lay down on the sofa; I forgot to tell them to wake me, and only woke at half-past eleven. My aunt was better. I drove home to my wife. She, poor thing, was quite worn out expecting me. I snatched a bite of something, embraced my little boy, reassured my wife and set off to call on you. You were not at home. At your flat I found Yevgeny Nikolaitch. When I got home I took up a pen, and here I am writing to you. Don't grumble and be cross to me, my true friend. Beat me, chop my guilty head off my shoulders, but don't deprive me of your affection. From your wife I learned that you will be at the Slavyanovs' this evening. I will certainly be there. I look forward with the greatest impatience to seeing you.

I remain, etc.

P.S.--We are in perfect despair about our little boy. Karl Fyodoritch prescribes rhubarb. He moans. Yesterday he did not know any one. This morning he did know us, and began lisping papa, mamma, boo.... My wife was in tears the whole morning.

IV
(FROM IVAN PETROVITCH TO PYOTR IVANITCH)

MY DEAR SIR, PYOTR IVANITCH!

I am writing to you, in your room, at your bureau; and before taking up my pen, I have been waiting for more than two and a half hours for you. Now allow me to tell you straight out, Pyotr Ivanitch, my frank opinion about this shabby incident. From your last letter I gathered that you were expected at the Slavyanovs', that you were inviting me to go there; I turned up, I stayed for five hours and there was no sign of you. Why, am I to be made a laughing-stock to people, do you suppose? Excuse me, my dear sir ... I came to you this morning, I hoped to find you, not imitating certain deceitful persons who look for people, God knows where, when they can be found at home at any suitably chosen time. There is no sign of you at home. I don't know what restrains me from telling you now the whole harsh truth. I will only say that I see you seem to be going back on your bargain regarding our agreement. And only now reflecting on the whole affair, I cannot but confess that I am absolutely astounded at the artful workings of your mind. I see clearly now that you have been cherishing your unfriendly design for a long time. This supposition of mine is confirmed by the fact that last week in an almost unpardonable way you took possession of that letter of yours addressed to me, in which you laid down yourself, though rather vaguely and incoherently, the terms of our agreement in regard to a circumstance of which I need not remind you. You are afraid of documents, you destroy them, and you try to make a fool of me. But I won't allow myself to be made a fool of, for no one has ever considered me one hitherto, and every one has thought well of me in that respect. I am opening my eyes. You try and put me off, confuse me with talk of Yevgeny Nikolaitch, and when with your letter of the seventh of this month, which I am still at a loss to understand, I seek a personal explanation from you, you make humbugging appointments, while you keep out of the way. Surely you do not suppose, sir, that I am not equal to noticing all this? You promised to reward me for my services, of which you are very well aware, in the way of introducing various persons, and at the same time, and I don't know how you do it, you contrive to borrow money from me in considerable sums without giving a receipt, as happened no longer ago than last week. Now, having got the money, you keep out of the way, and what's more, you repudiate the service I have done you in regard to Yevgeny Nikolaitch. You are probably reckoning on my speedy departure to Simbirsk, and hoping I may not have time to settle your business. But I assure you solemnly and testify on my word of honour that if it comes to that, I am prepared to spend two more months in Petersburg expressly to carry through my business, to attain my objects, and to get hold of you. For I, too, on occasion know how to get the better of people. In conclusion, I beg to inform you that if you do not give me a satisfactory explanation to-day, first in writing, and then personally face to face, and do not make a fresh statement in your letter of the chief points of the agreement existing between us, and do not explain fully your views in regard to Yevgeny Nikolaitch, I shall be compelled to have recourse to measures that will be highly unpleasant to you, and indeed repugnant to me also.

Allow me to remain, etc.

V
(FROM PYOTR IVANITCH TO IVAN PETROVITCH)

November 11.

MY DEAR AND HONOURED FRIEND, IVAN PETROVITCH!

I was cut to the heart by your letter. I wonder you were not ashamed, my dear but unjust friend, to behave like this to one of your most devoted friends. Why be in such a hurry, and without explaining things fully, wound me with such insulting suspicions? But I hasten to reply to your charges.

You did not find me yesterday, Ivan Petrovitch, because I was suddenly and quite unexpectedly called away to a death-bed. My aunt, Yefimya Nikolaevna, passed away yesterday evening at eleven o'clock in the night. By the general consent of the relatives I was selected to make the arrangements for the sad and sorrowful ceremony. I had so much to do that I had not time to see you this morning, nor even to send you a line. I am grieved to the heart at the misunderstanding which has arisen between us. My words about Yevgeny Nikolaitch uttered casually and in jest you have taken in quite a wrong sense, and have ascribed to them a meaning deeply offensive to me.

You refer to money and express your anxiety about it. But without wasting words I am ready to satisfy all your claims and demands, though I must remind you that the three hundred and fifty roubles I had from you last week were in accordance with a certain agreement and not by way of a loan.

In the latter case there would certainly have been a receipt. I will not condescend to discuss the other points mentioned in your letter. I see that it is a misunderstanding. I see it is your habitual hastiness, hot temper and obstinacy. I know that your goodheartedness and open character will not allow doubts to persist in your heart, and that you will be, in fact, the first to hold out your hand to me. You are mistaken, Ivan Petrovitch, you are greatly mistaken!

Although your letter has deeply wounded me, I should be prepared even to-day to come to you and apologise, but I have been since yesterday in such a rush and flurry that I am utterly exhausted and can scarcely stand on my feet. To complete my troubles, my wife is laid up; I am afraid she is seriously ill. Our little boy, thank God, is better; but I must lay down my pen, I have a mass of things to do and they are urgent. Allow me, my dear friend, to remain, etc.

VI

(FROM IVAN PETROVITCH TO PYOTR IVANITCH)

November 14.

DEAR SIR, PYOTR IVANITCH!

I have been waiting for three days, I tried to make a profitable use of them--meanwhile I feel that politeness and good manners are the greatest of ornaments for every one. Since my last letter of the tenth of this month, I have neither by word nor deed reminded you of my existence, partly in order to allow you undisturbed to perform the duty of a Christian in regard to your aunt, partly because I needed the time for certain considerations and investigations in regard to a business you know of. Now I hasten to explain myself to you in the most thoroughgoing and decisive manner.

I frankly confess that on reading your first two letters I seriously supposed that you did not understand what I wanted; that was how it was that I rather sought an interview with you and explanations face to face. I was afraid of writing, and blamed myself for lack of clearness in the expression of my thoughts on paper. You are aware that I have not the advantages of education and good manners, and that I shun a hollow show of gentility because I have learned from bitter experience how misleading appearances often are, and that a snake sometimes lies hidden under flowers. But you understood me; you did not answer me as you should have done because, in the treachery of your heart, you had planned beforehand to be faithless to your word of honour and to the friendly relations existing between us. You have proved this absolutely by your abominable conduct towards me of late, which is fatal to my interests, which I did not expect and which I refused to believe till the present moment. From the very beginning of our acquaintance you captivated me by your clever manners, by the subtlety of your behaviour, your knowledge of affairs and the advantages to be gained by association with you. I imagined that I had found a true friend and well-wisher. Now I recognise clearly that there are many people who under a flattering and brilliant exterior hide venom in their hearts, who use their cleverness to weave snares for their neighbour and for unpardonable deception, and so are afraid of pen and paper, and at the same time use their fine language not for the benefit of their neighbour and their country, but to drug and bewitch the reason of those who have entered into business relations of any sort with them. Your treachery to me, my dear sir, can be clearly seen from what follows.

In the first place, when, in the clear and distinct terms of my letter, I described my position, sir, and at the same time asked you in my first letter what you meant by certain expressions and intentions of yours, principally in regard to Yevgeny Nikolaitch, you tried for the most part to avoid answering, and confounding me by doubts and suspicions, you calmly put the subject aside. Then after treating me in a way which cannot be described by any seemly word, you began writing that you were wounded.

Pray, what am I to call that, sir? Then when every minute was precious to me and when you had set me running after you all over the town, you wrote, pretending personal friendship, letters in which, intentionally avoiding all mention of business, you spoke of utterly irrelevant matters; to wit, of the illnesses of your good lady for whom I have, in any case, every respect, and of how your baby had been dosed with rhubarb and was cutting a tooth. All this you alluded to in every letter with a disgusting regularity that was insulting to me. Of course I am prepared to admit that a father's heart may be torn by the sufferings of his babe, but why make mention of this when something different, far more important and interesting, was needed? I endured it in silence, but now when time has elapsed I think it my duty to explain myself. Finally, treacherously deceiving me several times by making humbugging appointments, you tried, it seems, to make me play the part of a fool and a laughing-stock for you, which I never intend to be. Then after first inviting me and thoroughly deceiving me, you informed me that you were called away to your suffering aunt who had had a stroke, precisely at five o'clock as you stated with shameful exactitude.

Luckily for me, sir, in the course of these three days I have succeeded in making inquiries and have learnt from them that your aunt had a stroke on the day before the seventh not long before midnight. From this fact I see that you have made use of sacred family relations in order to deceive persons in no way concerned with them. Finally, in your last letter you mention the death of your relatives as though it had taken place precisely at the time when I was to have visited you to consult about various business matters. But here the vileness of your arts and calculations exceeds all belief, for from trustworthy information which I was able by a lucky chance to obtain just in the nick of time, I have found out that your aunt died twenty-four hours later than the time you so impiously fixed for her decease in your letter. I shall never have done if I enumerate all the signs by which I have discovered your treachery in regard to me. It is sufficient, indeed, for any impartial observer that in every letter you style me, your true friend, and call me all sorts of polite names, which you do, to the best of my belief, for no other object than to put my conscience to sleep.

I have come now to your principal act of deceit and treachery in regard to me, to wit, your continual silence of late in regard to everything concerning our common interests, in regard to your wicked theft of the letter in which you stated, though in language somewhat obscure and not perfectly intelligible to me, our mutual agreements, your barbarous forcible loan of three hundred and fifty roubles which you borrowed from me as your partner without giving any receipt, and finally, your abominable slanders of our common acquaintance, Yevgeny Nikolaitch. I see clearly now that you meant to show me that he was, if you will allow me to say so, like a billy-goat, good for neither milk nor wool, that he was neither one thing nor the other, neither fish nor flesh, which you put down as a vice in him in your letter of the sixth instant. I knew Yevgeny Nikolaitch as a modest and well-behaved young man, whereby he may well attract, gain and deserve respect in society. I know also that every evening for the last fortnight you've put into your pocket dozens and sometimes even hundreds of roubles, playing games of chance with Yevgeny Nikolaitch. Now you disavow all this, and not only refuse to compensate me for what I have suffered, but have even appropriated money belonging to me, tempting me by suggestions that I should be partner in the affair, and luring me with various advantages which were to accrue. After having appropriated, in a most illegal way, money of mine and of Yevgeny Nikolaitch's, you decline to compensate me, resorting for that object to calumny with which you have unjustifiably blackened in my eyes a man whom I, by my efforts and exertions, introduced into your house. While on the contrary, from what I hear from your friends, you are still almost slobbering over him, and give out to the whole world that he is your dearest friend, though there is no one in the world such a fool as not to guess at once what your designs are aiming at and what your friendly relations really mean. I should say that they mean deceit, treachery, forgetfulness of human duties and proprieties, contrary to the law of God and vicious in every way. I take myself as a proof and example.

In what way have I offended you and why have you treated me in this godless fashion?

I will end my letter. I have explained myself. Now in conclusion. If, sir, you do not in the shortest possible time after receiving this letter return me in full, first, the three hundred and fifty roubles I gave you, and, secondly, all the sums that should come to me according to your promise, I will have recourse to every possible means to compel you to return it, even to open force, secondly to the protection of the laws, and finally I beg to inform you that I am in possession of facts, which, if they remain in the hands of your humble servant, may ruin and disgrace your name in the eyes of all the world. Allow me to remain, etc.

VII
(FROM PYOTR IVANITCH TO IVAN PETROVITCH)

November 15.

IVAN PETROVITCH!

When I received your vulgar and at the same time queer letter, my impulse for the first minute was to tear it into shreds, but I have preserved it as a curiosity. I do, however, sincerely regret our misunderstandings and unpleasant relations. I did not mean to answer you. But I am compelled by necessity. I must in these lines inform you that it would be very unpleasant for me to see you in my house at any time; my wife feels the same: she is in delicate health and the smell of tar upsets her. My wife sends your wife the book, _Don Quixote de la Mancha_, with her sincere thanks. As for the galoshes you say you left behind here on your last visit, I must regretfully inform you that they are nowhere to be found.

They are still being looked for; but if they do not turn up, then I will buy you a new pair.

I have the honour to remain your sincere friend,

VIII

On the sixteenth of November, Pyotr Ivanitch received by post two letters addressed to him. Opening the first envelope, he took out a carefully folded note on pale pink paper. The handwriting was his wife's. It was addressed to Yevgeny Nikolaitch and dated November the second. There was nothing else in the envelope. Pyotr Ivanitch read:

DEAR EUGÈNE,

Yesterday was utterly impossible. My husband was at home the whole evening.

Be sure to come to-morrow punctually at eleven. At half-past ten my husband is going to Tsarskoe and not coming back till evening. I was in a rage all night. Thank you for sending me the information and the correspondence.

What a lot of paper. Did she really write all that? She has style though; many thanks, dear; I see that you love me. Don't be angry, but, for goodness sake, come to-morrow.

A.

Pyotr Ivanitch tore open the other letter:

PYOTR IVANITCH,

I should never have set foot again in your house anyway; you need not have troubled to soil paper about it.

Next week I am going to Simbirsk. Yevgany Nikolaitch remains your precious and beloved friend. I wish you luck, and don't trouble about the galoshes.

IX

On the seventeenth of November Ivan Petrovitch received by post two letters addressed to him. Opening the first letter, he took out a hasty and carelessly written note. The handwriting was his wife's; it was addressed to Yevgeny Nikolaitch, and dated August the fourth. There was nothing else in the envelope. Ivan Petrovitch read:

* * * * *

Good-bye, good-bye, Yevgeny Nikolaitch! The Lord reward you for this too.

May you be happy, but my lot is bitter, terribly bitter! It is your choice.

If it had not been for my aunt I should not have put such trust in you. Do not laugh at me nor at my aunt. To-morrow is our wedding. Aunt is relieved that a good man has been found, and that he will take me without a dowry. I took a good look at him for the first time to-day. He seems good-natured.

They are hurrying me. Farewell, farewell.... My darling!! Think of me sometimes; I shall never forget you. Farewell! I sign this last like my first letter, do you remember?

TATYANA.

The second letter was as follows:

IVAN PETROVITCH,

To-morrow you will receive a new pair of galoshes. It is not my habit to filch from other men's pockets, and I am not fond of picking up all sorts of rubbish in the streets.

Yevgeny Nikolaitch is going to Simbirsk in a day or two on his grandfather's business, and he has asked me to find a travelling companion for him; wouldn't you like to take him with you?

The Glass Dog

Lyman Frank Baum

An accomplished wizard once lived on the top floor of a tenement house and passed his time in thoughtful study and studious thought. What he didn't know about wizardry was hardly worth knowing, for he possessed all the books and recipes of all the wizards who had lived before him; and, moreover, he had invented several wizardments himself.

This admirable person would have been completely happy but for the numerous interruptions to his studies caused by folk who came to consult him about their troubles (in which he was not interested), and by the loud knocks of the iceman, the milkman, the baker's boy, the laundryman and the peanut woman. He never dealt with any of these people; but they rapped at his door every day to see him about this or that or to try to sell him their wares. Just when he was most deeply interested in his books or engaged in watching the bubbling of a cauldron there would come a knock at his door. And after sending the intruder away he always found he had lost his train of thought or ruined his compound.

At length these interruptions aroused his anger, and he decided he must have a dog to keep people away from his door. He didn't know where to find a dog, but in the next room lived a poor glass-blower with whom he had a slight acquaintance; so he went into the man's apartment and asked: "Where can I find a dog?"

"What sort of a dog?" inquired the glass-blower.

"A good dog. One that will bark at people and drive them away. One that will be no trouble to keep and won't expect to be fed. One that has no fleas and is neat in his habits. One that will obey me when I speak to him. In short, a good dog," said the wizard.

"Such a dog is hard to find," returned the glass-blower, who was busy making a blue glass flower pot with a pink glass rosebush in it, having green glass leaves and yellow glass roses.

The wizard watched him thoughtfully.

"Why cannot you blow me a dog out of glass?" he asked, presently.

"I can," declared the glass-blower; "but it would not bark at people, you know."

"Oh, I'll fix that easily enough," replied the other. "If I could not make a glass dog bark I would be a mighty poor wizard."

"Very well; if you can use a glass dog I'll be pleased to blow one for you. Only, you must pay for my work."

"Certainly," agreed the wizard. "But I have none of that horrid stuff you call money. You must take some of my wares in exchange."

The glass-blower considered the matter for a moment.

"Could you give me something to cure my rheumatism?"

he asked.

"Oh, yes; easily."

"Then it's a bargain. I'll start the dog at once. What color of glass shall I use?"

"Pink is a pretty color," said the wizard, "and it's unusual for a dog, isn't it?"

"Very," answered the glass-blower; "but it shall be pink."

So the wizard went back to his studies and the glass-blower began to make the dog.

Next morning he entered the wizard's room with the glass dog under his arm and set it carefully upon the table. It was a beautiful pink in color, with a fine coat of spun glass, and about its neck was twisted a blue glass ribbon. Its eyes were specks of black glass and sparkled intelligently, as do many of the glass eyes worn by men.

The wizard expressed himself pleased with the glass-blower's skill and at once handed him a small vial.

"This will cure your rheumatism," he said.

"But the vial is empty!" protested the glass-blower.

"Oh, no; there is one drop of liquid in it," was the wizard's reply.

"Will one drop cure my rheumatism?" inquired the glass-blower, in wonder.

"Most certainly. That is a marvelous remedy. The one drop contained in the vial will cure instantly any kind of disease ever known to humanity. Therefore it is especially good for rheumatism. But guard it well, for it is the only drop of its kind in the world, and I've forgotten the recipe."

"Thank you," said the glass-blower, and went back to his room.

Then the wizard cast a wizzy spell and mumbled several very learned words in the wizardese language over the glass dog. Whereupon the little animal first wagged its tail from side to side, then winked his left eye knowingly, and at last began barking in a most frightful manner—that is, when you stop to consider the noise came from a pink glass dog. There is something almost astonishing in the magic arts of wizards; unless, of course, you know how to do the things yourself, when you are not expected to be surprised at them.

The wizard was as delighted as a school teacher at the success of his spell, although he was not astonished. Immediately he placed the dog outside his door, where it would bark at anyone who dared knock and so disturb the studies of its master.

The glass-blower, on returning to his room, decided not to use the one drop of wizard cure-all just then.

"My rheumatism is better to-day," he reflected, "and I will be wise to save the medicine for a time when I am very ill, when it will be of more service to me."

So he placed the vial in his cupboard and went to work blowing more roses out of glass. Presently he happened to think the medicine might not keep, so he started to ask the wizard about it. But when he reached the door the glass dog barked so fiercely that he dared not knock, and returned in great haste to his own room. Indeed, the poor man was quite upset at so unfriendly a reception from the dog he had himself so carefully and skillfully made.

The next morning, as he read his newspaper, he noticed an article stating that the beautiful Miss Mydas, the richest young lady in town, was very ill, and the doctors had given up hope of her recovery.

The glass-blower, although miserably poor, hard-working and homely of feature, was a man of ideas. He suddenly recollected his precious medicine, and determined to use it to better advantage than relieving his own ills. He dressed himself in his best clothes, brushed his hair and combed his whiskers, washed his hands and tied his necktie, blackened his hoes and sponged his vest, and then put the vial of magic cure-all in his pocket. Next he locked his door, went downstairs and walked through the streets to the grand mansion where the wealthy Miss Mydas resided.

The butler opened the door and said:

"No soap, no chromos, no vegetables, no hair oil, no books, no baking powder. My young lady is dying and we're well supplied for the funeral."

The glass-blower was grieved at being taken for a peddler.

"My friend," he began, proudly; but the butler interrupted him, saying:

"No tombstones, either; there's a family graveyard and

the monument's built."

"The graveyard won't be needed if you will permit me to speak," said the glass-blower.

"No doctors, sir; they've given up my young lady, and she's given up the doctors," continued the butler, calmly.

"I'm no doctor," returned the glass-blower.

"Nor are the others. But what is your errand?"

"I called to cure your young lady by means of a magical compound."

"Step in, please, and take a seat in the hall. I'll speak to the housekeeper," said the butler, more politely.

So he spoke to the housekeeper and the housekeeper mentioned the matter to the steward and the steward consulted the chef and the chef kissed the lady's maid and sent her to see the stranger. Thus are the very wealthy hedged around with ceremony, even when dying.

When the lady's maid heard from the glass-blower that he had a medicine which would cure her mistress, she said:

"I'm glad you came."

"But," said he, "if I restore your mistress to health she must marry me."

"I'll make inquiries and see if she's willing," answered the maid, and went at once to consult Miss Mydas.

The young lady did not hesitate an instant.

"I'd marry any old thing rather than die!" she cried. "Bring him here at once!"

So the glass-blower came, poured the magic drop into a

little water, gave it to the patient, and the next minute Miss Mydas was as well as she had ever been in her life.

"Dear me!" she exclaimed; "I've an engagement at the Fritters' reception to-night. Bring my pearl-colored silk, Marie, and I will begin my toilet at once. And don't forget to cancel the order for the funeral flowers and your mourning gown."

"But, Miss Mydas," remonstrated the glass-blower, who stood by, "you promised to marry me if I cured you."

"I know," said the young lady, "but we must have time to make proper announcement in the society papers and have the wedding cards engraved. Call to-morrow and we'll talk it over."

The glass-blower had not impressed her favorably as a husband, and she was glad to find an excuse for getting rid of him for a time. And she did not want to miss the Fritters' reception.

Yet the man went home filled with joy; for he thought his stratagem had succeeded and he was about to marry a rich wife who would keep him in luxury forever afterward.

The first thing he did on reaching his room was to smash his glass-blowing tools and throw them out of the window.

He then sat down to figure out ways of spending his wife's money.

The following day he called upon Miss Mydas, who was reading a novel and eating chocolate creams as happily as if she had never been ill in her life.

"Where did you get the magic compound that cured me?" she asked.

"From a learned wizard," said he; and then, thinking it would interest her, he told how he had made the glass dog for the wizard, and how it barked and kept everybody from bothering him.

"How delightful!" she said. "I've always wanted a glass dog that could bark."

"But there is only one in the world," he answered, "and it belongs to the wizard."

"You must buy it for me," said the lady.

"The wizard cares nothing for money," replied the glass-blower.

"Then you must steal it for me," she retorted. "I can never live happily another day unless I have a glass dog that can bark."

The glass-blower was much distressed at this, but said he would see what he could do. For a man should always try to please his wife, and Miss Mydas has promised to marry him within a week.

On his way home he purchased a heavy sack, and when he passed the wizard's door and the pink glass dog ran out to bark at him he threw the sack over the dog, tied the opening with a piece of twine, and carried him away to his own room.

The next day he sent the sack by a messenger boy to Miss Mydas, with his compliments, and later in the afternoon he called upon her in person, feeling quite sure he would be received with gratitude for stealing the dog she so greatly desired.

But when he came to the door and the butler opened it, what was his amazement to see the glass dog rush out and begin barking at him furiously.

"Call off your dog," he shouted, in terror.

"I can't, sir," answered the butler. "My young lady has ordered the glass dog to bark whenever you call here. You'd better look out, sir," he added, "for if it bites you, you may have glassophobia!"

This so frightened the poor glass-blower that he went away hurriedly. But he stopped at a drug store and put his last dime in the telephone box so he could talk to Miss Mydas without being bitten by the dog.

"Give me Pelf 6742!" he called.

"Hello! What is it?" said a voice.

"I want to speak with Miss Mydas," said the glass-blower.

Presently a sweet voice said: "This is Miss Mydas. What is it?"

"Why have you treated me so cruelly and set the glass dog on me?" asked the poor fellow.

"Well, to tell the truth," said the lady, "I don't like your looks. Your cheeks are pale and baggy, your hair is coarse and long, your eyes are small and red, your hands are big and rough, and you are bow-legged."

"But I can't help my looks!" pleaded the glass-blower; "and you really promised to marry me."

"If you were better looking I'd keep my promise," she returned. "But under the circumstances you are no fit mate for me, and unless you keep away from my mansion I shall set my glass dog on you!" Then she dropped the 'phone and would have nothing more to say.

The miserable glass-blower went home with a heart bursting with disappointment and began tying a rope to the bedpost by which to hang himself.

Some one knocked at the door, and, upon opening it, he saw the wizard.

"I've lost my dog," he announced.

"Have you, indeed?" replied the glass-blower tying a knot in the rope.

"Yes; some one has stolen him."

"That's too bad," declared the glass-blower, indifferently.

"You must make me another," said the wizard.

"But I cannot; I've thrown away my tools."

"Then what shall I do?" asked the wizard.

"I do not know, unless you offer a reward for the dog."

"But I have no money," said the wizard.

"Offer some of your compounds, then," suggested the glass-blower, who was making a noose in the rope for his head to go through.

"The only thing I can spare," replied the wizard, thoughtfully, "is a Beauty Powder."

"What!" cried the glass-blower, throwing down the rope, "have you really such a thing?"

"Yes, indeed. Whoever takes the powder will become the most beautiful person in the world."

"If you will offer that as a reward," said the glass-blower, eagerly, "I'll try to find the dog for you, for above everything else I long to be beautiful."

"But I warn you the beauty will only be skin deep," said the wizard.

"That's all right," replied the happy glass-blower; "when I lose my skin I shan't care to remain beautiful."

"Then tell me where to find my dog and you shall have the powder," promised the wizard.

So the glass-blower went out and pretended to search, and by-and-by he returned and said:

"I've discovered the dog. You will find him in the mansion of Miss Mydas."

The wizard went at once to see if this were true, and, sure enough, the glass dog ran out and began barking at him. Then the wizard spread out his hands and chanted a magic spell which sent the dog fast asleep, when he picked him up and carried him to his own room on the top floor of the tenement house.

Afterward he carried the Beauty Powder to the glass-blower as a reward, and the fellow immediately swallowed it and became the most beautiful man in the world.

The next time he called upon Miss Mydas there was no dog to bark at him, and when the young lady saw him she fell in love with his beauty at once.

"If only you were a count or a prince," she sighed, "I'd willingly marry you."

"But I am a prince," he answered; "the Prince of Dogblowers."

"Ah!" said she; "then if you are willing to accept an allowance of four dollars a week I'll order the wedding cards engraved."

The man hesitated, but when he thought of the rope hanging from his bedpost he consented to the terms.

So they were married, and the bride was very jealous of her husband's beauty and led him a dog's life. So he managed to get into debt and made her miserable in turn.

As for the glass dog, the wizard set him barking again by means of his wizardness and put him outside his door. I suppose he is there yet, and am rather sorry, for I should like to consult the wizard about the moral to this story.

Ma'ame Pélagie

Kate Chopin

I.

When the war began, there stood on Côte Joyeuse an imposing mansion of red brick, shaped like the Pantheon. A grove of majestic live-oaks surrounded it.

Thirty years later, only the thick walls were standing, with the dull red brick showing here and there through a matted growth of clinging vines. The huge round pillars were intact; so to some extent was the stone flagging of hall and portico. There had been no home so stately along the whole stretch of Côte Joyeuse. Every one knew that, as they knew it had cost Philippe Valmet sixty thousand dollars to build, away back in 1840. No one was in danger of forgetting that fact, so long as his daughter Pélagie survived. She was a queenly, white-haired woman of fifty. "Ma'ame Pélagie," they called her, though she was unmarried, as was her sister Pauline, a child in Ma'ame Pélagie's eyes; a child of thirty-five. The two lived alone in a three-roomed cabin, almost within the shadow of the ruin. They lived for a dream, for Ma'ame Pélagie's dream, which was to rebuild the old home.

It would be pitiful to tell how their days were spent to accomplish this end; how the dollars had been saved for thirty years and the picayunes hoarded; and yet, not half enough gathered! But Ma'ame Pélagie felt sure of twenty years of life before her, and counted upon as many more for her sister. And what could not come to pass in twenty—in forty—years?

Often, of pleasant afternoons, the two would drink their black coffee, seated upon the stone-flagged portico whose canopy was the blue sky of Louisiana. They loved to sit there in the silence, with only each other and the sheeny, prying lizards for company, talking of the old times and planning for the new; while light breezes stirred the tattered vines high up among the columns, where owls nested.

"We can never hope to have all just as it was, Pauline," Ma'ame Pélagie would say; "perhaps the marble pillars of the salon will have to be replaced by wooden ones, and the crystal candelabra left out. Should you be willing, Pauline?"

"Oh, yes, Sesœur, I shall be willing." It was always, "Yes, Sesœur," or "No, Sesœur," "Just as you please, Sesœur," with poor little Mam'selle Pauline. For what did she remember of that old life and that old splendor? Only a faint gleam here and there; the half-consciousness of a young, uneventful existence; and then a great crash. That meant the nearness of war; the revolt of slaves; confusion ending in fire and flame through which she was borne safely in the strong arms of Pélagie, and carried to the log cabin which was still their home. Their brother, Léandre, had known more of it all than Pauline, and not so much as Pélagie. He had left the management of the big plantation with all its memories and traditions to his older sister, and had gone away to dwell in cities. That was many years ago. Now, Léandre's business called him frequently and upon long journeys from home, and his motherless daughter was coming to stay with her aunts at Côte Joyeuse.

They talked about it, sipping their coffee on the ruined portico. Mam'selle Pauline was terribly excited; the flush that throbbed into her pale, nervous face showed it; and she locked her thin fingers in and out incessantly.

"But what shall we do with La Petite, Sesœur? Where shall we put her? How shall we amuse her? Ah, Seigneur!"

"She will sleep upon a cot in the room next to ours," responded Ma'ame Pélagie, "and live as we do. She knows how we live, and why we live; her father has told her. She knows we have money and could squander it if we chose. Do not fret, Pauline; let us hope La Petite is a true Valmet."

Then Ma'ame Pélagie rose with stately deliberation and went to saddle? her horse, for she had yet to make her last daily round through the fields; and Mam'selle Pauline threaded her way slowly among the tangled grasses toward the cabin.

The coming of La Petite, bringing with her as she did the pungent atmosphere of an outside and dimly known world, was a shock to these two, lining their dream-life.

The girl was quite as tall as her aunt Pélagie, with dark eyes that reflected joy as a still pool reflects the light of stars; and her rounded cheek was tinged like the pink crèpe myrtle. Mam'selle Pauline kissed her and trembled. Ma'ame Pélagie looked into her eyes with a searching gaze, which seemed to seek a likeness of the past in the living present.

And they made room between them for this young life.

II.

La Petite had determined upon trying to fit herself to the strange, narrow existence which she knew awaited her at Côte Joyeuse. It went well enough at first. Sometimes she followed Ma'ame Pélagie into the fields to note how the cotton was opening, ripe and white; or to count the ears of corn upon the hardy stalks. But oftener she was with her aunt Pauline, assisting in household offices, chattering of her brief past, or walking with the older woman arm-in-arm under the trailing moss of the giant oaks.

Mam'selle Pauline's steps grew very buoy-ant that summer, and her eyes were sometimes as bright as a bird's, unless La Petite were away from her side, when they would lose all other light but one of uneasy expectancy. The girl seemed to love her well in return, and called her endearingly Tan'-tante. But as the time went by, La Petite became very quiet,—not listless, but thoughtful, and slow in her movements. Then her cheeks began to pale, till they were tinged like the creamy plumes of the white crèpe myrtle that grew in the ruin.

One day when she sat within its shadow, between her aunts, holding a hand of each, she said: "Tante Pélagie, I must tell you something, you and Tan'tante." She spoke low, but clearly and firmly. "I love you both,—please remember that I love you both. But I must go away from you. I can't live any longer here at Côte Joyeuse."

A spasm passed through Mam'selle Pauline's delicate frame. La Petite could feel the twitch of it in the wiry fingers that were intertwined with her own. Ma'ame Pélagie remained unchanged and motionless. No human eye could penetrate so deep as to see the satisfaction which her soul felt. She said: "What do you mean, Petite? Your father has sent you to us, and I am sure it is his wish that you remain."

"My father loves me, tante Pélagie, and such will not be his wish when he knows. Oh!" she continued with a restless movement, "it is as though a weight were pressing me backward here. I must live another life; the life I lived before. I want to know things that are happening from day to day over the world, and hear them talked about. I want my music, my books, my companions. If I had known no other life but this one of privation, I suppose it would be different. If I had to live this life, I should make the best of it. But I do not have to; and you know, tante Pélagie, you do not need to. It seems to me," she added in a whisper, "that it is a sin against myself. Ah, Tan'tante!—what is the matter with Tan'tante?"

It was nothing; only a slight feeling of faintness, that would soon pass. She entreated them to take no notice; but they brought her some water and fanned her with a palmetto leaf.

But that night, in the stillness of the room, Mam'selle Pauline sobbed and would not be comforted. Ma'ame Pélagie took her in her arms.

"Pauline, my little sister Pauline," she entreated, "I never have seen you like this before. Do you no longer love me? Have we not been happy together, you and I?"

"Oh, yes, Sesœur."

"Is it because La Petite is going away?"

"Yes, Sesœur."

"Then she is dearer to you than I!" spoke Ma'ame Pélagie with sharp resentment. "Than I, who held you and warmed you in my arms the day you were born; than I, your mother, father, sister, everything that could cherish you. Pauline, don't tell me that."

Mam'selle Pauline tried to talk through her sobs.

"I can't explain it to you, Sesœur. I don't understand it myself. I love you as I have always loved you; next to God. But if La Petite goes away I shall die. I can't understand,—help me, Sesœur. She seems —she seems like a saviour; like one who had come and taken me by the hand and was leading me somewhere—somewhere I want to go."

Ma'ame Pélagie had been sitting beside the bed in her peignoir and slippers. She held the hand of her sister who lay there, and smoothed down the woman's soft brown hair. She said not a! word, and the silence was broken only by Ma'mselle Pauline's continued sobs. Once Ma'ame Pélagie arose to drink of orange-flower water, which she gave to her sister, as she would have offered it to a nervous, fretful child. Almost an hour passed before Ma'ame Pélagie spoke again. Then she said:—
"Pauline, you must cease that sobbing, now, and sleep. You will make yourself ill. La Petite will not go away. Do you hear me? Do you understand? She will stay, I promise you."

Mam'selle Pauline could not clearly comprehend, but she had great faith in the word of her sister, and soothed by the promise and the touch of Ma'ame Pélagie's strong, gentle hand, she fell asleep.

III.

Ma'ame Pélagie, when she saw that her sister slept, arose noiselessly and stepped outside upon the low-roofed narrow gallery. She did not linger there, but with a step that was hurried and agitated, she crossed the distance that divided her cabin from the ruin.

The night was not a dark one, for the sky was clear and the moon resplendent. But light or dark would have made no difference to Ma'ame Pélagie. It was not the first time she had stolen away to the ruin at night-time, when the whole plantation slept; but she never before had been there with a heart so nearly broken. She was going there for the last time to dream her dreams; to see the visions that hitherto had crowded her days and nights, and to bid them farewell.

There was the first of them, awaiting her upon the very portal; a robust old white-haired man, chiding her for returning home so late. There are guests to be entertained. Does she not know it? Guests from the city and from the near plantations. Yes, she knows it is late. She had been abroad with Félix, and they did not notice how the time was speeding. Félix is there; he will explain it all. He is there beside her, but she does not want to hear what he will tell her father.

Ma'ame Pélagie had sunk upon the bench where she and her sister so often came to sit. Turning, she gazed in through the gaping chasm of the window at her side. The interior of the ruin is ablaze. Not with the moonlight, for that is faint beside the other one—the sparkle from the crystal candelabra, which negroes, moving noiselessly and respectfully about, are lighting, one after the other. How the gleam of them reflects and glances from the polished marble pillars!

The room holds a number of guests. There is old Monsieur Lucien Santien, leaning against one of the pillars, and laughing at something which Monsieur Lafirme is telling him, till his fat shoulders shake. His son Jules is with him—Jules, who wants to marry her. She laughs. She wonders if Félix has told her father yet. There is young Jerome Lafirme playing at checkers upon the sofa with Léandre. Little Pauline stands annoying them and disturbing the game. Léandre reproves her. She begins to cry, and old black Clémentine, her nurse, who is not far off, limps across the room to pick her up and carry her away. How sensitive the little one is! But she trots about and takes care of herself better than she did a year or two ago, when she fell upon the stone hall floor and raised a great "bo-bo" on her forehead. Pélagie was hurt and angry enough about it; and she ordered rugs and buffalo robes to be brought and laid thick upon the tiles, till the little one's steps were surer.

"Il ne faut pas faire mal à Pauline."

She was saying it aloud—"faire mal à Pauline."

But she gazes beyond the salon, back into the big dining hall, where the white crèpe myrtle grows. Ha! how low that bat has circled. It has struck Ma'ame Pélagie full on the breast. She does not know it. She is beyond there in the dining hall, where her father sits with a group of friends over their wine. As usual they are talking politics. How tiresome! She has heard them say "la guerre" oftener than once. La guerre. Bah! She and Félix have something pleasanter to talk about, out under the oaks, or back in the shadow of the oleanders.

But they were right! The sound of a cannon, shot at Sumter, has rolled across the' Southern States, and its echo is heard along the whole stretch of Côte Joyeuse.

Yet Pélagie does not believe it. Not till La Ricaneuse stands before her with bare, black arms akimbo, uttering a volley of vile abuse and of brazen impudence. Pélagie wants to kill her. But yet she will not believe. Not till Félix comes to her in the chamber above the dining hall —there where that trumpet vine hangs—comes to say good-by to her. The hurt which the big brass buttons of his new gray uniform pressed into the tender flesh of her bosom has never left it. She sits upon the sofa, and he beside her, both speechless with pain. That room would not have been altered. Even the sofa would have been there in the same spot, and Ma'ame Pélagie had meant all along, for thirty years, all along, to lie there upon it some day when the time came to die.

But there is no time to weep, with the enemy at the door. The door has been no barrier. They are clattering through the halls now, drinking the wines, shattering the crystal and glass, slashing the portraits.

One of them stands before her and tells her to leave the house. She slaps his face. How the stigma stands out red as blood upon his blanched cheek!

Now there is a roar of fire and the flames are bearing down upon her motionless figure. She wants to show them how a daughter of Louisiana can perish before her conquerors. But little Pauline clings to her knees in an agony of terror. Little Pauline must be saved.

"Il ne faut pas faire mal à Pauline."

Again she is saying it aloud—"faire mal à Pauline."

The night was nearly spent; Ma'ame Pélagie had glided from the bench upon which she had rested, and for hours lay prone upon the stone flagging, motionless. When she dragged herself to her feet it was to walk like one in a dream. About the great, solemn pillars, one after the other, she reached her arms, and pressed her cheek and her lips upon the senseless brick.

"Adieu, adieu!" whispered Ma'ame Pélagie.

There was no longer the moon to guide her steps across the familiar pathway to the cabin. The brightest light in the sky was Venus, that swung low in the east. The bats had ceased to beat their wings about the ruin. Even the mocking-bird that had warbled for hours in the old mulberry-tree had sung himself asleep. That darkest hour before the day was mantling the earth. Ma'ame Pélagie hurried through the wet, clinging grass, beating aside the heavy moss that swept across her face, walking on toward the cabin—toward Pauline. Not once did she look back upon the ruin that brooded like a huge monster—a black spot in the darkness that enveloped it.

IV.

Little more than a year later the transformation which the old Valmet place had undergone was the talk and wonder of Côte Joyeuse. One would have looked in vain for the ruin; it was no longer there; neither was the log cabin. But out in the open, where the sun shone upon it, and the breezes blew about it, was a shapely structure fashioned from woods that the forests of the State had furnished. It rested upon a solid foundation of brick.

Upon a corner of the pleasant gallery sat Léandre smoking his afternoon cigar, and chatting with neighbors who had called. This was to be his pied à terre now; the home where his sisters and his daughter dwelt. The laughter of young people was heard out under the trees, and within the house where La Petite was playing upon the piano. With the enthusiasm of a young artist she drew from the keys strains that seemed marvelously beautiful to Mam'selle Pauline, who stood enraptured near her. Mam'selle Pauline had been touched by the re-creation of Valmet. Her cheek was as full and almost as flushed as La Petite's. The years were falling away from her.

Ma'ame Pélagie had been conversing with her brother and his friends. Then she turned and walked away; stopping to listen awhile to the music which La Petite was making. But it was only for a moment. She went on around the curve of the veranda, where she found herself alone. She stayed there, erect, holding to the banister rail and looking out calmly in the distance across the fields.

She was dressed in black, with the white kerchief she always wore folded across her bosom. Her thick, glossy hair rose like a silver diadem from her brow. In her deep, dark eyes smouldered the light of fires that would never flame. She had grown very old. Years instead of months seemed to have passed over her since the night she bade farewell to her visions.

Poor Ma'ame Pélagie! How could it be different! While the outward pressure of a young and joyous existence had forced her footsteps into the light, her soul had stayed in the shadow of the ruin.

The Nose

Nicholas Gogol

I

On the 25th March, 18—, a very strange occurrence took place in St Petersburg. On the Ascension Avenue there lived a barber of the name of Ivan Jakovlevitch. He had lost his family name, and on his sign-board, on which was depicted the head of a gentleman with one cheek soaped, the only inscription to be read was, "Blood-letting done here." On this particular morning he awoke pretty early. Becoming aware of the smell of fresh-baked bread, he sat up a little in bed, and saw his wife, who had a special partiality for coffee, in the act of taking some fresh-baked bread out of the oven.

"To-day, Prasskovna Ossipovna," he said, "I do not want any coffee; I should like a fresh loaf with onions."

"The blockhead may eat bread only as far as I am concerned," said his wife to herself; "then I shall have a chance of getting some coffee." And she threw a loaf on the table.

For the sake of propriety, Ivan Jakovlevitch drew a coat over his shirt, sat down at the table, shook out some salt for himself, prepared two onions, assumed a serious expression, and began to cut the bread. After he had cut the loaf in two halves, he looked, and to his great astonishment saw something whitish sticking in it. He carefully poked round it with his knife, and felt it with his finger.

"Quite firmly fixed!" he murmured in his beard. "What can it be?"

He put in his finger, and drew out—a nose!

Ivan Jakovlevitch at first let his hands fall from sheer astonishment; then he rubbed his eyes and began to feel it. A nose, an actual nose; and, moreover, it seemed to be the nose of an acquaintance! Alarm and terror were depicted in Ivan's face; but these feelings were slight in comparison with the disgust which took possession of his wife.

"Whose nose have you cut off, you monster?" she screamed, her face red with anger. "You scoundrel! You tippler! I myself will report you to the police! Such a rascal! Many customers have told me that while you were shaving them, you held them so tight by the nose that they could hardly sit still." But Ivan Jakovlevitch was more dead than alive; he saw at once that this nose could belong to no other than to Kovaloff, a member of the Municipal Committee whom he shaved every Sunday and Wednesday.

"Stop, Prasskovna Ossipovna! I will wrap it in a piece of cloth and place it in the corner. There it may remain for the present; later on I will take it away."

"No, not there! Shall I endure an amputated nose in my room? You understand nothing except how to strop a razor. You know nothing of the duties and obligations of a respectable man. You vagabond! You good-for-nothing! Am I to undertake all responsibility for you at the police-office? Ah, you soap-smearer! You blockhead! Take it away where you like, but don't let it stay under my eyes!" Ivan Jakovlevitch stood there flabbergasted. He thought and thought, and knew not what he thought.

"The devil knows how that happened!" he said at last, scratching his head behind his ear. "Whether I came home drunk last night or not, I really don't know; but in all probability this is a quite extraordinary occurrence, for a loaf is something baked and a nose is something different. I don't understand the matter at all." And Ivan Jakovlevitch was silent. The thought that the police might find him in unlawful possession of a nose and arrest him, robbed him of all presence of mind. Already he began to have visions of a red collar with silver braid and of a sword—and he trembled all over.

At last he finished dressing himself, and to the accompaniment of the emphatic exhortations of his spouse, he wrapped up the nose in a cloth and issued into the street.

He intended to lose it somewhere—either at somebody's door, or in a public square, or in a narrow alley; but just then, in order to complete his bad luck, he was met by an acquaintance, who showered inquiries upon him. "Hullo, Ivan Jakovlevitch! Whom are you going to shave so early in the morning?" etc., so that he could find no suitable opportunity to do what he wanted. Later on he did let the nose drop, but a sentry bore down upon him with his halberd, and said, "Look out! You have let something drop!" and Ivan Jakovlevitch was obliged to pick it up and put it in his pocket.

A feeling of despair began to take possession of him; all the more as the streets became more thronged and the merchants began to open their shops. At last he resolved to go to the Isaac Bridge, where perhaps he might succeed in throwing it into the Neva.

But my conscience is a little uneasy that I have not yet given any detailed information about Ivan Jakovlevitch, an estimable man in many ways.

Like every honest Russian tradesman, Ivan Jakovlevitch was a terrible drunkard, and although he shaved other people's faces every day, his own was always unshaved. His coat (he never wore an overcoat) was quite mottled, i.e. it had been black, but become brownish-yellow; the collar was quite shiny, and instead of the three buttons, only the threads by which they had been fastened were to be seen.

Ivan Jakovlevitch was a great cynic, and when Kovaloff, the member of the Municipal Committee, said to him, as was his custom while being shaved, "Your hands always smell, Ivan Jakovlevitch!" the latter answered, "What do they smell of?" "I don't know, my friend, but they smell very strong." Ivan Jakovlevitch after taking a pinch of snuff would then, by way of reprisals, set to work to soap him on the cheek, the upper lip, behind the ears, on the chin, and everywhere.

This worthy man now stood on the Isaac Bridge. At first he looked round him, then he leant on the railings of the bridge, as though he wished to look down and see how many fish were swimming past, and secretly threw the nose, wrapped in a little piece of cloth, into the water. He felt as though a ton weight had been lifted off him, and laughed cheerfully. Instead, however, of going to shave any officials, he turned his steps to a building, the sign-board of which bore the legend "Teas served here," in order to have a glass of punch, when suddenly he perceived at the other end of the bridge a police inspector of imposing exterior, with long whiskers, three-cornered hat, and sword hanging at his side. He nearly fainted; but the police inspector beckoned to him with his hand and said, "Come here, my dear sir." Ivan Jakovlevitch, knowing how a gentleman should behave, took his hat off quickly, went towards the police inspector and said, "I hope you are in the best of health."

"Never mind my health. Tell me, my friend, why you were standing on the bridge."

"By heaven, gracious sir, I was on the way to my customers, and only looked down to see if the river was flowing quickly."

"That is a lie! You won't get out of it like that. Confess the truth."

"I am willing to shave Your Grace two or even three

times a week gratis," answered Ivan Jakovlevitch.

"No, my friend, don't put yourself out! Three barbers are busy with me already, and reckon it a high honour that I let them show me their skill. Now then, out with it! What were you doing there?"

Ivan Jakovlevitch grew pale. But here the strange episode vanishes in mist, and what further happened is not known.

II

Kovaloff, the member of the Municipal Committee, awoke fairly early that morning, and made a droning noise—"Brr! Brr!"—through his lips, as he always did, though he could not say why. He stretched himself, and told his valet to give him a little mirror which was on the table. He wished to look at the heat-boil which had appeared on his nose the previous evening; but to his great astonishment, he saw that instead of his nose he had a perfectly smooth vacancy in his face. Thoroughly alarmed, he ordered some water to be brought, and rubbed his eyes with a towel. Sure enough, he had no longer a nose! Then he sprang out of bed, and shook himself violently! No, no nose any more! He dressed himself and went at once to the police superintendent.

But before proceeding further, we must certainly give the reader some information about Kovaloff, so that he may know what sort of a man this member of the Municipal Committee really was. These committee-men, who obtain that title by means of certificates of learning, must not be compared with the committee-men appointed for the Caucasus district, who are of quite a different kind. The learned committee-man—but Russia is such a wonderful country that when one committee-man is spoken of all the others from Riga to Kamschatka refer it to themselves. The same is also true of all other titled officials. Kovaloff had been a Caucasian committee-man two years previously, and could not forget that he had occupied that position; but in order to enhance his own importance, he never called himself "committee-man" but "Major." "Listen, my dear," he used to say when he met an old woman in the street who sold shirt-fronts; "go to my house in Sadovaia Street and ask 'Does Major Kovaloff live here?' Any child can tell you where it is."

Accordingly we will call him for the future Major Kovaloff. It was his custom to take a daily walk on the Neffsky Avenue. The collar of his shirt was always remarkably clean and stiff. He wore the same style of whiskers as those that are worn by governors of districts, architects, and regimental doctors; in short, all those who have full red cheeks and play a good game of whist. These whiskers grow straight across the cheek towards the nose.

Major Kovaloff wore a number of seals, on some of which were engraved armorial bearings, and others the names of the days of the week. He had come to St

Petersburg with the view of obtaining some position corresponding to his rank, if possible that of vice-governor of a province; but he was prepared to be content with that of a bailiff in some department or other. He was, moreover, not disinclined to marry, but only such a lady who could bring with her a dowry of two hundred thousand roubles. Accordingly, the reader can judge for himself what his sensations were when he found in his face, instead of a fairly symmetrical nose, a broad, flat vacancy.

To increase his misfortune, not a single droshky was to be seen in the street, and so he was obliged to proceed on foot. He wrapped himself up in his cloak, and held his handkerchief to his face as though his nose bled. "But perhaps it is all only my imagination; it is impossible that a nose should drop off in such a silly way," he thought, and stepped into a confectioner's shop in order to look into the mirror.

Fortunately no customer was in the shop; only small shop-boys were cleaning it out, and putting chairs and tables straight. Others with sleepy faces were carrying fresh cakes on trays, and yesterday's newspapers stained with coffee were still lying about. "Thank God no one is here!" he said to himself. "Now I can look at myself leisurely." He stepped gingerly up to a mirror and looked.

"What an infernal face!" he exclaimed, and spat with disgust. "If there were only something there instead of the nose, but there is absolutely nothing."

He bit his lips with vexation, left the confectioner's, and resolved, quite contrary to his habit, neither to look nor smile at anyone on the street. Suddenly he halted as if rooted to the spot before a door, where something extraordinary happened. A carriage drew up at the entrance; the carriage door was opened, and a gentleman in uniform came out and hurried up the steps. How great was Kovaloff's terror and astonishment when he saw that it was his own nose!

At this extraordinary sight, everything seemed to turn round with him. He felt as though he could hardly keep upright on his legs; but, though trembling all over as though with fever, he resolved to wait till the nose should return to the carriage. After about two minutes the nose actually came out again. It wore a gold-embroidered uniform with a stiff, high collar, trousers of chamois leather, and a sword hung at its side. The hat, adorned with a plume, showed that it held the rank of a state-councillor. It was obvious that it was paying "duty-calls." It looked round on both sides, called to the coachman "Drive on," and got into the carriage, which drove away.

Poor Kovaloff nearly lost his reason. He did not know what to think of this extraordinary procedure. And indeed how was it possible that the nose, which only yesterday he had on his face, and which could neither walk nor drive, should wear a uniform. He ran after the carriage, which fortunately had stopped a short way off before the Grand Bazar of Moscow. He hurried towards it and pressed through a crowd of beggar-women with their faces bound up, leaving only two openings for the eyes, over whom he had formerly so often made merry.

There were only a few people in front of the Bazar. Kovaloff was so agitated that he could decide on nothing, and looked for the nose everywhere. At last he saw it standing before a shop. It seemed half buried in its stiff collar, and was attentively inspecting the wares displayed.

"How can I get at it?" thought Kovaloff. "Everything—the uniform, the hat, and so on—show that it is a state-councillor. How the deuce has that happened?"

He began to cough discreetly near it, but the nose paid him not the least attention.

"Honourable sir," said Kovaloff at last, plucking up courage, "honourable sir."

"What do you want?" asked the nose, and turned round.

"It seems to me strange, most respected sir—you should know where you belong—and I find you all of a sudden—where? Judge yourself."

"Pardon me, I do not understand what you are talking about. Explain yourself more distinctly."

"How shall I make my meaning plainer to him?" Then plucking up fresh courage, he continued, "Naturally—besides I am a Major. You must admit it is not befitting that I should go about without a nose. An old apple-woman on the Ascension Bridge may carry on her business without one, but since I am on the look out for a post; besides in many houses I am acquainted with ladies of high position—Madame Tchektyriev, wife of a state-councillor, and many others. So you see—I do not know, honourable sir, what you——" (here the Major shrugged his shoulders). "Pardon me; if one regards the matter from the point of view of duty and honour—you will yourself understand——" "I understand nothing," answered the nose. "I repeat, please explain yourself more distinctly."

"Honourable sir," said Kovaloff with dignity, "I do not know how I am to understand your words. It seems to me the matter is as clear as possible. Or do you wish—but you are after all my own nose!"

The nose looked at the Major and wrinkled its forehead. "There you are wrong, respected sir; I am myself. Besides, there can be no close relations between us. To judge by the buttons of your uniform, you must be in quite a different department to mine." So saying, the nose turned away.

Kovaloff was completely puzzled; he did not know what to do, and still less what to think. At this moment he heard the pleasant rustling of a lady's dress, and there approached an elderly lady wearing a quantity of lace, and by her side her graceful daughter in a white dress which set off her slender figure to advantage, and wearing a light straw hat. Behind the ladies marched a tall lackey with long whiskers.

Kovaloff advanced a few steps, adjusted his cambric collar, arranged his seals which hung by a little gold chain, and with smiling face fixed his eyes on the graceful lady, who bowed lightly like a spring flower, and raised to her brow her little white hand with transparent fingers. He smiled still more when he spied under the brim of her hat her little round chin, and part of her cheek faintly tinted with rose-colour. But suddenly he sprang back as though he had been scorched. He remembered that he had nothing but an absolute blank in place of a nose, and tears started to his eyes. He turned round in order to tell the gentleman in uniform that he was only a state-councillor in appearance, but really a scoundrel and a rascal, and nothing else but his own nose; but the nose was no longer there. He had had time to go, doubtless in order to continue his visits.

His disappearance plunged Kovaloff into despair. He went back and stood for a moment under a colonnade, looking round him on all sides in hope of perceiving the nose somewhere. He remembered very well that it wore a hat with a plume in it and a gold-embroidered uniform; but he had not noticed the shape of the cloak, nor the colour of the carriages and the horses, nor even whether a lackey stood behind it, and, if so, what sort of livery he wore. Moreover, so many carriages were passing that it would have been difficult to recognise one, and even if he had done so, there would have been no means of stopping it.

The day was fine and sunny. An immense crowd was passing to and fro in the Neffsky Avenue; a variegated stream of ladies flowed along the pavement. There was his acquaintance, the Privy Councillor, whom he was accustomed to style "General," especially when strangers were present. There was Iarygin, his intimate friend who always lost in the evenings at whist; and there another Major, who had obtained the rank of committee-man in the Caucasus, beckoned to him.

"Go to the deuce!" said Kovaloff sotto voce. "Hi! coachman, drive me straight to the superintendent of police." So saying, he got into a droshky and continued to shout all the time to the coachman "Drive hard!"

"Is the police superintendent at home?" he asked on entering the front hall.

"No, sir," answered the porter, "he has just gone out."

"Ah, just as I thought!"

"Yes," continued the porter, "he has only just gone out; if you had been a moment earlier you would perhaps have caught him."

Kovaloff, still holding his handkerchief to his face, re-entered the droshky and cried in a despairing voice "Drive on!"

"Where?" asked the coachman.

"Straight on!"

"But how? There are cross-roads here. Shall I go to the right or the left?"

This question made Kovaloff reflect. In his situation it

was necessary to have recourse to the police; not because the affair had anything to do with them directly but because they acted more promptly than other authorities. As for demanding any explanation from the department to which the nose claimed to belong, it would, he felt, be useless, for the answers of that gentleman showed that he regarded nothing as sacred, and he might just as likely have lied in this matter as in saying that he had never seen Kovaloff.

But just as he was about to order the coachman to drive to the police-station, the idea occurred to him that this rascally scoundrel who, at their first meeting, had behaved so disloyally towards him, might, profiting by the delay, quit the city secretly; and then all his searching would be in vain, or might last over a whole month. Finally, as though visited with a heavenly inspiration, he resolved to go directly to an advertisement office, and to advertise the loss of his nose, giving all its distinctive characteristics in detail, so that anyone who found it might bring it at once to him, or at any rate inform him where it lived. Having decided on this course, he ordered the coachman to drive to the advertisement office, and all the way he continued to punch him in the back—"Quick, scoundrel! quick!" "Yes, sir!" answered the coachman, lashing his shaggy horse with the reins.

At last they arrived, and Kovaloff, out of breath, rushed into a little room where a grey-haired official, in an old coat and with spectacles on his nose, sat at a table holding his pen between his teeth, counting a heap of copper coins.

"Who takes in the advertisements here?" exclaimed Kovaloff.

"At your service, sir," answered the grey-haired functionary, looking up and then fastening his eyes again on the heap of coins before him.

"I wish to place an advertisement in your paper——"

"Have the kindness to wait a minute," answered the official, putting down figures on paper with one hand, and with the other moving two balls on his calculating-frame.

A lackey, whose silver-laced coat showed that he served in one of the houses of the nobility, was standing by the table with a note in his hand, and speaking in a lively tone, by way of showing himself sociable. "Would you believe it, sir, this little dog is really not worth twenty-four kopecks, and for my own part I would not give a farthing for it; but the countess is quite gone upon it, and offers a hundred roubles' reward to anyone who finds it. To tell you the truth, the tastes of these people are very different from ours; they don't mind giving five hundred or a thousand roubles for a poodle or a pointer, provided it be a good one." The official listened with a serious air while counting the number of letters contained in the note. At either side of the table stood a number of housekeepers, clerks and porters, carrying notes. The writer of one wished to sell a barouche, which had been brought from Paris in 1814 and had been very little used; others wanted to dispose of a strong droshky which wanted one spring, a spirited horse seventeen years old, and so on. The room where these people were collected was very small, and the air was very close; but Kovaloff was not affected by it, for he had covered his face with a handkerchief, and because his nose itself was heaven knew where.

"Sir, allow me to ask you—I am in a great hurry," he said at last impatiently.

"In a moment! In a moment! Two roubles, twenty-four kopecks—one minute! One rouble, sixty-four kopecks!" said the grey-haired official, throwing their notes back to the housekeepers and porters. "What do you wish?" he said, turning to Kovaloff.

"I wish—" answered the latter, "I have just been swindled and cheated, and I cannot get hold of the perpetrator. I only want you to insert an advertisement to say that whoever brings this scoundrel to me will be well rewarded." "What is your name, please?"

"Why do you want my name? I have many lady friends—Madame Tchektyriev, wife of a state-councillor, Madame Podtotchina, wife of a Colonel. Heaven forbid that they should get to hear of it. You can simply write 'committee-man,' or, better, 'Major.'" "And the man who has run away is your serf."

"Serf! If he was, it would not be such a great swindle! It

is the nose which has absconded."

"H'm! What a strange name. And this Mr Nose has stolen from you a considerable sum?"

"Mr Nose! Ah, you don't understand me! It is my own nose which has gone, I don't know where. The devil has played a trick on me."

"How has it disappeared? I don't understand."

"I can't tell you how, but the important point is that now it walks about the city itself a state-councillor. That is why I want you to advertise that whoever gets hold of it should bring it as soon as possible to me. Consider; how can I live without such a prominent part of my body? It is not as if it were merely a little toe; I would only have to put my foot in my boot and no one would notice its absence. Every Thursday I call on the wife of M. Tchektyriev, the state-councillor; Madame Podtotchina, a Colonel's wife who has a very pretty daughter, is one of my acquaintances; and what am I to do now? I cannot appear before them like this." The official compressed his lips and reflected. "No, I cannot insert an advertisement like that," he said after a long pause.

"What! Why not?"

"Because it might compromise the paper. Suppose everyone could advertise that his nose was lost. People already say that all sorts of nonsense and lies are inserted."

"But this is not nonsense! There is nothing of that sort in my case."

"You think so? Listen a minute. Last week there was a case very like it. An official came, just as you have done, bringing an advertisement for the insertion of which he paid two roubles, sixty-three kopecks; and this advertisement simply announced the loss of a black-haired poodle. There did not seem to be anything out of the way in it, but it was really a satire; by the poodle was meant the cashier of some establishment or other." "But I am not talking of a poodle, but my own nose; i.e. almost myself."

"No, I cannot insert your advertisement."

"But my nose really has disappeared!"

"That is a matter for a doctor. There are said to be people who can provide you with any kind of nose you like. But I see that you are a witty man, and like to have your little joke."

"But I swear to you on my word of honour. Look at my face yourself."

"Why put yourself out?" continued the official, taking a pinch of snuff. "All the same, if you don't mind," he added with a touch of curiosity, "I should like to have a look at it."

The committee-man removed the handkerchief from before his face.

"It certainly does look odd," said the official. "It is perfectly flat like a freshly fried pancake. It is hardly credible."

"Very well. Are you going to hesitate any more? You see

it is impossible to refuse to advertise my loss. I shall be particularly obliged to you, and I shall be glad that this incident has procured me the pleasure of making your acquaintance." The Major, we see, did not even shrink from a slight humiliation.

"It certainly is not difficult to advertise it," replied the official; "but I don't see what good it would do you. However, if you lay so much stress on it, you should apply to someone who has a skilful pen, so that he may describe it as a curious, natural freak, and publish the article in the Northern Bee" (here he took another pinch) "for the benefit of youthful readers" (he wiped his nose), "or simply as a matter worthy of arousing public curiosity." The committee-man felt completely discouraged. He let his eyes fall absent-mindedly on a daily paper in which theatrical performances were advertised. Reading there the name of an actress whom he knew to be pretty, he involuntarily smiled, and his hand sought his pocket to see if he had a blue ticket— for in Kovaloff's opinion superior officers like himself should not take a lesser-priced seat; but the thought of his lost nose suddenly spoilt everything.

The official himself seemed touched at his difficult position. Desiring to console him, he tried to express his sympathy by a few polite words. "I much regret," he said, "your extraordinary mishap. Will you not try a pinch of snuff? It clears the head, banishes depression, and is a good preventive against hæmorrhoids." So saying, he reached his snuff-box out to Kovaloff, skilfully concealing at the same time the cover, which was adorned with the portrait of some lady or other.

This act, quite innocent in itself, exasperated Kovaloff. "I don't understand what you find to joke about in the matter," he exclaimed angrily. "Don't you see that I lack precisely the essential feature for taking snuff? The devil take your snuff-box. I don't want to look at snuff now, not even the best, certainly not your vile stuff!" So saying, he left the advertisement office in a state of profound irritation, and went to the commissary of police. He arrived just as this dignitary was reclining on his couch, and saying to himself with a sigh of satisfaction, "Yes, I shall make a nice little sum out of that." It might be expected, therefore, that the committee-man's visit would be quite inopportune.

This police commissary was a great patron of all the arts and industries; but what he liked above everything else was a cheque. "It is a thing," he used to say, "to which it is not easy to find an equivalent; it requires no food, it does not take up much room, it stays in one's pocket, and if it falls, it is not broken." The commissary accorded Kovaloff a fairly frigid reception, saying that the afternoon was not the best time to come with a case, that nature required one to rest a little after eating (this showed the committee-man that the commissary was acquainted with the aphorisms of the ancient sages), and that respectable people did not have their noses stolen.

The last allusion was too direct. We must remember that Kovaloff was a very sensitive man. He did not mind anything said against him as an individual, but he could not endure any reflection on his rank or social position. He even believed that in comedies one might allow attacks on junior officers, but never on their seniors.

The commissary's reception of him hurt his feelings so much that he raised his head proudly, and said with dignity, "After such insulting expressions on your part, I have nothing more to say." And he left the place.

He reached his house quite wearied out. It was already growing dark. After all his fruitless search, his room seemed to him melancholy and even ugly. In the vestibule he saw his valet Ivan stretched on the leather couch and amusing himself by spitting at the ceiling, which he did very cleverly, hitting every time the same spot. His servant's equanimity enraged him; he struck him on the forehead with his hat, and said, "You good-for-nothing, you are always playing the fool!" Ivan rose quickly and hastened to take off his master's cloak.

Once in his room, the Major, tired and depressed, threw himself in an armchair and, after sighing a while, began to soliloquise:

"In heaven's name, why should such a misfortune befall me? If I had lost an arm or a leg, it would be less insupportable; but a man without a nose! Devil take it!—what is he good for? He is only fit to be thrown out of the window. If it had been taken from me in war or in a duel, or if I had lost it by my own fault! But it has disappeared inexplicably. But no! it is impossible," he continued after reflecting a few moments, "it is incredible that a nose can disappear like that—quite incredible. I must be dreaming, or suffering from some hallucination; perhaps I swallowed, by mistake instead of water, the brandy with which I rub my chin after being shaved. That fool of an Ivan must have forgotten to take it away, and I must have swallowed it." In order to find out whether he were really drunk, the Major pinched himself so hard that he unvoluntarily uttered a cry. The pain convinced him that he was quite wide awake. He walked slowly to the looking-glass and at first closed his eyes, hoping to see his nose suddenly in its proper place; but on opening them, he started back. "What a hideous sight!" he exclaimed.

It was really incomprehensible. One might easily lose a button, a silver spoon, a watch, or something similar; but a loss like this, and in one's own dwelling!

After considering all the circumstances, Major Kovaloff felt inclined to suppose that the cause of all his trouble should be laid at the door of Madame Podtotchina, the Colonel's wife, who wished him to marry her daughter. He himself paid her court readily, but always avoided coming to the point. And when the lady one day told him point-blank that she wished him to marry her daughter, he gently drew back, declaring that he was still too young, and that he had to serve five years more before he would be forty-two. This must be the reason why the lady, in revenge, had resolved to bring him into disgrace, and had hired two sorceresses for that object. One thing was certain—his nose had not been cut off; no one had entered his room, and as for Ivan Jakovlevitch—he had been shaved by him on Wednesday, and during that day and the whole of Thursday his nose had been there, as he knew and well remembered. Moreover, if his nose had been cut off he would naturally have felt pain, and doubtless the wound would not have healed so quickly, nor would the surface have been as flat as a pancake.

All kinds of plans passed through his head: should he bring a legal action against the wife of a superior officer, or should he go to her and charge her openly with her treachery?

His reflections were interrupted by a sudden light, which shone through all the chinks of the door, showing that Ivan had lit the wax-candles in the vestibule. Soon Ivan himself came in with the lights. Kovaloff quickly seized a handkerchief and covered the place where his nose had been the evening before, so that his blockhead of a servant might not gape with his mouth wide open when he saw his master's extraordinary appearance.

Scarcely had Ivan returned to the vestibule than a stranger's voice was heard there.

"Does Major Kovaloff live here?" it asked.

"Come in!" said the Major, rising rapidly and opening

the door.

He saw a police official of pleasant appearance, with grey whiskers and fairly full cheeks—the same who at the commencement of this story was standing at the end of the Isaac Bridge. "You have lost your nose?" he asked.

"Exactly so."

"It has just been found."

"What—do you say?" stammered Major Kovaloff.

Joy had suddenly paralysed his tongue. He stared at the police commissary on whose cheeks and full lips fell the flickering light of the candle.

"How was it?" he asked at last.

"By a very singular chance. It has been arrested just as it was getting into a carriage for Riga. Its passport had been made out some time ago in the name of an official; and what is still more strange, I myself took it at first for a gentleman. Fortunately I had my glasses with me, and then I saw at once that it was a nose. I am shortsighted, you know, and as you stand before me I cannot distinguish your nose, your beard, or anything else. My mother-in-law can hardly see at all." Kovaloff was beside himself with excitement. "Where is it? Where? I will hasten there at once."

"Don't put yourself out. Knowing that you need it, I have brought it with me. Another singular thing is that the principal culprit in the matter is a scoundrel of a barber living in the Ascension Avenue, who is now safely locked up. I had long suspected him of drunkenness and theft; only the day before yesterday he stole some buttons in a shop. Your nose is quite uninjured." So saying, the police commissary put his hand in his pocket and brought out the nose wrapped up in paper.

"Yes, yes, that is it!" exclaimed Kovaloff. "Will you not stay and drink a cup of tea with me?"

"I should like to very much, but I cannot. I must go at once to the House of Correction. The cost of living is very high nowadays. My mother-in-law lives with me, and there are several children; the eldest is very hopeful and intelligent, but I have no means for their education."

After the commissary's departure, Kovaloff remained for some time plunged in a kind of vague reverie, and did not recover full consciousness for several moments, so great was the effect of this unexpected good news. He placed the recovered nose carefully in the palm of his hand, and examined it again with the greatest attention.

"Yes, this is it!" he said to himself. "Here is the heat-boil on the left side, which came out yesterday." And he nearly laughed aloud with delight.

But nothing is permanent in this world. Joy in the second moment of its arrival is already less keen than in the first, is still fainter in the third, and finishes by coalescing with our normal mental state, just as the circles which the fall of a pebble forms on the surface of water, gradually die away. Kovaloff began to meditate, and saw that his difficulties were not yet over; his nose had been recovered, but it had to be joined on again in its proper place.

And suppose it could not? As he put this question to himself, Kovaloff grew pale. With a feeling of indescribable dread, he rushed towards his dressing-table, and stood before the mirror in order that he might not place his nose crookedly. His hands trembled.

Very carefully he placed it where it had been before. Horror! It did not remain there. He held it to his mouth and warmed it a little with his breath, and then placed it there again; but it would not hold.

"Hold on, you stupid!" he said.

But the nose seemed to be made of wood, and fell back on the table with a strange noise, as though it had been a cork. The Major's face began to twitch feverishly. "Is it possible that it won't stick?" he asked himself, full of alarm. But however often he tried, all his efforts were in vain.

He called Ivan, and sent him to fetch the doctor who occupied the finest flat in the mansion. This doctor was a man of imposing appearance, who had magnificent black whiskers and a healthy wife. He ate fresh apples every morning, and cleaned his teeth with extreme care, using five different tooth-brushes for three-quarters of an hour daily.

The doctor came immediately. After having asked the Major when this misfortune had happened, he raised his chin and gave him a fillip with his finger just where the nose had been, in such a way that the Major suddenly threw back his head and struck the wall with it. The doctor said that did not matter; then, making him turn his face to the right, he felt the vacant place and said "H'm!" then he made him turn it to the left and did the same; finally he again gave him a fillip with his finger, so that the Major started like a horse whose teeth are being examined. After this experiment, the doctor shook his head and said, "No, it cannot be done. Rather remain as you are, lest something worse happen. Certainly one could replace it at once, but I assure you the remedy would be worse than the disease." "All very fine, but how am I to go on without a nose?" answered Kovaloff. "There is nothing worse than that. How can I show myself with such a villainous appearance? I go into good society, and this evening I am invited to two parties. I know several ladies, Madame Tchektyriev, the wife of a state-councillor, Madame Podtotchina—although after what she has done, I don't want to have anything to do with her except through the agency of the police. I beg you," continued Kovaloff in a supplicating tone, "find some way or other of replacing it; even if it is not quite firm, as long as it holds at all; I can keep it in place sometimes with my hand, whenever there is any risk. Besides, I do not even dance, so that it is not likely to be injured by any sudden movement. As to your fee, be in no anxiety about that; I can well afford it." "Believe me," answered the doctor in a voice which was neither too high nor too low, but soft and almost magnetic, "I do not treat patients from love of gain. That would be contrary to my principles and to my art. It is true that I accept fees, but that is only not to hurt my patients' feelings by refusing them. I could certainly replace your nose, but I assure you on my word of honour, it would only make matters worse. Rather let Nature do her own work. Wash the place often with cold water, and I assure you that even without a nose, you will be just as well as if you had one. As to the nose itself, I advise you to have it preserved in a bottle of spirits, or, still better, of warm vinegar mixed with two spoonfuls of brandy, and then you can sell it at a good price. I would be willing to take it myself, provided you do not ask too much."

"No, no, I shall not sell it at any price. I would rather it were lost again."

"Excuse me," said the doctor, taking his leave. "I hoped to be useful to you, but I can do nothing more; you are at any rate convinced of my good-will." So saying, the doctor left the room with a dignified air.

Kovaloff did not even notice his departure. Absorbed in a profound reverie, he only saw the edge of his snow-white cuffs emerging from the sleeves of his black coat.

The next day he resolved, before bringing a formal action, to write to the Colonel's wife and see whether she would not return to him, without further dispute, that of which she had deprived him.

The letter ran as follows:

"To Madame Alexandra Podtotchina,

"I hardly understand your method of action. Be sure that by adopting such a course you will gain nothing, and will certainly not succeed in making me marry your daughter. Believe me, the story of my nose has become well known; it is you and no one else who have taken the principal part in it. Its unexpected separation from the place which it occupied, its flight and its appearances sometimes in the disguise of an official, sometimes in proper person, are nothing but the consequence of unholy spells employed by you or by persons who, like you, are addicted to such honourable pursuits. On my part, I wish to inform you, that if the above-mentioned nose is not restored to-day to its proper place, I shall be obliged to have recourse to legal procedure.

"For the rest, with all respect, I have the honour to be your humble servant,

"Platon Kovaloff."

The reply was not long in coming, and was as follows:

"Major Platon Kovaloff,—

"Your letter has profoundly astonished me. I must confess that I had not expected such unjust reproaches on your part. I assure you that the official of whom you speak has not been at my house, either disguised or in his proper person. It is true that Philippe Ivanovitch Potantchikoff has paid visits at my house, and though he has actually asked for my daughter's hand, and was a man of good breeding, respectable and intelligent, I never gave him any hope.

"Again, you say something about a nose. If you intend to imply by that that I wished to snub you, i.e. to meet you with a refusal, I am very astonished because, as you well know, I was quite of the opposite mind. If after this you wish to ask for my daughter's hand, I should be glad to gratify you, for such has also been the object of my most fervent desire, in the hope of the accomplishment of which, I remain, yours most sincerely, "Alexandra Podtotchina."

"No," said Kovaloff, after having reperused the letter, "she is certainly not guilty. It is impossible. Such a letter could not be written by a criminal." The committee-man was experienced in such matters, for he had been often officially deputed to conduct criminal investigations while in the Caucasus. "But then how and by what trick of fate has the thing happened?" he said to himself with a gesture of discouragement. "The devil must be at the bottom of it." Meanwhile the rumour of this extraordinary event had spread all over the city, and, as is generally the case, not without numerous additions. At that period there was a general disposition to believe in the miraculous; the public had recently been impressed by experiments in magnetism. The story of the floating chairs in Koniouchennaia Street was still quite recent, and there was nothing astonishing in hearing soon afterwards that Major Kovaloff's nose was to be seen walking every day at three o'clock on the Neffsky Avenue. The crowd of curious spectators which gathered there daily was enormous. On one occasion someone spread a report that the nose was in Junker's stores and immediately the place was besieged by such a crowd that the police had to interfere and establish order. A certain speculator with a grave, whiskered face, who sold cakes at a theatre door, had some strong wooden benches made which he placed before the window of the stores, and obligingly invited the public to stand on them and look in, at the modest charge of twenty-four kopecks. A veteran colonel, leaving his house earlier than usual expressly for the purpose, had the greatest difficulty in elbowing his way through the crowd, but to his great indignation he saw nothing in the store window but an ordinary flannel waistcoat and a coloured lithograph representing a young girl darning a stocking, while an elegant youth in a waistcoat with large lappels watched her from behind a tree. The picture had hung in the same place for more than ten years. The colonel went off, growling savagely to himself, "How can the fools let themselves be excited by such idiotic stories?" Then another rumour got abroad, to the effect that the nose of Major Kovaloff was in the habit of walking not on the Neffsky Avenue but in the Tauris Gardens. Some students of the Academy of Surgery went there on purpose to see it. A high-born lady wrote to the keeper of the gardens asking him to show her children this rare phenomenon, and to give them some suitable instruction on the occasion.

All these incidents were eagerly collected by the town wits, who just then were very short of anecdotes adapted to amuse ladies. On the other hand, the minority of solid, sober people were very much displeased. One gentleman asserted with great indignation that he could not understand how in our enlightened age such absurdities could spread abroad, and he was astonished that the Government did not direct their attention to the matter. This gentleman evidently belonged to the category of those people who wish the Government to interfere in everything, even in their daily quarrels with their wives.

But here the course of events is again obscured by a veil.

III

Strange events happen in this world, events which are sometimes entirely improbable. The same nose which had masqueraded as a state-councillor, and caused so much sensation in the town, was found one morning in its proper place, i.e. between the cheeks of Major Kovaloff, as if nothing had happened.

This occurred on 7th April. On awaking, the Major looked by chance into a mirror and perceived a nose. He quickly put his hand to it; it was there beyond a doubt!

"Oh!" exclaimed Kovaloff. For sheer joy he was on the point of performing a dance barefooted across his room, but the entrance of Ivan prevented him. He told him to bring water, and after washing himself, he looked again in the glass. The nose was there! Then he dried his face with a towel and looked again. Yes, there was no mistake about it!

"Look here, Ivan, it seems to me that I have a heat-boil on my nose," he said to his valet.

And he thought to himself at the same time, "That will be a nice business if Ivan says to me 'No, sir, not only is there no boil, but your nose itself is not there!'"

But Ivan answered, "There is nothing, sir; I can see no boil on your nose."

"Good! Good!" exclaimed the Major, and snapped his fingers with delight.

At this moment the barber, Ivan Jakovlevitch, put his head in at the door, but as timidly as a cat which has just been beaten for stealing lard.

"Tell me first, are your hands clean?" asked Kovaloff when he saw him.

"Yes, sir."

"You lie."

"I swear they are perfectly clean, sir."

"Very well; then come here."

Kovaloff seated himself. Jakovlevitch tied a napkin under his chin, and in the twinkling of an eye covered his beard and part of his cheeks with a copious creamy lather.

"There it is!" said the barber to himself, as he glanced

at the nose. Then he bent his head a little and examined it from one side. "Yes, it actually is the nose—really, when one thinks——" he continued, pursuing his mental soliloquy and still looking at it. Then quite gently, with infinite precaution, he raised two fingers in the air in order to take hold of it by the extremity, as he was accustomed to do.

"Now then, take care!" Kovaloff exclaimed.

Ivan Jakovlevitch let his arm fall and felt more embarrassed than he had ever done in his life. At last he began to pass the razor very lightly over the Major's chin, and although it was very difficult to shave him without using the olfactory organ as a point of support, he succeeded, however, by placing his wrinkled thumb against the Major's lower jaw and cheek, thus overcoming all obstacles and bringing his task to a safe conclusion.

When the barber had finished, Kovaloff hastened to dress himself, took a droshky, and drove straight to the confectioner's. As he entered it, he ordered a cup of chocolate. He then stepped straight to the mirror; the nose was there!

He returned joyfully, and regarded with a satirical expression two officers who were in the shop, one of whom possessed a nose not much larger than a waistcoat button.

After that he went to the office of the department where he had applied for the post of vice-governor of a province or Government bailiff. As he passed through the hall of reception, he cast a glance at the mirror; the nose was there! Then he went to pay a visit to another committee-man, a very sarcastic personage, to whom he was accustomed to say in answer to his raillery, "Yes, I know, you are the funniest fellow in St Petersburg." On the way he said to himself, "If the Major does not burst into laughter at the sight of me, that is a most certain sign that everything is in its accustomed place."

But the Major said nothing. "Very good!" thought Kovaloff.

As he returned, he met Madame Podtotchina with her daughter. He accosted them, and they responded very graciously. The conversation lasted a long time, during which he took more than one pinch of snuff, saying to himself, "No, you haven't caught me yet, coquettes that you are! And as to the daughter, I shan't marry her at all." After that, the Major resumed his walks on the Neffsky Avenue and his visits to the theatre as if nothing had happened. His nose also remained in its place as if it had never quitted it. From that time he was always to be seen smiling, in a good humour, and paying attentions to pretty girls.

IV

Such was the occurrence which took place in the northern capital of our vast empire. On considering the account carefully we see that there is a good deal which looks improbable about it. Not to speak of the strange disappearance of the nose, and its appearance in different places under the disguise of a councillor of state, how was it that Kovaloff did not understand that one cannot decently advertise for a lost nose? I do not mean to say that he would have had to pay too much for the advertisement—that is a mere trifle, and I am not one of those who attach too much importance to money; but to advertise in such a case is not proper nor befitting.

Another difficulty is—how was the nose found in the baked loaf, and how did Ivan Jakovlevitch himself—no, I don't understand it at all!

But the most incomprehensible thing of all is, how authors can choose such subjects for their stories. That really surpasses my understanding. In the first place, no advantage results from it for the country; and in the second place, no harm results either.

All the same, when one reflects well, there really is something in the matter. Whatever may be said to the contrary, such cases do occur—rarely, it is true, but now and then actually.

Out Of Season

Ernest Miller Hemingway

On the four lira he had earned by spading the hotel garden he got quite drunk. He saw the young gentleman coming down the path and spoke to him mysteriously. The young gentleman said he had not eaten yet but would be ready to go as soon as lunch was finished. Forty minutes or an hour.

At the cantina near the bridge they trusted him for three more grappas because he was so confident and mysterious about his job for the afternoon. It was a windy day with the sun coming out from behind clouds and then going under in sprinkles of rain. A wonderful day for trout fishing.

The young gentleman came out of the hotel and asked him about the rods. Should his wife come behind with the rods? Yes, said Peduzzi, let her follow us. The young gentleman went back into the hotel and spoke to his wife. He and Peduzzi started down the road. The young gentleman had a musette over his shoulder. Peduzzi saw the wife, who looked as young as the young gentleman and was wearing mountain boots and a blue beret, start out to follow them down the road carrying the fishing rods unjointed one in each hand. Peduzzi didn't like her to be way back there. Signorina, he called, winking at the young gentleman, come up here and walk with us.

Signora come up here. Let us all walk together. Peduzzi wanted them all three to walk down the street of Cortina together.

The wife stayed behind, following rather sullenly. Signorina, Peduzzi called tenderly, come up here with us. The young gentleman looked back and shouted something. The wife stopped lagging behind, and walked up.

Everyone they met walking through the main street of the town Peduzzi greeted elaborately. Buon' di Arturo! Tipping his hat. The bank clerk stared at him from the door of the Fascist café. Groups of three and four people standing in front of the shops stared at the three. The workmen in their stone-powdered jackets working on the foundations of the new hotel looked up as they passed. Nobody spoke or gave any sign to them except the town beggar, lean and old with a spittle thickened beard, who lifted his hat as they passed.

Peduzzi stopped in front of a store with the window full of bottles and brought his empty grappa bottle from an inside pocket of his old military coat. A little to drink, some marsala for the Signora, something, something to drink. He gestured with the bottle. It was a wonderful day. Marsala, you like marsala, Signorina? A little marsala?

The wife stood sullenly. You'll have to play up to this, she said. I can't understand a word he says. He's drunk isn't he?

The young gentleman appeared not to hear Peduzzi. He was thinking what in hell makes him say Marsala. That's what Max Beerbohm drinks.

Geld, Peduzzi said finally, taking hold of the young gentleman's sleeve. Lire. He smiled reluctant to press the subject but needing to bring the young gentleman into action.

The young gentleman took out his pocket book and gave him a ten lire note. Peduzzi went up the steps to the door of the Speciality of Domestic and Foreign Wines shop. It was locked.

It is closed until two, someone passing in the street said scornfully. Peduzzi came down the steps. He felt hurt. Never mind, he said, we can get it at the Concordia.

They walked down the road to the Concordia three abreast. On the porch of the Concordia where the rusty bobsleds were stacked the young gentleman said, Was wollen sie? Peduzzi handed him the ten lira note folded over and over. Nothing, he said, Anything. He was embarrassed. Marsala maybe. I don't know. Marsala?

The door of the Concordia shut on the young gentleman and the wife. Three marsalas, said the y. g. to the girl behind the pastry counter. Two you mean? she asked. No, he said, one for a vecchio. Oh, she said, a vecchio, and laughed getting down the bottle. She poured out the three muddy looking drinks into three glasses. The wife was sitting at a table under the line of newspapers on sticks. The y. g. put one of the marsalas in front of her.

You might as well drink it, he said. Maybe it'll make you feel better. She sat and looked at the glass. The y. g. went outside the door with a glass for Peduzzi but could not see him.

I don't know where he is, he said coming back into the pastry room carrying the glass.

He wanted a quart of it, said the wife.

How much is a quarter litre, the y. g. asked the girl.

Of the bianco? One lira.

No, of the marsala. Put these two in too, he said giving her his own glass and the one poured for Peduzzi. She filled the quarter litre wine measure with a funnel. A bottle to carry it, said the y. g.

She went to hunt for a bottle. It all amused her.

I'm sorry you feel so rotten Tiny, he said, I'm sorry I talked the way I did at lunch. We were both getting at the same thing from different angles.

It doesn't make any difference, she said. None of it makes any difference.

Are you too cold, he asked. I wish you'd worn another sweater.

I've got on three sweaters.

The girl came in with a very slim brown bottle and poured the marsala into it. The y. g. paid five lira more. They went out of the door. The girl was amused. Peduzzi was walking up and down at the other end out of the wind and holding the rods.

Come on, he said, I will carry the rods. What difference

does it make if anybody sees them. No one will trouble us. No one will make any trouble for me in Cortina. I know them at the municipio. I have been a soldier. Everybody in this town likes me. I sell frogs. What if it is forbidden to fish? Not a thing. Nothing. No trouble. Big trout I tell you. Lots of them.

They were walking down the hill toward the river. The town was in back of them. The sun had gone under and it was sprinkling rain. There, said Peduzzi, pointing to a girl in the doorway of a house they passed. My daughter.

His doctor, the wife said, has he got to show us his doctor?

He said his daughter, said the y. g.

The girl went into the house as Peduzzi pointed.

They walked down the hill across the fields and then turned to follow the river bank. Peduzzi talked rapidly with much winking and knowingness. As they walked three abreast the wife caught his breath across the wind. Once he nudged her in the ribs. Part of the time he talked in D'Ampezzo dialect and sometimes in Tyroler German dialect. He could not make out which the young gentleman and his wife understood the best so he was being bi-lingual. But as the young gentleman said Ja Ja Peduzzi decided to talk altogether in Tyroler. The young gentleman and the wife understood nothing.

Everybody in the town saw us going through with these rods. We're probably being followed by the game police now. I wish we weren't in on this damn thing. This damned old fool is so drunk too.

Of course you haven't got the guts to just go back, said the wife. Of course you have to go on.

Why don't you go back? Go on back Tiny.

I'm going to stay with you. If you go to jail we might as well both go.

They turned sharp down the bank and Peduzzi stood his coat blowing in the wind gesturing at the river. It was brown and muddy. Off on the right there was a dump heap.

Say it to me in Italian, said the young gentleman

Un' mezz' ora. Piu d' un' mezz' ora.

He says it's at least a half an hour more. Go on back Tiny. You're cold in this wind anyway. It's a rotten day and we aren't going to have any fun anyway.

All right, she said, and climbed up the grassy bank.

Peduzzi was down at the river and did not notice her till she was almost out of sight over the crest. Frau! he shouted. Frau! Fraulein! You're not going? She went on over the crest of the hill.

She's gone! said Peduzzi. It shocked him.

He took off the rubber bands that held the rod segments together and commenced to joint up one of the rods.

But you said it was half an hour further.

Oh yes. It is good half an hour down. It is good here too.

Really?

Of course. It is good here and good there too.

The y. g. sat down on the bank and jointed up a rod, put on the reel and threaded the line through the guides. He felt uncomfortable and afraid that any minute a gamekeeper or a posse of citizens would come over the bank from the town. He could see the houses of the town and the campanile over the edge of the hill. He opened his leader box. Peduzzi leaned over and dug his flat hard thumb and forefinger in and tangled the moistened leaders.

Have you some lead?

No.

You must have some lead. Peduzzi was excited. You must have piombo. Piombo. A little piombo. Just here. Just above the hook or your bait will float on the water. You must have it. Just a little piombo.

Have you got some?

No. He looked through all his pockets desperately. Sifting through the cloth dirt in the linings of his inside military pockets. I haven't any. We must have piombo.

We can't fish then, said the y. g. and unjointed the rod, reeling the line back through the guides. We'll get some piombo and fish tomorrow.

But listen caro, you must have piombo. The line will lie flat on the water. Peduzzi's day was going to pieces before his eyes. You must have piombo. A little is enough. Your stuff is all clean and new but you have no lead. I would have brought some. You said you had everything.

The y. g. looked at the stream discoloured by the melting snow. I know, he said, we'll get some piombo and fish tomorrow.

At what hour in the morning? Tell me that.

At seven.

The sun came out. It was warm and pleasant. The young gentleman felt relieved. He was no longer breaking the law. Sitting on the bank he took the bottle of marsala out of his pocket and passed it to Peduzzi. Peduzzi passed it back. The y. g. took a drink of it and passed it to Peduzzi again. Peduzzi passed it back again. Drink, he said, drink. It's your marsala. After another short drink the y. g. handed the bottle over. Peduzzi had been watching it closely. He took the bottle very hurriedly and tipped it up. The grey hairs in the folds of his neck oscillated as he drank his eyes fixed on the end of the narrow brown bottle. He drank it all. The sun shone while he drank. It was wonderful. This was a great day after all. A wonderful day.

Senta caro! In the morning at seven. He had called the young gentleman caro several times and nothing had happened. It was good marsala. His eyes glistened. Days like this stretched out ahead. It would begin again at seven in the morning.

They started to walk up the hill toward the town. The y. g. went on ahead. He was quite a way up the hill. Peduzzi called to him.

Listen caro can you let me take five lira for a favour?

For today? asked the young gentleman frowning.

No, not today. Give it to me today for tomorrow. I will provide everything for tomorrow. Pane, salami, formaggio, good stuff for all of us. You and I and the signora. Bait for fishing, minnows, not worms only. Perhaps I can get some marsala. All for five lira. Five lira for a favour.

The young gentleman looked through his pocket book and took out a two lira note and two ones.

Thank you caro. Thank you, said Peduzzi in the tone of one member of the Carleton Club accepting the Morning Post from another. This was living. He was through with the hotel garden, breaking up frozen manure with a dung fork. Life was opening out.

Until seven o'clock then caro, he said, slapping the y. g. on the back. Promptly at seven.

I may not be going, said the young gentleman putting his purse back in his pocket.

What, said Peduzzi. I will have minnows Signor. Salami, everything. You and I and the Signora. The three of us.

I may not be going, said the y. g., very probably not. I will leave word with the padrone at the hotel office.

How the Camel Got His Hump

Joseph Rudyard Kipling

NOW this is the next tale, and it tells how the Camel got his big hump.

In the beginning of years, when the world was so new and all, and the Animals were just beginning to work for Man, there was a Camel, and he lived in the middle of a Howling Desert because he did not want to work; and besides, he was a Howler himself. So he ate sticks and thorns and tamarisks and milkweed and prickles, most 'scruciating idle; and when anybody spoke to him he said 'Humph!' Just 'Humph!' and no more.

Presently the Horse came to him on Monday morning, with a saddle on his back and a bit in his mouth, and said, 'Camel, O Camel, come out and trot like the rest of us.'

'Humph!' said the Camel; and the Horse went away and told the Man.

Presently the Dog came to him, with a stick in his mouth, and said, 'Camel, O Camel, come and fetch and carry like the rest of us.'

'Humph!' said the Camel; and the Dog went away and told the Man.

Presently the Ox came to him, with the yoke on his neck and said, 'Camel, O Camel, come and plough like the rest of us.'

'Humph!' said the Camel; and the Ox went away and told the Man.

At the end of the day the Man called the Horse and the Dog and the Ox together, and said, 'Three, O Three, I'm very sorry for you (with the world so new-and-all); but that Humph-thing in the Desert can't work, or he would have been here by now, so I am going to leave him alone, and you must work double-time to make up for it.'

That made the Three very angry (with the world so new-and-all), and they held a palaver, and an _indaba_, and a _punchayet_, and a pow-wow on the edge of the Desert; and the Camel came chewing milkweed _most_ 'scruciating idle, and laughed at them. Then he said 'Humph!' and went away again.

Presently there came along the Djinn in charge of All Deserts, rolling in a cloud of dust (Djinns always travel that way because it is Magic), and he stopped to palaver and pow-pow with the Three.

'Djinn of All Deserts,' said the Horse, '_is_ it right for any one to be idle, with the world so new-and-all?'

'Certainly not,' said the Djinn.

'Well,' said the Horse, 'there's a thing in the middle of your Howling Desert (and he's a Howler himself) with a long neck and long legs, and he hasn't done a stroke of work since Monday morning. He won't trot.'

'Whew!' said the Djinn, whistling, 'that's my Camel, for all the gold in Arabia! What does he say about it?'

'He says "Humph!"' said the Dog; 'and he won't fetch and carry.'

'Does he say anything else?'

[THIS is the picture of the Djinn making the beginnings of the Magic that brought the Humph to the Camel. First he drew a line in the air with his finger, and it became solid; and then he made a cloud, and then he made an egg--you can see them both at the bottom of the picture--and then there was a magic pumpkin that turned into a big white flame. Then the Djinn took his magic fan and fanned that flame till the flame turned into a magic by itself. It was a good Magic and a very kind Magic really, though it had to give the Camel a Humph because the Camel was lazy. The Djinn in charge of All Deserts was one of the nicest of the Djinns, so he would never do anything really unkind.]

'Only "Humph!"; and he won't plough,' said the Ox.

'Very good,' said the Djinn. 'I'll humph him if you will kindly wait a minute.'

The Djinn rolled himself up in his dust-cloak, and took a bearing across the desert, and found the Camel most 'scruciatingly idle, looking at his own reflection in a pool of water.

'My long and bubbling friend,' said the Djinn, 'what's this I hear of your doing no work, with the world so new-and-all?'

'Humph!' said the Camel.

The Djinn sat down, with his chin in his hand, and began to think a Great Magic, while the Camel looked at his own reflection in the pool of water.

'You've given the Three extra work ever since Monday morning, all on account of your 'scruciating idleness,' said the Djinn; and he went on thinking Magics, with his chin in his hand.

'Humph!' said the Camel.

'I shouldn't say that again if I were you,' said the Djinn; 'you might say it once too often. Bubbles, I want you to work.'

[HERE is the picture of the Djinn in charge of All Deserts guiding the Magic with his magic fan. The camel is eating a twig of acacia, and he has just finished saying "humph" once too often (the Djinn told him he would), and so the Humph is coming. The long towelly-thing growing out of the thing like an onion is the Magic, and you can see the Humph on its shoulder. The Humph fits on the flat part of the Camel's back. The Camel is too busy looking at his own beautiful self in the pool of water to know what is going to happen to him.

Underneath the truly picture is a picture of the World-so-new-and-all.

There are two smoky volcanoes in it, some other

mountains and some stones and a lake and a black island and a twisty river and a lot of other things, as well as a Noah's Ark. I couldn't draw all the deserts that the Djinn was in charge of, so I only drew one, but it is a most deserty desert.]

And the Camel said 'Humph!' again; but no sooner had he said it than he saw his back, that he was so proud of, puffing up and puffing up into a great big lolloping humph.

'Do you see that?' said the Djinn. 'That's your very own humph that you've brought upon your very own self by not working. To-day is Thursday, and you've done no work since Monday, when the work began. Now you are going to work.'

'How can I,' said the Camel, 'with this humph on my back?'

'That's made a-purpose,' said the Djinn, 'all because you missed those three days. You will be able to work now for three days without eating, because you can live on your humph; and don't you ever say I never did anything for you. Come out of the Desert and go to the Three, and behave. Humph yourself!'

And the Camel humphed himself, humph and all, and went away to join the Three. And from that day to this the Camel always wears a humph (we call it 'hump' now, not to hurt his feelings); but he has never yet caught up with the three days that he missed at the beginning of the world, and he has never yet learned how to behave.

The Camel's hump is an ugly lump
Which well you may see at the Zoo;
But uglier yet is the hump we get
From having too little to do.

Kiddies and grown-ups too-oo-oo,
If we haven't enough to do-oo-oo,
We get the hump—
Cameelious hump—
The hump that is black and blue!

We climb out of bed with a frouzly head
And a snarly-yarly voice.
We shiver and scowl and we grunt and we growl
At our bath and our boots and our toys;

And there ought to be a corner for me
(And I know there is one for you)
When we get the hump—
Cameelious hump—
The hump that is black and blue!

The cure for this ill is not to sit still,
Or frowst with a book by the fire;
But to take a large hoe and a shovel also,
And dig till you gently perspire;

And then you will find that the sun and the wind,
And the Djinn of the Garden too,
Have lifted the hump—
The horrible hump—
The hump that is black and blue!

I get it as well as you-oo-oo—
If I haven't enough to do-oo-oo—
We all get hump—
Cameelious hump—
Kiddies and grown-ups too!